breathe
in,
cash
out

breathe
in,
cash
out

a novel

MADELEINE
HENRY

ATRIA PAPERBACK

new york london toronto sydney new delhi

ATRIA
PAPERBACK

An Imprint of Simon & Schuster, Inc.
1230 Avenue of the Americas
New York, NY 10020

First Atria Paperback edition July 2020

ATRIA PAPERBACK and colophon are registered trademarks of Simon & Schuster, Inc.

For information about special discounts for bulk purchases, please contact Simon & Schuster Special Sales at 1-866-506-1949 or business@simonandschuster.com.

The Simon & Schuster Speakers Bureau can bring authors to your live event. For more information or to book an event, contact the Simon & Schuster Speakers Bureau at 1-866-248-3049 or visit our website at www.simonspeakers.com.

Interior design by Kyle Kabel

Manufactured in the United States of America

1   3   5   7   9   10   8   6   4   2

The Library of Congress has cataloged the hardcover edition as follows:

Names: Henry, Madeleine, author.
Title: Breathe in, cash out : a novel / Madeleine Henry.
Description: New York : Atria Books, 2019. |
Identifiers: LCCN 2019002246 (print) | LCCN 2019003211 (ebook) |
ISBN 9781982114558 (eBook) | ISBN 9781982114534 (hardback) |
ISBN 9781982114541 (paperback) Subjects: | BISAC: FICTION / Contemporary Women. | FICTION / Humorous.
Classification: LCC PS3608.E5736 (ebook) |
LCC PS3608.E5736 B74 2019 (print) | DDC 813/.6—dc23
LC record available at https://lccn.loc.gov/2019002246

ISBN 978-1-9821-1453-4
ISBN 918-1-9821-1454-1 (pbk)
ISBN 978-1-9821-1455-8 (ebook)

To my barista

"'If you fuckin' buy this bond in a fuckin' trade, you're fuckin' fucked.' And 'If you don't pay fuckin' attention to the fuckin' two-year, you get your fuckin' face ripped off.'"

—Michael Lewis,
Liar's Poker

"I offer you peace. I offer you love. I offer you friendship. I see your beauty. I hear your need. I feel your feelings. My wisdom flows from the Highest Source. I salute that Source in you. Let us work together for unity and love."

—Gandhi

prologue

"Are you okay?" Skylar asks.

I've seen her flawless features—long blond hair, bright blue eyes, nonexistent pores—pop up on my Instagram feed hundreds of times, and she's always come across as effortlessly happy. But right now, she looks concerned.

I'm trying to explain to my Instagram-famous yoga idol that despite cashing checks from the notorious Anderson Shaw (the most prestigious investment bank on Wall Street), which pays me an absurd amount of money to do things that require no skill except surviving in a constant state of panic—ASAP, NOW, !, FIRE DRILL, MORE TO COME, FWD: FWD: FWD: PLS DO TX—I'm doing the best I can on my spiritual journey.

And yes, I accidentally slept with my boss last night, but I have so many problems right now that I am writing that one off completely.

All I want is to be a yoga teacher. I just need enough money to get started, so I'm waiting for my year-end bonus. In the meantime, yeah, it's pretty lonely and soul-crushing to be the only person on my floor who's not down to sign their dream away for a seven-figure salary, and who will exit this hellhole of an industry in a thoroughly *fuck you* way. Like, not only am I leaving you, suckers, but I am leaving for a profession with antithetical values—not only does this job not work for me, but the *spirit* of your company is *wrong*. On top of it all, I am so out of shape that it's not even funny. I don't have muscle definition anywhere on my body. I am a human tube. A *tube*.

Meanwhile, Skylar sits across from me, looking as serene and in touch with her inner peace as she does on Instagram. She has no idea that I'm doing more aerobics in my head right now than I have done with my body in months. I want to impress her because she is *the* Skylar Smith, the thirty-something yogi with 200K followers at @SkylarSmithYoga, and she actually stands for something. She uses her account as a platform to promote love for mankind with heartfelt captions that have made me cry. She is a vision of who I want to be.

I'm just . . . in transition.

How do I explain that?

chapter 1

The night before . . .

I am five coffees deep and drowsy. I rest in a split on my yoga mat as the women around me massage their own shoulders and luxuriate in slow head circles before the midnight class begins. Finally, a break.

One bare foot stamps my mat.

"Apologies."

He strides past, leaving a temporary heel print on the vinyl. *Apologies,* muttered unintentionally and deadpan like a reflexive *bless you* to someone you don't know on the subway. He unrolls his own yoga mat—one of the slippery two-dollar rentals—right beside me, leaving only inches between us. *Great.* In order to do a decent side crow or rock-star pose, I'm going to trespass on this asshole's airspace. And he on mine.

He pretzels into a cross-legged seat, palms on his knees. His legs are thick and hairy beneath black spandex-and-mesh shorts. It's not the typical yoga body. If his muscles were any bigger, they might be trashy. As they are now, his chest and arms fill his NANTUCKET TRIATHLON shirt perfectly. His face is sharp, and he's not wearing a wedding ring. For a second, I imagine climbing onto his lap.

I stand and align the long edges of my mat perpendicular to the front of the room. Better. Arranging shapes is a habit of mine. For the past two years, I've spent half of my time as an investment banking analyst aligning text boxes of bullshit in PowerPoint.

"Do you have the time?" he asks.

"Yes," I say. I like being deliberately vague.

He smirks. He is probably twice my age, judging from the patches of gray hair. Yoga tries to balance opposites, especially the masculine with the feminine, and the people you usually see in studios are evidence: lean, muscled women and flexible, necklace-wearing men. This stranger does not fit the mold. From his wide jaw to his massive feet, he is all man. The only man here.

"I'm Mark." He extends a wide-fingered hand. I like big.

"Allegra," I say, taking his.

I smile invitingly at Mark.

"You're not one of those crazy yogis, are you?" he asks.

I laugh a little from shock.

"What do you mean?" I ask.

"Young and beautiful?" he says. "Can't be trusted."

"Yeah, totally," I say sarcastically. "Just one of those yogi ass-holes, I guess."

"Just rotten," he says.

We laugh, and he winks. That was forward. His eyes drift down my body and back up again. Now I'm sure he's hitting on me. If he weren't so handsome, the advance in a *yoga studio* would put me off, but good-looking men can get away with overconfidence.

"Come to *sukhasana*, or any comfortable seat," the teacher coos, "and let us take a moment to set our intention for practice today." She leads us in an *omm* as we set our intentions, but I already know mine. I am going to yoga-fuck this Mark from my mat for the next hour.

Savasana, or corpse pose, is always last. After stretching out muscles useless to office life—the pelvic psoas as I twist my torso into triangle pose, the glottis in my throat as I make my breath hotter and faster in "breath of fire"—we lie in complete relaxation. We're invited to experience death in corpse pose. It lasts up to fifteen minutes, usually in complete darkness and silence. It's considered poor etiquette to get up and leave in the middle of *savasana*, which would disturb the experience of death, obviously. Good yogis leave before or after.

I glance toward Mark for a cue. We lie next to each other, close enough, sweaty enough, and breathless enough that we could have just had sex. He is staring at me. His liquid-soft brown eyes are unblinking and hungry. My groin blushes hot, and I am instantly wet. I roll my hips slightly from side to side, and his gaze drifts down to the top of my yoga pants. I close my eyes, enjoying the deliciousness of being exactly what he wants. Yoga, when done correctly, quiets the mind. Whether it's the yoga that did it or Mark, my inner monologue has stopped, and I feel only desire for him.

When class is finally over, we push our mats into jelly-roll coils. Other students shuffle, whisper thank-yous, and zip up their coats to head home. Thinking of the Ashtanga series makes me think of the series of poses that Mark and I will cycle through tonight.

* * *

I wake up in Mark's Midtown studio the way one-night stands always end. We are back-to-back, with a wide strip of space between us as a reminder of what he owes me: absolutely nothing. The sex was good. It wasn't like getting Groundhog Day–slammed by some twenty-something who thinks he's the shit because at some point he rubs your clitoris. Mark kissed slowly. His oral was soft and specific. I actually came. He held my legs straight up, perpendicular to my waist, and just stared at my genitals while we fucked.

Genitals is exactly the right word to use here, because the sex wasn't personal. Well, except for the one moment when he groaned that I was "fucking amazing at yoga."

Alarm sounds jingle from Mark's phone.

He lumbers out of bed toward the bathroom. Shower water hits marble. Sitting up, I see the place has a first-apartment feel: barely any furniture, and what's there looks secondhand. It's a little understated for someone paying forty dollars for an hour of yoga. I fish my phone out of my gym bag and scroll through the mailbox: fifty-two new work emails since I last checked six hours ago. It's 8:12 a.m.

"Legz," he says.

His playful tone suggests the z.

"Markz," I parrot.

He emerges, lower body toweled and bare chest defined beneath a white tee.

"Coffee?" he asks.

"No, thanks," I say. I do want coffee, but being given something so soon after sex makes it feel like a payment.

"I have Colombian beans," he says. "I'll grind them right now."

"No, really."

"You're right, dinner is much better than coffee," he says. I can't help but smile. "All right, all right. You win. You beat me down. Dinner it is."

"Wow, you give up so easy."

"I know, right? I'll cook. Red or white?"

"Neither, I don't really drink."

"Well, that's what you get for meeting a girl at a yoga class," he says. "I had a feeling my next girlfriend would be a do-gooder."

"Oh my God."

"Too much charm?" he asks. "I know. I'm cursed."

I head to the bathroom and change quickly, no time for a shower. I give myself a once-over, nervous enough that I might actually like this alpha asshole. My blond hair looks dry and stiff at the ends from too much flat-ironing. I finger-brush away a couple of clumps and rub the ends to grease them with the natural oils from my hands. My light eyebrows, almost as pale as my skin, disappear into my forehead. In my T.J. Maxx suit, I look like Taylor Swift would if she had a day job as a tax attorney.

Mark and I step over a paper copy of the *Wall Street Journal* outside his door and ride the elevator down. He is dressed sharply in a suit—so sharply that I do a double take. His gleaming loafers look like new Berlutis that could cost up to two thousand dollars. We pass a Pink store, where his crisp dress shirt matches the one in the window display. His blue jacket fits perfectly, as if he is a Patrick Bateman double. To top it all off, his skin is better than mine. His face is clear and moisturized to the point of actual dewiness.

"Are you an actor or something?" I ask.

"No, why?"

"Your suit," I say, gesturing.

Is nicer than your apartment.

"Just showing you my range," he says.

He raises his hand to hail me a cab.

"Oh, no thanks," I say. Anderson Shaw's headquarters shines just a couple of blocks away. "I'll walk."

"I insist," he says. "My treat."

"No, really," I say.

"All right," he says. "See you tonight."

He lowers his hand to grab my ass.

"Goodbye now," he says.

We start to walk in the same direction and I pretend not to notice. Phone in hand, I sift through emails, back in my default state of skimming and replying "Will do." I only look up at the final intersection, where I stand face-to-face with Anderson's headquarters on the other side of the street. Mark is still beside me, zoned into his phone as well. Green light. We meet each other's eyes as we cross the street. He looks puzzled until it dawns on him, and instantly, all of his ass-cupping warmth vanishes.

He picks up his pace. My mouth stays shock-locked in one surprise *O*. Mark *who*? Mark fucking *who*? I slow my walk until he is three or four paces ahead. My heart clogs my throat. Yellow cabs whiz past me to unload today's batch of bankers, traders, and equity researchers. Mark's coattails almost blend into the ID-swiping crowd of backs in the lobby, but I keep my eyes on him.

He passes the first bank of elevators. The second and final bank leads only to the fifteenth floor, a transportation hub known as the Sky Lobby. On either side of me, elevators are constantly arriving or leaving. They obey Anderson's unspoken rule where, once a car is half-full, someone will thumb-jab the door-close button two hard, *fuck you* times. The self-selected *fuck you*–er of Mark's elevator acts fast. The shining silver doors close.

Hundreds of suits roll through the palatial Sky Lobby. The right side of the enormous atrium is a seamless floor-to-ceiling window overlooking Manhattan. The left side is lined with more elevator banks where, instead of hitting buttons inside the elevator, you enter your floor number into a calculator-type keypad stationed to one side of the bank and are assigned to an elevator—F6, or G8, as the case may be. Mark's head bobs through the crowd to my bank. I am just seconds behind him. Limply, I press the same numbers he did, vaguely noting that the buttons are still warm from his fingertips. We are assigned to the same elevator headed to the same floor: thirty-five, dedicated to Healthcare banking.

There aren't many devout yogis in my line of work—and I won't be here for long. The plan is to complete a two-hundred-hour yoga-teacher training and then teach full-time after my two-year analyst contract expires (T-minus two months to go). I've been dedicated to a serious yoga practice since college, but I signed with Anderson before I decided to turn the hobby into a job. Hence my current situation. For now, I live as much as I can by credos like "All you need is less" while pulling all-nighters and nodding along in whose-dick-is-bigger conversations comparing deals and bonuses.

I am a second-year investment banking analyst at Anderson Shaw. On my résumé, that means I build financial models from scratch, strategize for powerhouse executives, and prepare materials for the M&A deals headlining the *Wall Street Journal*. In reality, I spend up to twenty-four hours a day changing the colors on stacked bar charts, making my bosses feel better about themselves, and, as of last night, literally fucking a coworker.

Half of my job is making "pitch books." Senior bankers carry these to sales meetings with clients in order to convince the CEO on the other side of the table to do some kind of deal. Bankers pitch all kinds of deals: buy a company in the same sector "for scale," or buy a company in a different sector "to diversify," and then use proceeds to fuel more deals in a never-ending flywheel of shit for me to do. To create the sales pitch, we make line graphs, schematics, and financial model outputs. Then we work on the deal itself, once the CEO agrees, *Yes, we would be a better company if we had half as much cash on the balance sheet. Who wants that much cash anyway? Not fucking us.*

At the moment, I'm waiting with Mark and another analyst for F3. Those phonetics sum it up: F3. Eff me. The analyst between us is known for always looking like a complete mess. Her black eyeliner is constantly smudged as if she's been wearing the same makeup for weeks or crying about some work-related catastrophe. Today, her skirt is beyond wrinkled, again.

"Rough night?" she asks me.

Mark's eyes dart toward us.

"Sort of," I say.

If *she* thinks *I* look bad, then I am so fucked. The three of us file into the elevator and blink up to the thirty-fifth floor. Everyone laser-eyes their phone.

The doors open, and Mark and I split in opposite directions. I head to the pantry for coffee. Every banking floor looks the same: shared desks down one side and window offices down the other.

It has the feel of a two-lane highway where one lane is made of dirt and the other is paved and tree-lined. Each of the shared desks seats four—two facing two, without any physical divider—and is known as a "pod," meant for analysts, associates, and vice presidents. The all-glass offices are for senior vice presidents and managing directors.

I throw the coffee back like an eight-ounce shot and head to my desk. Turns out, Mark's office is right before Real Estate, the only other group on thirty-five, and out of sight from my pod on the other side of the floor. His broad back faces me as he takes in the view from his power nest. He grabs his hips, elbows wide, and juts his pelvis forward. I scurry unnoticed to safety.

Fuck. It is 9 a.m. and I am living in a nightmare. I am never here this early, and no other desk-dweller is either. I wait for the three other bankers in my pod: there's Chloe, the emotionless fake blonde from Dartmouth who Instagrammed herself on a partner's G5 with the hashtag #likeaG5; Puja, the heiress whose father owns one of the biggest private banks in India, and who grew up using a credit card with her last name—the bank's name—printed on the front; and Tripp, the devil-may-care associate known for keeping an earbud in his right ear and watching Netflix on one of his two computer screens all day. This is a habit he began as an intern while sitting next to a vice president.

At the desk, I navigate to Anderson Shaw's internal facebook. There is one Mark in Healthcare: Mark Thomas Swift, whose profile picture matches Markz's exactly. He just transferred into HG from Equity Capital Markets, another Anderson Shaw banking group, as a managing director. Today is his first day.

I immediately start to internet-stalk Mark: Google, Facebook, Instagram, LinkedIn, Twitter, fucking everything. He has a couple of photos on New York Social Diary, but those thumbnails are too small to reveal much. His Facebook is private. LinkedIn corroborates his AS employment, but otherwise his profile is empty, like that of anyone who's not looking for another job. At least his Instagram is public. His posts are geotagged—the Loeb Boathouse, Lincoln Center, and the Metropolitan Museum of Art, all for black-tie events. I hover over a picture of him standing alone and illuminated by floor lights at Avenue. The caption reads: "Charity—#Yellowstone #JayGatz." Did he just compare himself to the Great Gatsby? I'm more concerned he felt the need to abbreviate "Gatsby" like a college bro. As I scroll deeper into summertime posts, the geotags become Jackson Hole, Aspen, and Montauk Point. It is a hyperbolically sceney Instagram. I don't think he has been anywhere expensive without taking a picture of it.

You know what? This guy doesn't give a shit about yoga.

Fingernails rap my desk, finding the only wooden oasis in the mess of papers.

"Hello," Mark says.

He doesn't look me in the eye. He seems to be checking if anyone else is around, and no one is. Junior people are commuting or sleeping, and senior people are tucked into their glass enclaves. Mark walks around to stand behind my monitors, which display in a horizontally tiled sequence: his Instagram, LinkedIn, Facebook, and Google-searched name. Every analyst has two desktop monitors, and his internet identity is smeared across both of mine. I corner-X out of every window as fast as humanly possible.

"Allegra," he says.

"Yes?" I squeak.

"Let's be mature about this," he says. He strides away.

What does that even mean? He turns the corner, leaving me alone with his ambiguous decree. Should that go on my to-do list for, like, my job? I open Microsoft Outlook to get on with the day. Now, on top of everything else, I feel an urge to reflect on my fucking life. Like, how did things get this out of control? Maybe Mark was right when he called me rotten. Maybe I'll never be the yogi I want to be and, really, at my *core*, I'm just an Anderson piece of shit.

chapter 2

No one grows up wanting to be an investment banker. Anyone who says they did is lying. One of the most common questions to prepare for analyst interviews is: What does an investment banker do? And the truth is, no one fucking knows.

Most people are just here to make millions. The standard track is: two years of banking and then move to the "buy side"—i.e., investing—where you can earn an annual $450K at the entry level at age twenty-five. If you leave banking for a hedge fund and rise to the top—requiring you to roll sevens with your lucky-dice hand every day for a decade—you will get compensated on a "2 and 20" incentive structure. That means you take home 2 percent of the money you manage plus 20 percent of the profits every year. So, if you manage $1 billion, you will make $20 million a year no matter what, even if all you do is play solitaire.

If hedge funds aren't your thing, then there's private equity—OMG, more finance! *Hell* yeah—where you buy and sell companies not available on the stock market. This also earns you millions at the top and offers the experience of sitting down all day just *knowing* that your bank account is growing. This is cool because then you can buy expensive things you won't have time to use, but you can tell other people that you own these things.

If you turn out to be a complete fuckup at banking, then you probably won't get a hedge fund or private equity job, but that's okay. There's always business development at a Fortune 500 company waiting for you. This totally decent profession with a sustainable lifestyle carries great shame as an exit option. It's fewer hours, less technical, less pay, and people are happier. The combination is disgraceful on Wall Street.

But believe me when I say that not *everyone* goes into banking for the money. Some people just got swept up in Ivy League social pressure. I went to Princeton, where about half the graduating class matriculates into finance or consulting annually.

The process unfolds like clockwork. Every fall, big banks and consulting firms flock to campus in droves. First-round interviews for all bulge brackets take place during the same week. You know who is interviewing, because you see them walking around in suits, and the cast of characters attending these interviews is gossiped about extensively at school. Everyone knows who gets called back, who gets cut, and when. If someone with a 3.8 GPA gets even a first-round at Anderson Shaw, people freak out and google how rich their parents are. The events of interview season are up for public consumption, and the job hunt becomes a competitive social game where small differences are overblown. Anderson is the best bank, and the gap between it and second place is, like, fucking cosmic.

Now, as my peers climb to the next ladder rung—buy side, whatever—I won't join them. I seriously do not belong.

*   *   *

My dad raised me. Mom died of bone cancer when I was eight, after six rounds of chemo and twenty-one hospital stays in ten months. She was a dancer turned dance instructor and had long blond hair like me. She stayed devoted to dancing—ballet, jazz, modern—in a local troupe until she got sick. I used to watch them rehearse after school. She moved in spectacular ways, as if she channeled powers from out of this world. For her to lose control of her body was hard on everyone.

Dad is strong at sixty, the same height and weight as DC Comics' Superman, at six foot three and 235 pounds, as he says. He has all of Mom's strength, expressed differently. He talks like a fucking sailor, and when I was young it made him happy whenever I talked like him or won anything. In general, he thinks the world is way too politically correct and way too sensitive: he wasn't going to raise a wimp. Mom was warmer, but they shared a strong work ethic and sense of family: we were the Cobbs, and no one could mess with us.

After Mom passed away, I just wanted Dad to be happy again. One way to do that, I learned, was by excelling. No matter what I achieved—straight As, sports games—my success brought him joy. Plus, he relished coaching me. So achievement became the only space where we really connected. It may have looked like he was pushing me too much, or was too firm, but that's just how he showed love. I showed love for him in return by engaging. Our bond is deep but, at the same time, forged entirely over my potential.

On weekends, he'd run the back roads around us in Princeton, New Jersey, while I biked next to him. We'd shoot the shit about whoever we were passing and about my future: Princeton and then Anderson Shaw was always the dream plan. Best college, best job. Princeton was coincidentally the college closest to home, but he never said that out loud. Even though Dad is much smarter than I am, he never had a steady career. Instead, he had a series of odd jobs—management consultant, fitness instructor—and he only actively managed his savings by the time I got to high school. I felt like his purpose.

It wasn't until eighth grade that I glimpsed our limits. I got my period and didn't tell him. He noticed my oddly light load of laundry that night. The next morning, over cold cereal, he told me "facts" about the "female" body in complete sentences. Later that year, we were watching a movie after dinner, and a sex scene came on. He cleared his throat. "That," he said. He paused. "Is sex." But talking about Princeton and Anderson was seamless. Those conversations fed our relationship and excited him about the future.

To this day, he thinks I'm a career banker.

Wherever there's a ton of money to be made, there's cutthroat competition. Your best shot of getting into Anderson is a summer internship in college. Anderson makes most of its interns offers, and thus fills out its incoming class of new analysts. If you miss that chance, you're basically fucked forever.

Leading up to the internship interview gauntlet, Dad helped me cram. *What does an investment banking analyst fucking do? All right, that. What is the weighted average cost of capital? All right, that formula with words I've never seen before.* We figured out what Anderson wants in an intern through my lunches with Princeton alumni who worked there. For instance, Anderson's is a team-based culture, so I should talk about how much I love working on teams. Whenever possible, I should say the word *team.*

We knew that I might get fucked with. One interviewer was known to stay silent for the first ten minutes just to see how candidates would react to unexpected stress. Dad made me a reading list of a dozen books and I read them all, including one entirely about credit default swaps. I learned how to do things like calculate a company's unlevered beta to the S&P. Finally, we reached Anderson's Super Day. I'd endured final-round interviews with two other banks that week already and had not been to class in a month.

A week later, an alum and head of the Princeton recruiting effort at AS called me with the news: Anderson Shaw wanted to extend me an offer for their ten-week summer internship. I'd always had two names in my head—Princeton, Anderson—and finally, we'd done it. I called Dad immediately; he'd never been so happy.

By week two of the internship, I wanted out. There is a big difference between knowing you will spend a hundred hours a week doing bullshit work for rich, selfish assholes, and then actually fucking doing it.

Analysts who will be in finance forever and analysts quitting tomorrow are indistinguishable in terms of how much they complain about the job. Hating your life is part of the culture. *How are you? "So fucking miserable." Yeah, same. "Okay, cool, see you later."* In that dialogue, one person will bank for life, and the other is actually having an identity crisis. Which is which? No one knows.

Dad and I didn't talk much that summer because of my schedule, but we texted every day. Given the masturbating-to-misery norm of banking, when I would complain to Dad about how awful the job was, my point was not made that I didn't want to be there. He would text back, Proud of you. He adopted Anderson's use of the word *team*. Sometimes, he texted back, Proud of team.

I got Anderson's full-time offer at the end of the summer and had forty-eight hours to respond. As I finally taxied home that night from the train station, I planned to tell Dad in person that I would turn it down. He still lived in the two-bedroom in Princeton, New Jersey, where I'd grown up. It's on a block of houses that look the same, each with a patch of lawn. When I pulled up, all of our neighbors were waiting outside the house for me, and Dad beamed front and center on the sidewalk. The whole block knew I worked at Anderson. Dad and I hugged—it was good to be home—and he pointed out to the neighbors how pale I was in August, how unexercised, how miserable. These were signs of having made it. We, the Cobbs, had made it.

Dad and I had deep-dish pizza for dinner. I nibbled nervously at our kitchen table. As a warm-up, I started by saying that the only reason to be an Anderson analyst was for the money. But with the thrift he'd passed onto me by example, piles of cash would be abstractions: Dad's the kind of guy who turns the thermostat down in rooms while I'm sitting in them, just to save. I never wanted fancy things.

"I mean, there's no other reason to be there," I say. He laughs for no reason. He's just happy.

"It's too fucking awful," I say.

"Fucking Anderson," he says, smiling. "I love it."

I haven't made my point.

"You're too skinny," he says. "Eat."

"I'm trying to talk to you," I say.

"Talk with your mouth full," he says.

"Do you know most analysts leave Anderson after two years?" I ask.

"Leave?" He doesn't understand. "Wimps."

No. Banking isn't what it used to be in the 1980s. These days, every analyst leaves banking for the buy side after two years, for better pay and better hours. There is a U-curve of talent that peaks at analyst level and then at the top with managing directors. Career bankers aren't as smart. If they could cut it elsewhere, they would. I realized this over the summer. Now, I am up against his image of the brand from forty years ago.

"Cobbs are not wimps," he says.

I stare at the refrigerator behind him, speckled with magnets of me. They are portraits commemorating my participation in sports teams, mostly middle school softball and soccer. Dad coached most of those teams.

"You're not thinking of turning them down, are you?" he asks. I pause. He lowers his pizza to his plate.

"No, of course not," I say. "Other people leave. I'm just explaining."

He starts eating again, slowly. I reach for a fork and poke at my own slice of pizza.

Dad looks at me skeptically.

"Sorry, I'm just not that hungry," I say.

"Allegra?" he says.

"Yeah?"

"Proud of you."

I took the yoga class that changed my life senior fall, after I signed the two-year contract with Anderson. I'd been cramming for midterms all morning and impulsively signed up for the class as a break. It turned out to be ninety minutes straight of an instructor telling me calmly that I actually mattered. Like, *Listen to your body. Take it easy. Breathe. Do less. Have fun. Trust yourself. Feel the love around you.*

It was fucking incredible.

I'd always been active. I played a team sport every season growing up. That was in addition to some after-school gymnastics, yoga, and dance. But yoga never really spoke to me until that moment. I had to be stressed out of my mind, on the verge of taking responsibility for myself in the "real world," before I finally paid attention to what I liked instead of to what everyone else was doing.

Dad didn't know much about yoga. Over Thanksgiving break, when I mentioned that I was doing hot yoga classes almost every day near school, he googled "girls hot yoga" in front of me. His search returned what could be seen as a gallery of strippers in sexually provocative poses.

"No, but it's athletic," I tried to explain.

He grunted.

I thought to bring up dance as a reference point because he'd always respected Mom's art. Mom could hold a perfect split while leaping across a stage. She practiced on her own every day, even as a full-time teacher. She endured muscle tears and bloody feet. The way he admired dance, maybe he could understand at least the physical part of yoga. But of course, I couldn't mention Mom, because her memory hurt him. Besides, most yoga doesn't look as difficult.

So I was just honest.

"Yoga is the only thing I've ever done where I feel like my full self," I said. "I don't just care about my mind. I care about my body, and I feel like I have a soul, and yoga studios are the only places I know that nurture all three."

He was silent.

"Dad?" I asked. "Hello?"

"All the rich kids at Princeton have you talking like we're rich."

"I know we're not rich," I said.

"Well, then stop acting like it," he snapped.

I showed my surprise.

"Sorry, sorry," he apologized. "Work out all you want before Anderson."

He Xed out of the "girls hot yoga" search. I was frustrated. I wasn't trying to run away from responsibility—I just never cared about prestige or power the way Dad did. I cared more about my inner life.

I wanted to do and be around yoga as much as possible, and eventually that sparked the idea: teach. Meanwhile, the more I practiced, the more I poured energy into part of my life where Dad couldn't relate. We grew apart by omission until he emailed me an article describing the American Yoga Championship, a competition judging yoga postures. "Yoga for Cobbs!!!" he wrote. Dad's follow-up emails with more information were so animated that I looked into it.

Every year, American Yoga holds regional qualifiers across the country that prelude a national finale. Each round requires the athlete to perform a choreographed yoga flow in five minutes, followed by ten mandatory and two optional poses. The contest unfolds onstage before a panel of judges. A brief written test follows, where contestants write about the benefits of each posture. I entered, and Dad and I grew closer while I trained. He sent me workouts for shoulder strength and researched judges' criteria. I knew he had been a little aimless now that he wasn't coaching me, but here he was again, ignited by purpose. In his mind, I was still the Allegra he knew, kicking yoga ass. Anderson, now yoga gold. The Cobbs.

But the more we trained, the farther I got from what I'd loved about yoga in the first place. Dad supplied me with a steady stream of quotes to keep me in a "winner's mind-set," including, "Winners do what losers won't." That became my practice mantra. By the time I realized how off-track we were from the spirit of yoga, teaching us to relax, quitting no longer made sense. After all, the competition is respected. I figured it might help me get my footing in the yoga world after Anderson. So I prepared. I competed. I did my absolute best. And, out of the thousand other people who competed that year—there are no entry-level requirements—I earned the women's gold.

Now, two years later, banking has nearly sucked dry my yoga soul. I try to practice, but working at Anderson makes that tough on every level. I haven't told anyone my plan to quit and teach—I haven't even picked a training program, because that feels like abandoning Dad. I imagine him on the sofa alone, wearing his necklace chain strung with his wedding ring, watching the game.

So here I am, in transition. I am neither full banker nor full yogi and don't mesh seamlessly with either group. The closer I get to the end of my contract, the more I catch myself missing Mom. She was just over five feet tall and, in a lot of ways, a helpful contrast to Dad. She saw dance as much more than a sport. She thought expressing your inner life was important. I don't know what she would say to me now, but I feel like she would understand, or at least make me feel less fucking ridiculous.

chapter 3

Assistants trickle in before the rest of the analysts. There is one for every five or so bankers, shared across levels. My assistant, Trixie, sits at the desk around the corner. Her back is just barely in sight, like a shark fin. Her tightly coiled gray perm swims in and out of view. Mornings are usually peaceful, but not today. Today, I fucked my boss.

"Hey, Alfredo."

It's Tripp. He changes my nickname every time we talk—I don't think he actually knows my name. A lot of people don't like Tripp—they say he's a "privileged clownshit" or something. The fact that he's attractive makes him even less popular on a floor full of quants who need this job to get any ass at all. Tripp sits down next to me looking like the Hugo Boss brand personified: tall, strong jaw, and floppy brown hair.

"Late night?" he asks. "Or early morning?"

I don't know. There is no sun in hell.

"Late night," I decide. Which I regret, because *today*, I have one meeting I actually fucking care about.

"Broo-tahl," he says. That's his word for everything, a variation on the pronunciation of "brutal." *How is your new team? "Broo-tahl." How is your day? "Broo-tahl."* Tripp once appeared on an episode of *NYC Elite*, a reality show, where in his one minute on screen, he says "Broo-tahl" three times. During the other fifty-five seconds, Tripp manages to kiss his brother's girlfriend on national TV at some club in the Hamptons. Sometimes he replays this clip—volume on—at the pod and makes a *score* fist when he kisses her. Like, *Yeah. That's me.*

Tripp is the one I get along with best on the floor. We clicked early, ever since he raised his hand during a presentation on Anderson's principles at new-banker training and asked about the Wi-Fi because "Snapchat isn't working." We've endured this banking torture side by side for two years now, and he's basically my fraternity brother, hazed by the same 24/7 onslaught of ridiculous bullshit.

Tripp tries to chat, but today, I ignore him. Our conversations get stupid fast, and I need to focus. Yesterday Tripp swore he could "own" me at every sport, and for the rest of the afternoon while we worked, I named a series of different sports, and he responded just with: *"Own." Soccer? "Own." Football? "Own." Basketball? "Are you even serious? Own."* I can't get sucked back into that shit. My life is a garbage fire. Tripp asks me what it's like to be the blond April Ludgate, and I roll my eyes.

"April," he says, "play nice."

"I'm working," I say.

"You sleep last night?" he asks.

Yeah, around.

"A bit," I say.

"Broo-tahl."

Typing hides silence. Most of the work I do here is mindless and could even be automated within the next ten years. Does Anderson really need thinking, feeling, self-aware human beings to make these fucking tables? How about *no*. Today, my to-do list is brainless enough that I can beat myself up while being productive. I mean, what the fuck? How is this my real, actual life?

I send an order for a dozen stock price charts to India—analysts outsource as many graphs as possible to an unsung group in Bangalore. Those usually come back in need of resizing, different axes, or *something* that sucks the life out of me like a dementor, but those are problems for Future Allegra. I fix other bullshit, drink three cups of black coffee, and will time to pass until it's 10:55 a.m. Finally, I grab my phone on my way to the lobby. My heart rate just outpaces the steady buzzing of new emails. I switch alerts to silent and zigzag through oncoming waves of suits toward the revolving-door exit. Time to meet her.

Fifteen minutes later, I fidget nervously by the Shake Shack next to Anderson. I'm sure I was on time ten minutes ago, but maybe real yogis don't think about time the same way us corporate people do. Is she coming?

I am waiting for Skylar Smith, a thirty-something yogi with 200K followers on her expertly curated Instagram. I've followed her account for years. Like those of most InstaYogis, her feed is mostly pictures of herself in yoga poses. Her gallery began as a series of yoga flow videos she made in her own kitchen. She wore socks and taped herself by propping her phone against her sneaker.

I found her account before she got famous while browsing by

hashtag #yoga. She only had a few thousand followers back then, and they were apparently all dudes asking for some more of that cow pose. It was yoga obscurity, but I really liked her feed. She posted every night after work—she held odd jobs as a waitress, a temp, a personal trainer, and so on. In her captions, she wrote about her personal life or some yoga philosophy she was thinking about. I looked forward to her posts every day because she was relatable and real. She seemed like a normal, working person who acknowledged that life is tough but that yoga helped her. And she was self-taught, like me.

A couple of her videos went viral and, now, the yoga world watches her flows. It helped that Skylar is a beautiful blonde. Still, I think she deserves every bit of recognition she's had. It makes me happy to see someone with a good heart work the system.

Like all big InstaYogis, she models for high-end yoga clothing brands. This is paradoxical, but whatever. *The Yoga Sutras*, an authoritative yoga text, says we should strive for *aparigraha*, or "non-possessiveness." That means do not covet worldly goods. *So, like,* aparigraha *and let go of everything—except these fucking leggings, ladies. And this strappy-ass sports bra, because purple is* in. Not that I judge, of course. I just had sex with my boss and direct-deposit checks from the birthplace of capitalism.

Advertising aside, her content still resonates. She seems as sweet and dedicated to her practice as always, just with a bigger platform. She posts twice a day, morning and night, and I still look forward to her pictures. Sometimes, when I'm in a sour mood, I write off her posts as stupidly precious, like, *Oh* really, *you're just so* happy—but most of the time, she reminds me there's a better life out there somewhere.

American Yoga's annual national competition brought us

together. There was an article about past winners just published in *Mindfulness* magazine, probably to promote the next championship. There still aren't many entrants, because a lot of people think a "yoga competition" is an oxymoron. In any case, I was named among the winners as "the Anderson Shaw Yogi," and the blurb about me said I was from Princeton, New Jersey, won the gold two years ago, and now worked at Anderson Shaw. Beside this were two photos of my finalist poses. Skylar emailed my work address last week and attached the piece. It was the single best thing ever to happen in that inbox.

She wrote:

Allegra,

I'm writing to introduce myself. My name is Skylar Smith (about me: @SkylarSmithYoga).

I just read "The Anderson Shaw Yogi" and wanted to pass on a brief message.

I teach my students that we are here to love and everything else is secondary. So to practice what I preach, I am reaching out.

I saw your photos in *Mindfulness* and really admire your skills and energy. :) You show the balance and joy I aspire to teach every day. You are so grounded in your body, in a practice celebrating the beautiful human spirit.

Please keep doing what you love! It inspires people you don't even know. You are good.

If ever you want to connect or flow, I am here.

Warmly,

Skylar

So here we are, now, on the brink of a lifestyle collision.

Or did I get seriously yoga punk'd?

I putz around her Instagram, even though I know it extremely well. In her latest post, she holds her back leg up in Lord of the Dance pose as the rising sun peeks through the keyhole of her raised hand. The Sanskrit tattoo on her visible ribs—*ananda*, for "utter bliss"—sparkles in the exact center of the picture. She's fucking beaming, as always. Meanwhile, I tell three separate lunch groups in business casual, *Sorry, I'm saving this seat. Hey, I heard that. There are actually lots of open seats outside, and it's a pretty nice day for al fresco. Yeah, fuck you, too.*

"Hi!"

Skylar.

"Hi," I say.

Skylar sits across from me and crosses her nimble legs Indian style. She smiles easily and looks so friendly that I instantly relax. In person, she projects an energy every bit as nice as it appears on Instagram. Some people really are—what's the word—happy? Sometimes I forget those people exist.

She wears a long-sleeve white thermal tee and lavender yoga pants. She interlaces her fingers on the table, drawing attention to her toned arms, shoulders, and core that alluringly suggest a lifestyle of movement. Her face is even more stunning in real life, which I should have expected from a public figure. She rocked a pixie haircut last year, the ultimate test of an attractive face.

Now, her thick blond hair has grown out below her shoulders. Her slight tan makes her blue eyes sparkle. I return her smile. Behind her, dark suits zoom through the tenth item on their to-do list: *Eat.*

"Thank you so much for making the time," she says. "You must be so busy."

She gestures at the throng of speed walkers. I recognize one of the girls booking it back to the office as the Wharton grad known for handing out business cards that said STUDENT at senior-year networking events when she was just a freshman.

"Thank *you* for making the trip," I say.

From your two-bedroom in the East Village. She posts photos and videos from her living room fairly often. It has light-yellow walls and a beige sofa that looks insanely comfortable. Her last post from home had the caption: "Love yourself. Love other people. Love your world. Give and receive love freely. Love knows no bounds." I liked it while I was in line at Starbucks.

"How are you?" she asks.

"Really great right now," I say. "How are you?"

"Wonderful," she says.

I actually believe her, unlike all the falsely positive assholes I work with. Skylar and I continue to smile at each other. There is so much enthusiasm—I can feel the energy—and yet not a single word flows between us.

But now where do we go from here? I already know everything about her. From her "What I Eat in a Day" YouTube video, I know she wakes up at 4 a.m., eats vegan, and makes fake ice cream by freezing mashed bananas. I know she takes all of her own pictures for Instagram, with the exception of a long stretch taken by her photographer boyfriend, Jordan, until they broke up a few months ago. Skylar's peppy younger sister, Rosie, and mom regularly appear in her photos. Their family brims with love.

"I'm a huge fan," I admit.

"Same!" she says.

"Wow," I say earnestly. "That is extremely flattering."

I've also bought Skylar's videos. She sells thirty-minute yoga classes online, and each is a flow sequence inspired by a theme, like acceptance or friendship. I bought a five-pack of her classes for fifty dollars after she emailed me and watched half of one on the subway to work. I wanted to finish it, but I lost service underground and when I resurfaced, I got assigned to an emergency leveraged buyout that required me to stay up for forty-eight hours straight. I cried at my desk, not because I was sad, but because I had stared at the screen for so long by the end that I stopped blinking regularly and my eyes needed to moisten themselves.

"I loved your thirty-minute flow on forgiveness," I say.

The first fifteen minutes were the best.

"Thank you so much," she says.

"Are you teaching nearby today?" I ask.

"No, I'm just here to meet you!" she says. "Then private lessons this afternoon."

"Wow," I say. "You are living my dream."

I force a laugh, but I'm sincere.

"What's it like on the other side?" I ask.

She laughs as if I'm kidding and changes the subject.

"So, the article in *Mindfulness* was a bit short," she says. "It says you work here, of course, but not much else, I'm afraid."

"Right," I say. I guess celebrities apologize for *not* knowing someone they meet for the first time. "I mean, when you work at Anderson, that's about all there is to you. So, you know more than you think."

"Anderson Shaw *and* yoga," she says. "Such a crazy combination."

A yin-and-yang symbol decorated the page next to my profile, suggesting harmony between the two poles of my background. I remember rolling my eyes when I saw it.

"I mean, whatever you combine Anderson with, that's always going to be a tough mix," I say. "Because Anderson is like a forest fire."

She looks confused.

"Meaning, it wrecks everything in its path," I say.

"I see," she says without conviction, as if she doesn't really see. "Honestly, I just want to emphasize, like I wrote in my email, how much respect I have for you. Your practice is so beautiful. Those poses at American Yoga. . . . You made them look easy."

"Thank you."

"Did you have a mentor or teacher help you in particular?" she asks.

"I'm mostly self-taught," I say.

She brightens.

"Good for you," she says.

"Thank you," I say. "I'm looking forward to practicing more next year."

"Now is always the perfect time," she says.

I smile. "Right," I say. "Will do."

She scrunches her brow. "That's not an order!"

"Oh, I know," I say. "Sorry. Bad habit. It's how I talk at work. And I work *a lot,* so sometimes the lines blur." I make squiggly lines with my hands.

"Sure, life ebbs and flows," she excuses me.

"Yeah," I agree hesitantly.

"So, what changes are in store for you next year?" she asks.

"Um." I stutter.

I've never put my plan out into the world out loud.

"I'm going to quit my job, once I save up enough money. Then training," I manage. "Then teaching."

That's vague as shit.

"Oh!" she says. "Amazing. Which studio?"

Skylar gazes at me, radiating kindness, and I realize that this is my chance to share my dreams with someone who would really understand. And this person is *Skylar*. It's surreal. A pain throbs suddenly in my shoulders, and I tilt my head sharply to the side to crack my cervical vertebrae in three loud pops. I massage my neck. My back and shoulders are stiff from sleeping on Mark's fucking bed. Every time he moved, I jerked awake.

"Are you okay?" she asks.

Skylar looks concerned.

"Yeah it's just . . ."

I slept with my boss last night.

I trail off to avoid the confession and avert my eyes. In the Shake Shack line, I spy the analyst so meticulous that she tweezes her legs instead of shaving them. She asked everyone with a private equity firm offer what their compensation package was last year. I notice our table shake from my jittering knee and grab my kneecap.

"You seem a bit tense," she says gently.

"I know," I say. "I'm sorry."

The momentary escape that Skylar provided from my daily life is fading, and my mind resumes its normal state: despair. Who knows what HR nightmare this whole Mark disaster could create. And that's not even the biggest problem in the broader scheme of my imploding life. I have no job to jump to, but I will quit this one in two months. I want to make a living in a career that values *aparigraha*. The person I vibe most with at work—Tripp—has "I am kind of a big deal" written in white font in his email signature and acts perpetually concussed. Now, I sit across from a complete stranger and yoga celebrity, and I feel like she *gets* me and has the *answers* to my *life*. I am off the deep end.

"Allegra?" she asks.

"Hm?" I reply.

"What are you thinking?" she asks.

I should just tell her. She's shared so much of herself with her fans, the least I can do is be honest when I'm having a meltdown in front of her. My gut says I can be me. Not the frat part that talks to Tripp in grunts and "bitchtits." Not the part that replies to M&A Google Alerts from Dad. Not the dried-to-a-raisin bitch sliver of me that croaks, *Yes, more,* to the most illogical stream of bullshit imaginable at work. They say, "When the student is ready, the teacher appears." Well, here Skylar fucking *is*.

"Whatever you're going through," she suggests, "it's weighing on you."

"I know."

Fuck.

"You can share it with me," she says.

"Well . . ." I say. "Okay."

She leans back an inch, surprised by my assertive tone.

"Sorry," I say. I'm abrasive. "I know your time is valuable, so I'll just say it. I'm in a transition. After this, I know I want to teach. I want to build a life around teaching yoga. I used to practice every day, and read the sutras, and I took care of my body. I had real relationships at the yoga studio at home. Then I got swept up in American Yoga. I had this intense coach, yada, yada, and now this. I will quit when my contract expires. Things snowballed, but . . ."

I pause and breathe.

"I don't know—there's way too much backstory for me to tell you everything, but I just fucked this guy last night, and turns out he's my boss," I say. "And it wasn't just some normal, lights-off, done-this-a-thousand-times kind of sex. This was, like, *memorable*. It was all flexible and stuff. And, totally separate issue, I'm under a lot of pressure from my dad. I just feel responsible for his happiness. Like, I'm not just choosing for *me*, I'm choosing for *us*. And I don't know how this happened, but I go to work every day and everything that Anderson values—money, power, speed—is not part of the yoga life, the life I actually want. Also, my body is just shit. Just absolute shit. My upper arms are water balloons. I don't even know who I am anymore."

Skylar looks stunned.

"Fuck," I say. "God, I'm so sorry." I point at my mouth. "Mouth."

"Okay," she says. Her tone suggests: *Slow down*. "What I'm hearing you say is that you lost your yoga way a bit." Pause. I can't tell if she's talking at a normal pace or much slower than average. "Do you still practice?"

"Well, mostly no. But that's only because I work a hundred hours a week."

Skylar had no idea how a bank works, so I started there. I told her that as an analyst, I was at the piss-bottom of the banking hierarchy.

I actually said "piss-bottom," which, for once, didn't sound entirely right or natural. (How am I ever going to be a yoga teacher if I can't even stop cursing in front of my fucking icon?) The next rung up: associate, then vice president, and, at the top, managing director.

An associate reviews analyst work and then sends the deck to the VP for comments. The comment-and-revision loop can continue for weeks before the presentation is ready for an MD to see. Long comment cycles—waiting on call at the desk for feedback, incorporating it in a "turn," and then repeating ad nauseam—partly explain the hours. And, of course, the all-nighters. I told her that junior bankers are basically not supposed to have hobbies, personal lives, or souls. The less you have going on outside of work, the more the upper levels like you. After a first-year broke up with his girlfriend for the sake of the job—over text, at his desk—I watched an MD literally pat him on the back. "Life is a series of trade-offs," the MD said.

On top of my schedule, there's no one in my life (read: my workplace) who appreciates yogi values. Meaning, living simply. Not identifying with belongings. A few days ago, for example, a group of second-years were making Keurig coffee in the pantry. One of the girls mentioned she was in a long-distance relationship with someone in New Zealand. Apparently, he lives near Rotorua and spends less than five dollars a day, and she really misses him. Analysts latched onto the middle part. *Five dollars?* They didn't believe anyone could live on so little. They asked for his name and, chortling, sent him cash over Venmo. In the description of each payment, they input a different day of the week. They sent him five dollars for "Monday" and then ten dollars for "weekend."

Skylar listened, which was intoxicating in its own right. The last time someone listened to me at work was—it's never fucking happened. Before my first client meeting, the MD assigned the VP, the associate, and me our roles. "Your job," he told the VP, "is to walk through the presentation. Your job"—to the associate—"is to answer any of their questions about the numbers. And your job"—to me, the analyst—"is to *shut* the *fuck* up." I mention that, too, as the finale to a long, winding answer to a question I'd almost forgotten. Skylar *mm*'s and squeezes my hand, as if I've just introduced myself to a support group. Have I?

"I am so sorry," Skylar says. "That sounds . . . inhumane."

"Yeah, basically," I say.

"For whatever it's worth," she continues, "I've been through something similar."

"Really?" I ask.

"Yes," she says. She leans back and reflects, looking more somber than I've ever seen her. "I was in a tough relationship. It reminds me a bit of what you're feeling. I was dating a photographer, and I thought we fell very deeply in love. I won't drag you through the details, but it turns out, in the end, he was just using me to help his career." I wince. "We dated for a couple of years. Looking back, I should have seen the signs. He always wanted to *be seen* with me, not just to be with me. He made sure he was credited in all my photos. I should have listened to my intuition sooner."

"I'm sorry," I say.

"Thank you. But the point is—I get it," she says. "Feeling used, disrespected. That's hard. It makes you want to be somewhere else. And that, I think, is suffering: really wanting to be somewhere else."

"That's exactly what I'm feeling."

"I can tell," she says.

She seems to wrestle with an idea.

"You know," she suggests, "maybe I could help. We could meet again, or a couple of times, just until you are in a better place."

I am floored. *Yes*, I want to say. But I need to wait a respectful amount of time before saying, *Yes*. I wait a few seconds.

"If that seems intrusive . . ." she starts.

Fuck. Too many seconds.

"Not at all," I interject.

"Good," she says. She smiles.

"Assuming you're not too busy," I say to be polite.

"That's so thoughtful of you," she says. "But part of what I do—and what I believe you are drawn to—is show compassion!" She laughs gently. "Right?"

"Right, of course," I say.

Yep, compassion for the needy. Now I feel bad. This poor woman. I'm such a mess that she feels compelled to get my life on track. Worse, my blink was to discourage her. I've become so corporate that I tried to talk the yogi in lotus out of doing some good in the world. Like, *You sure you're not too fucking busy? Yeah, okay*. I double-palm my forehead.

"Besides," she continues, "I've always reached out to others in the yoga community, one by one. I spread the beliefs of my practice, help people, and that comes back around to help me. I believe in what I do, and I try to do good where it is needed. And Allegra?" I lift my head up. "Your physical practice is so inspiring. I was blown away by some of your poses. I believe in you one hundred percent. More than that."

"Well then, yes," I say. "Definitely, thank you, yes."

She laughs. "Amazing," she says. She pauses, probably processing the massive shift in our relationship so soon. I can feel it, too. We are no longer on the same level, if we ever were. She's here to save my ass and she knows it. "Normally, whenever I take on a new student, I ask them to keep a journal for a day, so I can get a sense of their thoughts, feelings, and lifestyle. That might be helpful?" She looks back at me for my approval.

"For sure," I agree.

"Great," she says. "And you never know. Later on, if you do get to a better place, and we find ourselves in synch, maybe our relationship could grow into something more official. For now, the journal. It would be helpful just to have a baseline."

"Definitely," I say.

Wait—"official"? Could we actually work together? It's too good to be true, yet here she is, holding my hand in Shake Shack.

"Be completely honest," she says. "If you think 'piss-bottom,' write it!"

I laugh. There's no implication in her tone that I would lie, and I had no intention of doing so. I don't think I've told a lie since Anderson scared me shitless of the consequences during the month of new-banker training. That's when Human Resources told us that the most common reason for getting fired at Anderson is lying. After an hour of enduring HR's fear tactics, I left thinking, *Don't ever fucking think about it*.

"Of course," I say.

"Just for the rest of the day," she says. "What words are floating down your stream of consciousness? Does your inner critic have a tone? How are you sitting and breathing? What are your friends like and how do they make you feel? Take time out of the day to really turn inward. Find your voice and tell your story."

"For the rest of the day?" I ask. That could be a while. "Will do."

chapter 4

MINDFULNESS JOURNAL

12:02 p.m.

Okay feelings.
    My body is a disaster.
    Thank you for listening. Honestly. Can't say that enough.
    Okay, how am I sitting. I'm hunching forward. The back of my spine is curved like the profile of a cereal bowl, and my shoulders are hiked up to the bottoms of my ears. Just dropped my shoulders. Heard cracks. My torso is at a 45-degree angle to my legs, roughly. Sometimes my feet get numb from poor circulation.
    I know this is "bad posture." I had a professional tell me that. AS has an ergonomics guy who visits your workstation and makes recommendations. Erg Guy observed me and I sat like this in front of him because my body doesn't make other shapes anymore. At the end, he said that I was "asking for" neck and shoulder pain. I sort of just looked at him. Like, No, dude, I am doing my job and asking for a backrest. Thanks.

Anyway, now I'm pissed at Erg Guy all over again. Every-thing he said was a joke. He said that to move more, I could walk over to my colleagues and talk to them instead of IM'ing. My deskmate was right there, and he said, "Yeah, but what if you hate everyone you work with?" Erg Guy laughed. Then, he suggested I could take the stairs more often. Yeah. As you're aware, dude, there is a floor below us called the "Sky Lobby." We are above the Sky Lobby.

You know what ergonomics is? It's a department staffed with one guy who walks around and tells you how fucked you are. You say, "Thanks for your pamphlet on how my job is killing me. What can I do?" Then Erg Guy says, "Oh, do these ten things that are totally irreconcilable with your job."

Sorry.

Ugh. I'm so sorry. Not going to cross that out though because this is actually how I think. This is actually my life. This job makes me angry. I didn't used to be like this.

Anyway, I'm not always hunched forward, now that I think about it. Sometimes I lean back reclined all the way to the point where my arms are straight and I can keep typing. It's like being on an overnight airplane flight where you have to work the whole time. I basically alternate between these all day.

Except when I get up to get coffee . . .

I take deep breaths all the way back up to HG. For once, I'm trying to manage my excitement and not panic. I bring my attention to my expanding and contracting belly, to the present moment. Slowly, my insanely good fortune dawns on me.

Learn from *Skylar*?

She is a vision of who I want to be. Her contributions to yoga aside, she's nice in person—just as giving and genuine as her feed suggests. She listened and cared, and she didn't talk as if she were on a pedestal. Of course, she's *Skylar Smith*, but I felt respected. I had dignity in a human interaction. When she opened up about her past relationship, I was touched. She'd revealed as much to a blog I'd read, but in person, I saw how it affected her. It's like we connected. I connected with another human being.

I know I've been a complete yoga shit show recently. Now, with two months left before my quit date, here Skylar appears like the answer to my prayers. *Want a yoga guide? Hi, my name is @SkylarSmithYoga*. Someone steps on my foot, and I don't even fucking care. Making progress already.

As the elevator opens to the Sky Lobby, I recognize the foot-stepper as an analyst in Industrials. We had a conversation once where he was talking about one of the partners. "That guy has it all," he said. "Great tennis game, pretty wife, good-looking kids." *Yep, that's fucking everything.* We nod.

I transition back into work mode, more refreshed than five cups of coffee could've made me. I'm almost happy as I arrive at the glass door to HG. My ID card is clipped to the waistband of my skirt, so I have to lift my hip and aim it for the wall pad in order to unlock the door. The card swings and misses. For take two, I press my pelvis to the pad and rub until I hear the unlocking sound.

On the other side of the door, Harry—an associate and former editor in chief of the *Yale Daily News*, as he tells everyone—watches me. He smirks. Is he seriously waiting for me to open the door for him? The door locks on a timer as I consider this. With my phone in one hand, and a coffee in the other, I rub my hip against the wall pad again. The door unlocks. I hold it open as Harry crosses the threshold.

"You'd make a fine doorman," he says.

"Thanks," I say.

"Want a tip?" he asks.

"No," I say. "I've got it under control."

I drop my phone. He hands it to me. "Thanks," I say.

"Don't thank me," Harry says. "You've got it under control."

God, what an asshole. My spine zips straight up. Wait—fuck. Should I write that thought down in my journal? I could put horrifying spin on it for an entry: *I had to rub my ass across the door to open it, while some guy watched. Then he made a sarcastic remark, so I thought he was an asshole.*

Back at the desk, Tripp is watching *Evil Genius*. He's on a serial killer documentary kick in order to stay awake. He just finished Netflix's *The Staircase* but said it "wasn't blood enough." Now, on one of his computer monitors, the camera zooms gradually in on a mug shot of a horrifying woman in prison clothes. I don't even know what this show is about, but she definitely killed someone. A larger Excel window in the background frames the scene.

"Ace," Tripp greets me.

"Trace," I say.

I pull a graph-paper notebook out of my top drawer—my new journal. Typically, analysts use these things to keep track of their to-dos. Some have a different notebook for every client; others keep track of all live deals in the same one. Everyone has a different system, but we all use the archaic things. Sometimes I walk around the floor with one just to look busy. It's a flag to suggest *I'm headed to a meeting* and keeps people from talking to me. Tripp says he uses one as a dream journal.

"New client?" Tripp asks.

"Sort of."

Just don't lie.

12:09 p.m.

. . . Except when I get up to get coffee.

My deskmate is watching a movie about murder.

I put my pen down. Tripp startles as a throat is slit on-screen.

Chloe and Puja stand, and Chloe waves at Tripp to follow. It's their lunchtime, just after noon. Anderson's cafeteria gives 20 percent off everything before twelve and after 1:30 p.m. in order to stagger traffic evenly across midday eating hours. I don't know how the pod fell into this ritual, but it's as if they are intentionally going right when the discounts end.

I stay put, as always. Chloe and Puja asked me to join at first, but after enough no's, they stopped. I count myself among the discount crowd because I expect to take a 75 percent pay cut next year and I've had a twenty-five-year-long lesson in saving money from Dad. So I eat during the cheaper hours, scrounge around the HG pantry fridge on weekends, and cycle strategically through three work outfits. Every so often, the pod laughs off my 1:45 p.m. lunches as a quirk. Tripp still asks me every day if I want anything. I never really do, except one time I asked him for a fucking break and he got me a Kit Kat bar.

"Need anything?" Tripp asks.

"Nah."

"*Bueno*," he says.

They leave.

They return with their food. Chloe pulls the plastic lid off a chopped salad. God, I'm hungry. Normally, I pack a snack from home. *Right*.

Trixie walks past the pod as if she sensed my self-judgment from across the floor. She looks particularly uppity today in a light-pink cardigan with every button fastened. A few days ago, I said hey to her in the hallway by accident. In response, she pointed to the snag in my pantyhose and called it a "nice hooker rip." She said this with as much judgment as if she had caught me rubbing my keyboard up and down inside my dress pants while softly moaning expletives. I am afraid of my own assistant. I don't say hey now as she passes.

A blue rectangle materializes suddenly at the bottom right of one of my computer screens. It's an email from our manager, Jason Chase.

From: Jason Chase
To: Allegra Cobb
Thu 9 Nov 12:34 p.m.

Allegra, could you swing by?

Jason has one refrain: *Could you swing by?* It means that he is about to assign you to a new client and, depending on what transaction we are trying to push, an unknown amount of additional work. Getting put on a new company is called getting "staffed," and the manager is the "staffer."

"Jason needs me," I say.

"Ha," Chloe enunciates. "Then you'd better 'swing by.'"

"Thanks," I say.

"Ha," she repeats.

Is she incapable of actually laughing?

"Fuck dat," Tripp says.

"No, just fuck him," Puja says. "Then he won't staff you."

"*What?*" I ask, shocked.

"I said—" Puja starts.

"No, please, no," I say. "Tripp, can you tell me a joke or something?"

"Looks like we need a game," Tripp says. "One of our men is injured." He lights up and snaps both of his hands into thumb-and-index-finger guns. "I got it," he says. "Let's do Whose Life Sucks Most?"

I make a gag face.

"Shut it," he says. "You think your life sucks because you have to do something for your fucking job that you get paid for? Yeah, fucking right."

"I'll go first," Chloe says. "My job right now is literally to turn a PDF slide deck for an egg freezing company into a PowerPoint slide deck."

"God, is that it?" I ask.

"Yeah, no dice," Tripp says.

Chloe gawks to suggest, *What could be worse?* But I can guess where she's coming from. Chloe will join the über-elite KKR private equity group next year, where she will churn out financial models nonstop. Until she got the offer last fall, she wore KKR blinders. I was working alone at the pod one Sunday when she sat down, printed a hundred copies of her résumé, and then left without saying a word. Now she wants to learn as many technicals as possible before she starts. That means build as many financial models as she can. A task requiring her to resize shapes is going to feel like a waste.

"Puja?" Tripp prompts.

"Last night," Puja says, "I stayed until three a.m. because I had to add historicals for this model I'm building, and Research didn't have anything. So I had to pull everything manually from the filings back to 2005. Then I'm leaving, and I get into a taxi, and the driver was Indian and he starts lecturing me on how working for Anderson meant I wasn't siding with 'our people.'"

"Dayum," Tripp says.

"*Then*, this morning," she continues, "I had to spend thirty minutes with compliance because they surveilled my emails, and I'm not allowed to use the word *clusterfuck* when talking about a deal and, *apparently*, I said this deal I'm on is a clusterfuck ten times last night. And I've officially gained seven pounds since I've started here. Seven."

Holy shit, she went all in on this round. Get this girl a fucking trophy.

On top of all of that, Puja doesn't even want to be in this group. Her first choice had been for Consumer & Retail (CRG), an entirely separate industry, because "I love fashion." But, after extensive interviewing, her only offer was into Healthcare, one of the least popular groups. She only took the position because no reasonable person turns down Anderson. Now her most recent client sells colon cancer diagnostics. As Puja puts it, "I wanted Dolce. They gave me shit."

"You look great," Chloe says. "Really."

"Compliance can't touch me," Tripp says.

I roll my eyes. Tripp says he's too much of a celebrity for compliance to surveil him, all because of his one minute on *NYC Elite*. He messaged me on Anderson's internal instant messenger, "ASIM," the other day saying, *I am invinsible.* I asked, *You mean, invisible or invincible?* He said, *I mean in-vins-ible.*

"Compliance touches everyone," I say.

"Oh, you nasty," Tripp says. "Okay, it's my turn." He rolls up his sleeves with deliberately dramatic slowness. "I'm going to win this one."

"This isn't the kind of thing you want to win," I say.

"Shameless trash talk," he says. "You're a savage."

"Ha," Chloe says.

"I, as a twenty-nine-year-old, have to create a management presentation for a twenty-five-year-old client who has already graduated summa cum laude from Harvard and from Yale Law School, has become a partner at a hedge fund, and started his own company that he is going to sell for a billion dollars," Tripp says. "I was here until three thirty working on some other shit, and then right before I left, my analyst messaged me by accident that 'Tripp is such shit,' when he meant to message his buddy."

"Get out," Puja says. "Which analyst?"

"Mitch," Tripp says.

"Who's Mitch?" I ask.

"The one who went into a seizure last month," Tripp says. "So then I get home, and I wanted to watch a little TV to decompress. I tried to torrent *Pirates of the Caribbean* and accidentally downloaded a porno, like a huge-budget one, and it was way better than I thought it would be. Anyway, because my body clock is so fucked from this job, I watched the whole thing and only slept about an hour."

How are those fucking frozen eggs now, Chloe?

"Wow," Puja says.

"Beat that, A," Tripp says.

"No," I say. "You win."

"See?" he says. "Now go get staffed like a fuckin' champ."

I grab my yoga journal as I leave the pod. I will keep all notes in one book today—notes for AS, notes for Skylar—to keep suspicion to a minimum, and will type my baseline later. Armed, I walk the short trip to Jason's. He spots me through his all-glass office wall and waves me inside, smiling. I sit at his two-person round table.

"Hi, Jason."

"Hello, you," he says.

Like Skylar, Jason has resting smile-face. Unlike Skylar's, his is not a joyful smile. It's more of an *I'm sorry, please don't hate me* grin that makes him likable despite the fact that his only job is to assign work, usually a massive amount of it, due ASAP. Jason and I don't interact in any other capacity. I swing by, he names a new company for me to service forever, and then I leave.

Staffing HG can't take that much time for Jason, though. It's an office riddle: *What does Jason do all day?* Sometimes he just sits at his desk looking fucking un-busy as shit. We've spitballed theories at the pod. I've said he occupies himself by keeping his desktop from going to screen saver with carefully timed wrist flicks. It's considered an act of service for a VP to be the staffer for a year. Tripp says he would do it for half what they pay Jason.

"How are you doing?" Jason asks.

"Never better," I say.

Everyone here has to be high-energy and positive. Your attitude is rated by a group of higher-ups, and the lower your score,
the lower your bonus. One second-year analyst, Kim Jee, worked
his ass off last year, clocking a legendary number of hours on
headlining deals, only to get stiffed on his bonus because he never
smiled. A second-year analyst like me will receive a bonus of
somewhere between $70K to $120K depending on, among other
things, how euphoric I act as Jason continues to ruin my life.

"Great," he says. "I have a new company for you."

"Fantastic."

"Titan," he says. "Do you know it?"

"Yes, of course."

It's huge.

"There's absolutely nothing to do right now—we just want to
put the company on your radar," Jason says. "There may be a
meeting coming up in the next couple of weeks." He continues to
smile. "The associate on the team is Tripp Thompson. Vivienne
Wood is the senior VP, and Mark Swift is the MD."

Be cool. Becoolbecoolbecoolbecool.

"Swift," I parrot. "Haven't worked with him before."

"He's been with the client for years on the equity capital markets
side," Jason says. "I'm sure you two will enjoy working together."

Titan is an enormous managed care company. It makes about
$100 billion per year by reducing clients' healthcare costs. The
bigger the company, the bigger the deal, and bankers get paid
according to deal size. So Anderson will do a lot more free work
for them because we expect that goodwill to come back to us in
the form of zillions of fucking dollars when they buy, sell, or
restructure epic amounts of shit. Making this the second time I
have been fucked today.

I leave Jason's office. I don't think I can be mature about this. Mark heard me moan and whisper horrible, whorish things. He orgasm-grunted on me. I gagged with him in my mouth. I know the angles he saw me from (and I seriously don't look good from those). He went down on me, and I wasn't prepared for that, aesthetically. Show me an analyst who gets waxed regularly. I spend my whole analyst career here basically invisible to senior management, and now the one MD I want to avoid is on Titan with me.

I crumple into my office chair at a sideways momentum, so that it rolls into Tripp's chair like a bumper car.

"Welcome back," he says. "How'd it go?"

"Titan," I say.

"Noice," he says. "What do they do?"

"You're *on* it," I say.

"Oh, right, *Tetris*," he says.

"*Titan*," I say.

Tripp mouths the syllables until the lightbulb goes off. "Oh, *right*," he says. "But nothing's happening on Titan. Why are you freaking out?"

I force an unnatural laugh and straighten a stack of papers—old printouts covered with handwritten comments—that did not need to be straightened. I end up just pushing the stack into a left-leaning slant. I pull out my phone and check Instagram for some sanity-saving distraction. Skylar has posted a new photo with the caption, "Fall in love with taking care of yourself." *Oh my God, Skylar, please save me.*

"You guys hear about the new MD?" Puja asks. I scroll through the feed a bit faster.

"Yeah," Chloe and Tripp say at the same time.

"I'm on *Tetris* with him," Tripp says.

"*Titan,*" I say.

"Right," he says. "What'd I say?"

"Literally nothing," I say.

"I did an IPO with him last year," Chloe says. I scroll through Instagram even faster, until the square pictures form a continuous blur of color. "We were meeting in his office to go over some deck, and he sat at the head of the table and pumped some forearm-muscle-squeezer thing the whole time." She shakes her head. "I just remember thinking, *What a dick.*"

"I should get one of those," Tripp says.

"Throughout the whole meeting, he just kept pumping," Chloe says. "He must be obsessed with his body."

"You mean like Hubert?" Tripp asks. A laugh ripples across our pod. Hubert is a VP of investment banking lore. The story goes that, one day, this Hubert just stopped showing up to work and did everything remotely. He was on track to be fired, but that took a while because the administrative process of actually letting him go was bureaucratic and slow. After a few months, he returned to the office looking like an Olympian. Fat Hubert had been spending his days at SoulCycle, the indoor cycling studio. Now he is a SoulCycle instructor, and, as the legend goes, he looks fantastic.

"Hubert isn't real," Puja says.

"You don't know that," Tripp says.

"God, you're an idiot," Chloe says.

"So," I segue, "do you know anything else about this Mark?"

"Or Vivienne Wood?" Tripp asks.

"Tripp, you are on a team with her," I say. "You know her."

"Do you know how much shit I have on my plate?" Tripp asks. "You're lucky I even remember *your* name."

You don't.

"Well, guess we're about to find out," Tripp says, tapping my computer screen with his pen. A new message flashes in the bottom corner of my monitor. It's Vivienne's welcome email, a standard send-out from the MD or VP to any new team members. In this particular one, she notifies us of a meeting in one hour in Mark's office. Leaning very far left and using my keyboard, Tripp finger-pecks off a response to say that we will be there.

My baseline journal sits on my lap, daring me to add an honest update. *What's going on now, Allegra?* Well, right now, I'm remembering Mark's left hand on my shoulder and his right hand on my hip as I stood folded at the waist over the counter of his kitchenette. He did this weird thing where he drew a circle around my hip bone with his index finger and asked in a low voice if I liked that, and I totally did *not* but didn't say anything, because the rest was so good. Now that creepy hip bone circle is replaying in my head like a movie I can't unsee. Fuck, why do guys suck at dirty talk?

chapter 5

2:04 p.m.

Yep, this is a new low. Sitting in the office of the MD I slept with last night. We will be working together. He is late to our meeting.

    Don't want to look at anyone or anything in this room. Barely even looked at this VP when we met. Registered that she is some extremely pale, black-haired woman with a British accent. This is a "welcome meeting" she says, but honestly, she is the most unfriendly person I have ever met. Her last review must have told her to have better people skills or something.

    Waiting for the wrecking ball to hit.

    The air conditioner is loud.

Vivienne, Tripp, and I sit waiting for Mark in his office. Vivienne has twice assured us that he is coming. I journal and imagine him slicking his hair back with sink water from the men's bathroom and thinking about all the fun he's going to have innuendo-ing me at every meeting. *Thanks for being flexible on such short notice.*

But I doubt that'll happen—we'll probably do what MDs and analysts always do: ignore the shit out of each other.

My eyes stay squarely on the journal page in front of me.

"Team," Mark greets us as he enters.

My pen tears a small rip through the page.

Be calm, Allegra. Do not fucking emote.

"Hello, Mark," Vivienne says with the warmth of an ice cube. "Thank you so much for being available. I just wanted to get the team together for a brief hello. Not sure if everyone has worked together before."

"Okay," Mark says.

I hear Mark wheel himself to the head of the table.

"You with us, A?" Tripp asks.

I sense the attention on me like a spotlight and force myself to raise my head. Smile. Look at Vivienne, Tripp, and—Mark.

Now I see it. Glinting beneath fluorescent ceiling lights, the golden band is unmissable: Mark's wedding ring. *Wedding ring.* Wife symbol. What another woman has implicitly inscribed with the warning *Don't even fucking think about it.*

Looking around, I realize I am surrounded. Scattered among the deal toys covering every surface are silver-framed pictures of Mark with a glamorous brunette woman and children. And. Children. Well, that is fucking news. Pictures of them are every-where. I face a wall of portraits: photograph after photograph of the wife being waist-hugged by Mark on a European street corner, a Mediterranean beach, and in some Versailles-esque garden where he is in a tux and she is in a wedding dress with a train the size of an actual train. The two toddlers in their Christmas card—this is a family.

I zone back into my journal and add a line for Skylar.

2:05 p.m.

FYI that MD is someone's ~~husband~~ STET and dad.

I usually don't indulge in *woe is me* thinking—"You are the CEO of your own damn life," as Dad says—but come *on*. I have a one-night stand in good conscience, and now this? I had no idea he has a family. My thinking was, *Yeah. You. Anything. Now. Yoga studio? Middle-aged? I could be murdered? Let's fucking go. Take my clothes off.*

"Allegra, Tripp, have you met?" Vivienne asks.

"Yaw," Tripp says.

It's "nah," in "yes" form.

"We sit next to each other," I say.

"How lucky is she?" he asks.

No one answers.

"Let's do a round of introductions," Vivienne suggests. "In the spirit of HG's culture of a personal touch."

"Sure, of course," Mark says.

Is this personal-touch thing a joke? I've never seen this woman in my life, Tripp thinks we're in a *Tetris* meeting, and this morning, Mark and I literally said, *Goodbye now,* after fucking. Mark's unfocused eyes sweep the room without settling on any one of us. The stiff distance of his gaze echoes his sparse apartment: bare and unfurnished. It is convincingly as if we are strangers.

An expectant silence.

"I'll start," Mark says. "Name, school, hometown work for everyone? Mark, Yale, Riverdale, New York City."

"Hi," I say. "I'm Allegra. Princeton. From Princeton."

"Vivienne. Harvard. London."

"I'm Tripp," says Tripp. Somewhere, a whirring record wobbles itself slower and slower until a new pace entirely has been set, and it continues at half speed. "Went to Duke, go Blue Devils. Born and raised in Newport, Rhode Island. Went to St. George's for prep. Great surf scene."

"Great, moving on," Mark says. "This should be painless. Nothing to be done at the moment. Absolutely nothing. Titan has a board meeting next week—we are not presenting—and there may be some work coming out of that." He shrugs. "That, I believe, is the exhaustive update."

"They will be here for the conference tomorrow, too," Vivienne says.

Oh God. I know where this is going. She means the annual Anderson Shaw Healthcare Conference, attended by all large market cap companies. Last year, the staffer made all analysts sit in the back row to make it look oversubscribed, or interesting, or something.

"Yes, they will," Mark says. He is now looking at his phone.

"It might be a good idea to be prepared with a book of materials for Titan," Vivienne says. "Just in case you happen to get a few minutes with the CEO or the CFO. Then you'll have something to discuss."

Mark shrugs.

No, Vivienne. Stop.

"Honestly, I'm not sure I'll have any time with them," Mark says.

"We're happy to put something together," Vivienne says.

His office line rings. He spins round to answer, waving us out of the office. "Yes, my dear?" he asks into the receiver.

I am the other kind of dear: in headlights.

*   *   *

Judging by her initiative in Mark's office, Vivienne is very clearly trying to make MD. And judging by her people skills, she very clearly never will be. Senior vice president was a title invented for people too experienced to be VPs but missing intangible qualities needed for the next level. MDs deal mostly with clients, and that means you need softer skills and good relationships, not just technicals. Vivienne does not seem to get this. She may think she can be too productive *not* to promote, as if she can climb her way to the top on a stairway of unrequested decks. *Great.*

Tripp and I sit at the round marble table in her office with our open notebooks at the ready. My seat gives me a view through her glass walls right into Mark's office, where I watch him pack papers into a floppy brown leather briefcase. Headed home to the family.

"How are your other teams?" Vivienne asks.

"Busy," I say honestly.

"Great, so for the Titan materials," she says, "let's brainstorm?"

"Fantastic," Tripp says.

Mark exits his office and strides past us. I use my pen to write nonwords until he is out of sight. Meanwhile, Vivienne rattles off a list of possible topics for the completely unnecessary book of materials in an uninhibited stream of consciousness. Is she playing finance word association? I don't think I could recite the alphabet this quickly. My bottom-of-the-totem-pole muscle—which runs between my index finger tip and wrist—actually cramps as I scribe.

First, she wants an update on the economy. She starts spitting out titles for the slides we will present—such as "High M&A

Volumes"—which means, *Find the data to support that conclusion.*
Vivienne also wants to show how well the managed-care industry has done, using stock price charts. And the more she talks,
the more words she thinks of. She's pulling tasks out of a Mary
Poppins bag of shit for me to do instead of sleep. And Tripp is
"You bet!"-ing her every word. Now she wants slides on "strategic
alternatives," whose name is almost as specific as silence itself.
Turns out that means merger analyses with companies Titan
might want to buy. She runs down the list of names.

"Wait, those are all private companies, right?" I ask.

"Yes," Vivienne says. "So, because they don't publish financial
statements, you might have to do a little bit of digging."

Yeah, as in my grave.

"Oh, and one last thing," Vivienne says. "I have to attend a
closing dinner with clients tonight and then an event for the
Anderson Women's Group until about midnight, but then I can
send comments."

5:27 p.m.

*Soooooooooo . . . For a company that doesn't need any materi-
als, prepare a full book that they probably won't ever see. Include
merger analyses, some with made-up numbers. You just found
out about it now, but do it immediately, and let's check in at
midnight—before you spend the rest of the night on this.*

"Absolutely," Tripp says.

chapter 6

Finished another coffee.

For the record, I don't even know what I look like anymore. I just zoned out and my screen saver went to black. Then I stared at my reflection like, What the fuck? Me? I squinted. Couldn't believe it. Looks like I was wind-tunneled.

We are seconds from sending the deck to Vivienne at 11:30 p.m. I paste my merger model outputs into the PowerPoint file. Now, it's Tripp's turn to add his.

Imminently, Tripp and I will pick up our second dinner in the Sky Lobby and wait for Vivienne's comments. Every book that leaves Anderson is supposed to be formatted the same way: same color palette, font size, number of decimal places, and align the shit out of it. I have pulled all-nighters just reformatting, but Tripp cares less than most about it and about checking his analysts' work. This is part of why we get along—I want to leave the industry, and Tripp has what he calls "perspective."

Finally, Tripp adds his half and skims the full deck like it's an electronic flip-book before attaching it in an email to Vivienne. He signs the email "Aloha, Tripp" and forgets to add my name. We head down to pick up our food.

"You bringing your diary?" Tripp asks.

"No," I say.

Obviously he noticed.

"Tryna cope with the bullshit?" he asks.

"Actually, yes," I say. "Thanks for breakfast, by the way."

Tripp ordered us each a full eggs-bacon-and-pancakes breakfast. The rule is that Anderson will buy its bankers dinner every night up to twenty-five dollars, and then another twenty-five dollars' worth of food if you stay after midnight. But the aftermidnight rule is gray and you can only take advantage of it if you have a good relationship with your assistant. Tripp can buy whatever he wants because his assistant, Clarita, thinks she's always one personal favor away from taking him home. Clarita is forty-something and divorced. She baked him a chocolate cake for his birthday, which she has not done for anyone else. She says he is "so full of life."

"I have a question for you," Tripp says in the Sky Lobby.

"Shoot," I say.

I open Instagram, where Skylar's picture from this morning reminds me, "Fall in love with taking care of yourself." One day, I fucking will. The photo shows her meditating with her legs in lotus and her eyes closed. She smiles so warmly that I actually feel better just seeing this photo. *Like.*

I scroll through her profile and stop on one of her more touching posts from a few weeks ago. The video is of her doing a vinyasa flow in her kitchen. The caption:

@SkylarSmithYoga: I was shy, quiet

Spent most of my time alone

I just found it hard to relate. I was in my head.

Dreaming, thinking, doubting, feeling different.

Not at ease, I didn't belong. Not good enough.

Comparing.

Then I found yoga.

I was comfortable in yoga classes because it was

individual—but in a group. It made it easier to be with others.

"The wound is the place

where the light enters you." —Rumi

My struggles to form relationships helped me

appreciate connection. The connections I found in the studio.

I was deeply without, so now I savor.

I've built a life around helping other people.

"Love is the water of life.

Drink it down with heart and soul." —Rumi

However you choose to connect,

Spread love.

Love, Skye

I've already read the comments thread, where hundreds of people tell stories about when they felt like an outsider. It's a great post.

We enter the cafeteria, next to the Sky Lobby.

"One sec," he says.

We part ways to pick up our food. The cafeteria transforms every night after 8 p.m. The dozens of food stations—pizza, Mediterranean, sushi, chopped salad—are packed away, and the crowds are gone. Takeout plastic bags cover every surface, sorted by last name. I grab mine from the "A–C" section and scroll through the rest of my Instagram feed, which is filled with yoga.

Tripp and I reunite at the elevator bank.

"Your question?" I prompt.

"Right," he says. "So, where are you going after bonuses? Chloe was bugging me about it again today."

"Oh really," I say.

"Yeah, you're the only one she can't nail down," he says.

"No one knows about Puja, either," I say.

He gives me a *come on* look. Everyone knows Puja has been buy-side recruiting for two full years and doesn't have an offer yet, while almost all other second-years have jobs waiting for them. It's late in the cycle for her not to know where she's going. The longer before you lock down your exit, the more likely it is that you haven't made the cut.

"Anyway, I told Chloe I don't know," he says.

"Are you asking for *you*, or are you asking for Chloe?" I ask.

I eye him to say, *I'm onto you.* He surrender-palms me.

"I'm just starting drama," he says.

I laugh. I've considered telling the pod my plan, but the idea still makes me squirm. Admitting to my yoga dreams would be admitting that I'm abandoning these people on every level. Like, *Hey, see you in Aspen this March? "Not fucking happening." Want to join me at the Lobster Club? "How about no, no to your entire lifestyle, forever, starting now."* People refer to the jobs after banking as "exit options," but yoga is truly an escape, once and for all. I'm not as close with Chloe and Puja, but for some reason, I can't even tell Tripp. Goodbyes are tough.

"Chloe thinks you're doing a start-up in stealth mode," he says. "And that's why you won't say."

"Does she just gossip about me when I'm not there?" I ask.

"Nah," he says. "You're not that interesting."

"You really are starting drama, huh?" I say.

"*Obviously*," he says.

With bonuses approaching, the pod took bets last week on the order in which people would quit. I was in a meeting. Tripp told me that Chloe bet I would quit first because I have a "foot-out-the-door vibe." Apparently, I "get my shit done" but "there's a distance" to me. On the other end of the spectrum, everyone knows Tripp isn't quitting at all. Associates don't have as massive an exodus, anyway, and Tripp says he'll stick it out here until he meets a woman who will pay for his lifestyle. He wants to be a househusband so that he can work on his body all day.

"Fine, fine," he says. "I'll lay off."

I don't know how much longer I can avoid the question, though. We stop at the HG vending machine so he can buy Twizzlers.

"Twizzlers?" I ask. "How old are you?"

"Sree," he says.

He holds up two and a half fingers.

12:47 a.m.

The backstory with my dad is that he and I are very close. I've seen your posts with your Mom and Rosie, so I think you know where I'm coming from. Just that family is core to who we are. Idk. I think you said that once.

Just got a text from him. Thinking about home.

I put my pen down.

Dad's text: Do today what others won't, so tomorrow you do what others can't.

It's one of his winner's-mind-set phrases for me to apply to my job. The last he sent before that was Success requires sacrifice. Dad and I text or email every day, but we don't talk much by phone. Last time we really touched base, his latest idea was to write a daily summary of the markets, circulate it as an email newsletter around the block for a dollar, and grow that fee over time. He had the same idea a few years ago, and I made him a template to use in Word, but nothing ever came of it. I don't know how much time he spends trading every day, but I get the sense he watches more and more sports alone.

I've been planning how to tell Dad that I will quit. My best idea is to appeal to his appreciation of strength. He would never want me to take shit from anyone. Meanwhile, my job requires I wear a bitch mask 24/7. I say, *Yes, amazing*, to every absurd request. Analysts have to accept every assignment without question at any time of day, even if they are on the train to go to a funeral, which I know because it actually happened to Puja.

I have been collecting stories like that for when I finally break him the news. In March, for example, an MD asked me by email to drive for three hours one way during HG's annual ski trip in Jackson Hole so that I could take a picture of a client's storefront. He wanted to use that photo in a presentation. So I did. On the way back, it started to snow. In the end, the MD didn't use the photo. *Dad, do you see this isn't actually who you want me to be? Can't we do better than this?*

As I rehearse for the heart-to-heart, though, I know I'm avoiding the real issue. The real issue isn't how I will *deliver* the news to Dad, it's how the news will *change* our relationship. I don't know how to prepare for that part—what we have is fragile and a little awkward, but family is family, and I cherish it all the same. For now, I keep collecting anecdotes. It feels like I'm working toward something.

Vivienne calls Tripp at 1 a.m. Since we sent her the deck, we got caught in the dead zone known as "waiting for comments." People complain about bankers' hours, but what they don't usually say is that the hours are not correlated with amount of work. Even if you have no work, you can't leave the office before 9 p.m. unless you want to be ridiculed for having a bedtime or acting like an MD.

By now, Tripp has undone the top buttons on his dress shirt, and a few associates have gone home for the night. Behind us, two analysts take turns on an MD's putter, practicing their short game on one of the Styrofoam cups from the pantry. Apparently, whoever gets fewer balls in the cup has to take the SATs next weekend and publish the new score on his LinkedIn.

"Hey, Viv, how's it going?" Tripp asks.

"Hi, Vivienne," I fawn.

"Yes," she says. Partyish voices sound in the background. "Sorry, I've been tied up at the Women's Group event."

We get it. You have more important things to do than this assignment that you completely made up.

"No problemo," Tripp says.

"I have some comments," she says, crisp as winter. Tripp pretends to shiver, rubbing his hands up and down his biceps and mouthing *brrr*. That's funny. I would pound his fist if we weren't so deeply afraid.

Vivienne proceeds to comment so extensively as to dictate an entirely new and equally absurd, unrequested assignment. We did exactly as she asked; she just changed her mind. Vivienne wants us to use a different peer set for the stock price comparison and benchmarking charts, and then compute new merger analyses with CVS and Walmart.

Those mergers would be enormous and ridiculous, but they may encourage Titan to think about buying gigantic shit, and then we can all get paid more. I fall silent, but Tripp is enduringly positive and responds, "Awesome," "Sensational," and, "Brilliant." Vivienne ends with, "Thanks, team," before the line, like my morale, is suddenly dead.

"How does she live with herself?" Tripp asks. "Every day, she looks in the mirror, and she has to know, *I am Vivienne. I am this person.*"

"Hey," Chloe snaps.

"Oh my God, what?" Tripp asks.

"Are you only criticizing her because she's a woman?" Chloe asks.

Tripp rolls his head in an *I-can't-win* figure eight around his neck. To answer her, he points at the raised outlet on his desk, where his iPhone charger used to be. A half-eaten bag of Twizzlers now occupies the space.

"No, I don't want a Twizzler," Chloe says.

"I do," Puja says.

Tripp points again, calling attention to the fact that Vivienne asked to borrow his charger before she left for the closing dinner. She plopped it in her Louis Vuitton bag and took the fuck off.

"She stole my phone charger," Tripp says. He bites into another Twizzler and hands one to Puja. "Phone. *Charger.*"

"I'm working now," Chloe says.

"Whatever," he says. "I literally hate all of my VPs."

Tripp and I once sorted the HG VPs into categories of Douche, Double Douche, and Evil on a whiteboard in an MD's office one night. He thought this was so funny that he ASIMed me a picture of the list *for ya records*. I had to snap at him, *Compliance literally surveils everything, Tripp*. He ASIMed me, *In-vins-ible*.

"I mean, Will?" Tripp continues. "Asshat. Nick? Total asshat. Jim? Asshat. Viv? Asshat. She doesn't get special treatment." Chloe is absorbed in work again, but Tripp is happy at the chance to talk. "Quick follow-up question for you. So, French Revolution, did you feel bad for Louis the Fourteenth? Just curious."

"You don't understand the social context of working women," Chloe says.

"Obviously. The last time I touched a woman was months ago."

"So, Tripp, do you want to do Walmart?" I ask.

"Kill me now," he says.

"Tripp?" I ask.

The lull that follows is good for productivity.

Meanwhile, I side silently with Tripp. Hating VPs is a way of life. Cartooning the shit out of them is a form of therapy and frankly, other viewpoints wouldn't even make sense. Who would act this way? A human being? Not possible. So I imagine Vivienne showing 0.0 emotional response to ASPCA commercials and then having long talks with her four-hundred-dollar-an-hour psychologist about feeling empty. Chloe shakes her head randomly, as if she is still deeply offended by our lack of empathy for female investment bankers. But I know where Tripp is coming from. It's survival: Vivienne stole Tripp's phone charger, and Dad didn't raise a wimp.

*   *   *

4:10 a.m.

Finished another Skittles.

4:12 a.m.

Neck and shoulder pain.

"Will you quit your fucking diary entries?" Tripp asks.

I lay my pen down, parallel to the edge of my notebook. Tripp, Chloe, and I are the last three on the floor. Tripp mouths the words of his email to himself as he proofreads before finally hitting send. Meanwhile, Chloe's Excel shortcuts pitter-patter like rain. She's been pulling all-nighters for the past week on some $17 billion deal team, per her broadcasts.

I type my journal entries for Skylar. The novella is littered with junk food, sarcasm, and some tortured lusting for my boss—to the tune of, *I want him, I hate myself, I want him, I hate myself*—wrapping up only now, just after 4 a.m. I imagine Skylar opening the email while in lotus on her yoga mat, well rested and sipping ginger tea, dropping her mug lower with every additional anecdote. She thought I would be a quick fix, but I might have to start paying her. I can't afford her. Fuck. I'm self-conscious to reveal the shitstorm of my life to someone I respect but having *the* Skylar Smith as a mentor is too good to pass up.

I email the journal and stand.

"See you tomorrow," I tell Chloe.

"Later," she says. Her darting fingers draw attention to her nails, which are painted whitish pink. The color is chipped but nice. Getting that far on the continuum of physical presentation is frankly astounding. She's even wearing mascara.

"Nice mascara," I say.

"Thanks," she says.

"Who makes it?" I ask, out of curiosity.

"I forget," she says.

Right. She cares way too much about labels not to know.

"That's too bad," I say.

"You have a great face for makeup, you know," she says.

As I leave, I get the distinct impression that this is not a fucking compliment. *Thanks a lot, Chloe,* I imagine telling her. *Oh yeah, and I am going to a start-up in stealth mode after all. Our niche is outbidding KKR on every deal they ever fucking do.*

chapter 7

trudge to work four hours later, screening emails as I walk. My world is the size of an index card. I thumb out another *Will do.*

No one is staffed on only one company at once. Vivienne aside, I have five other psychos suddenly needing shit from me yesterday. Their projects include two deals—one, selling a company, and the other, issuing debt—and three industry updates. On one of my industry update teams, the guy in the associate role has turned over three times since we started working with the client a year ago. *Incredible* personal touch.

I stop beside the pretzel food cart that faces Anderson and wait for the light to turn. The stand is almost as much of a monument as the headquarters itself. The owner is always fucking here, and it's winter. I would wave, say hello, or *something,* but his bad attitude is as legendary as his cart's constant presence. He is sour and randomly spiteful.

I cross the street. Allegedly, I have one new personal email. I follow the alert to see if it's spam or a subscription leftover from college. Turns out a girl from Princeton High School emailed me for advice in deciding between Princeton, Harvard, and Yale. "Did

Princeton feel small?" she writes. Oh my God, I do not have time for this. If she can get into all three, she can figure that the fuck out while I devote all mental resources toward saving my own ass.

Another personal email arrives—from Skylar. She writes that she has so many thoughts in response to my journal, and that I can call, text, or email her whenever to talk about them. Her signature gives her cell number.

I call her right away.

"Hello?" she answers.

"Hi!" I say.

"Good morning," she says. She clears her throat. "Allegra?"

"Yes," I say. "Sorry, you said I could call."

"I did, of course," she says.

"Chop, chop."

I laugh.

"So, am I fucked or what?" I ask.

"Excuse me?" she asks.

God. "Right," I say. "I'm sorry."

She laughs.

"I mean, what did you think of the journal?"

"There was so much in there," she says. "Do you want to talk in person? Over the phone feels so impersonal."

"Okay," I say. "Tonight?"

There's a pause.

"Sorry, is that too soon?" I ask.

"Not at all," she says. "But before we talk about your journal, I would suggest you do a heartfelt-desire meditation. I can send you instructions. I think this will help center you and get you back in touch with your practice!"

"Before tonight?" I ask cautiously.

"Yes," she says. "The meditation is simple. If you tried it at your desk, no one would even notice. If you don't have time, no worries, but I really encourage you to take some time to refocus on *you*. And if you have any trouble with it at all, or if any part of it is confusing, just let me know. You know where to reach me!"

"Thank you, Skylar," I say.

She laughs. "Of course! I am here to help."

I know. Thank you.

"How about nine p.m. at Yoga Mala?" she asks.

"Perfect," I say instantly.

"Okay, see you tonight," she says.

"Morning, Tripp," I greet him.

"Whatever," he says.

"How'd you sleep?" I ask.

"You mean the one hour I lay in my bed and wanted to kill myself?" he asks.

"Yeah, that one," I say.

"It was shitty," he says.

Skylar's instructions arrive by text. Her iMessage maxes out the space allotted for a preview on my home screen. Guess I need more than four rows of help. My phone buzzes again with part two as I log into my desktop. The abrupt vibrations make her texts sound like defibrillator shocks trying to save me: *Clear. Clear.*

I read her long column of advice. She writes that meditating in lotus pose is optional, thank God, so *no*. Hopefully I can do this at my desk without suggesting I'm having a mental breakdown. "Get comfortable," she writes. "Relax your face and soften your shoulders. Breathe deeply, let your eyelids rest gently, and surrender to the now. For the next ten minutes, stay open. Let your deepest desire float from the bottom of your heart to the top of your mind. It will all become clear in the stillness. What does your heart say?"

Tripp's computer chimes, sending a whiplash shock down my spine. He tilts his monitor toward me so that I can see the email.

From: Mark Swift
To: Vivienne Wood, Tripp Thompson, Allegra Cobb
Fri 10 Nov 9:12 a.m.

Tx. Cut pages after macro and print 2 copies

—MS

Awesome. He wants a two-slide deck, and we basically gave him a novel. Almost at the exact same time, Tripp gets another alert, which we watch hit him in real time. It's Jason asking him to "swing by."

"This is oppressive," Tripp says. "I'm going to rebel."

"Do it," I urge.

"I will," he says. "I'm going to pee in the fucking corner."

Tripp leaves.

Okay, calm down. What do I want more than anything else?

I try to be as still as possible while the office warms up into daytime attack mode around me. It's not ideal, but there's no such thing as perfect. As I wait, what comes to mind is: Mark's last email. There was nothing special in there. In fact, it was so standard that a template for it could have come right out of an MD starter pack: *Skip the hello, abbreviate shit, and request or delete a massive amount of work.*

Fuck. He knew where to touch me. Before Mark, the last person

I had sex with was a pear-shaped man named Hillary—*Hillary*—two
months ago. We met on Hinge. Hillary wore a sweatshirt covered
in dog hair to meet me, and he asked to borrow a scrunchie for
his man bun, but I was like, whatever, this will still work. Meanwhile, Mark towers over me at six foot three, broad and sculpted
down to the tendon under a power suit. I linger on thoughts of
him. I'm getting aroused.

"Are you napping?" Tripp asks.

I jolt. "No," I say.

"I forgot my bitch book," he says.

Tripp leaves again with his dream journal. I text Skylar.

Me: Thank you 🙏. I am trying.

Me: And see you tonight!!

Great. This is already a disaster. I hang my head. Someone
asks me to think of my heartfelt desire, and I daydream about
my boss. Am I that lusty? Or lonely? The final thought feels
true. Yep, lonely. Last week, someone wrong-number texted
me, and I texted back. We had a conversation. Come on. Other
than that new contact—Lisa—the list of names in my most recent
Messages history are *VERIZON MSG You're out of data, Bldg
Super, Dad,* and an automated reminder to schedule a doctor's
appointment.

I don't really want to savor the taste of failure, so I try again.
*"Take some time to refocus on you. Relax your face and soften your
shoulders. Breathe deeply. . . . Stay open. . . . What does your heart
say?"* My thoughts keep drifting back to Mark. Okay, so my heartfelt desire is Mark. *Awesome.* I try to relax. Noises fade. A bit of
stillness does emerge. My thoughts congeal, and what feels truer

than wanting Mark is a pull to have something real with another human being.

Tripp collapses into his desk chair.

"What did Jason give you?" I ask.

"Death row," he mutters.

My phone buzzes. It's Skylar with instructions for the *so hum* meditation, which entails I repeat *so* on the inhale and *hum* on the exhale. *So hum* means "I am that," and it's a way to ask yourself who you are. I am explaining to Skylar that I will try my best, thank you again—and hopefully she can feel I'm sincere—when Outlook flashes a calendar alert on my left screen. A Team Titan meeting has just been scheduled to take place in Mark's office in two minutes. Vivienne stands beside me without warning or noise. She is the Ghost of Meetings Now.

"Now," she says.

"Absolutely," Tripp says.

I hold up a *one second* finger, which Vivienne regards with as much horror as if it were the middle finger. She walks off, and Tripp follows in her wake with a notebook. I finish my text to Skylar and proofread it as Tripp and Vivienne turn the corner. Their absence is an amplifying demand to join them.

Skylar: All is well

Skylar: Do what you can with what you have, where you are

Thank you, Skylar.

I grab my Titan notebook and speed-walk into Mark's office, where the team waits. Tripp's sleeves are rolled up to reveal grizzly, Viking-thick arm hair. Vivienne sits straight in a black pencil dress. Her dark bun of hair is pulled tighter than usual. The lights on the table's conference phone flash green to signal that someone—Mark—is on the line.

"Allegra, where were you?" Vivienne demands.

"I was—" I start.

"This is a fifty-billion-dollar client," she says. "This takes priority."

Tripp snaps his pen, which he's twirling in a circle with his index finger and thumb. I sit to Vivienne's right, straight across from him. Through the glass wall, I have a good view of Jason, who is doing absolutely fucking nothing at his desk.

"Is everyone here now?" Mark's voice asks.

Vivienne leans toward the speakerphone.

"Yes," she says.

"So I spoke to Dan"—the CFO—"and apparently they have been talking to Sierra regarding a potential merger," Mark says. He talks fast. "The CEOs got together, and they estimated billions in synergies. They want to introduce the idea to the board at the meeting next week."

Impossible.

Tripp stops twirling his pen. Sierra is another managed care company worth about $30 billion. The fees due to Anderson if this deal went through would be enormous. Senior people are paid in accord with group performance. An MD like Mark, making 5 percent of the group's revenue each year, could make $5 million from this deal alone. This just became my most important team.

"Dan wants a merger analysis with Sierra for the board meeting next week," Mark says. "Their meeting will take place over two days in Arizona. I'd like to be able to brief and prep Dan in advance. I leave Monday, so I'll need the materials by Monday morning. I hope none of you had weekend plans."

"Of course," Vivienne says. "We'll start right away."

I almost roll my eyes at her use of the word *we*.

"Anything from the junior team?" Mark asks.

Is Mark talking to me? Tripp clears his throat and falls silent. His throat-clearing segued to nothing.

"Just excited to be a part of the team," I say.

"We're happy to have you, Amanda," Mark says.

"It's Allegra."

Did he actually forget? Or is he teasing me?

"Right," he says. "Have a great weekend, team."

Jason starts to circle the floor at 8:30 p.m. Most seats are still full. Because it's Friday, he looks everyone in the eye and asks when they plan to go home. He points his finger and chides us in a sort-of-serious, sort-of-kidding tone to obey Safe Saturdays.

This rule is one of the lifestyle initiatives that Anderson rolled out in order to keep fewer analysts from quitting. The rule means analysts and associates are banned from the headquarters from 9 p.m. on Friday until 6 a.m. on Sunday. In theory, this makes our weekends more predictable and allows us to make plans with other human beings. In practice, this means working from home. You are allowed in the office if you get a "pass," or written permission from the head of the group. Tonight, Team Titan has a pass, but somehow I will make time to see Skylar.

Tripp and I have been doing shit for Vivienne all afternoon. Instead of the *so hum*, I worked on a megamerger so Vivienne and Mark can buy bigger houses in the Hamptons. The more Tripp and I get into it, the more I see that this deal could be fucking enormous.

This isn't cherry-picking data for unrequested discussion materials at Vivienne's command. This is league tables. This is *WSJ*. People like Mark will give serious shits about it. This will take over everything.

So I was right to be scared by Vivienne's check-in. She summoned me with a two-word email ("my office")—what?—and invited me to sit at her round table with an index finger so straight I realized she may not have knuckles. From her office chair, she proceeded to call me "Analyst" instead of Allegra and demanded that this team be my first priority. Behind her, the broad spine of a dictionary of usage stuck out on her bookshelf. The thing was weathered, as if it had fallen into a bathtub, or she took it to the beach, or she'd read it a thousand fucking times.

"I completely understand," I said.

"If you don't, I will make a *note* of it," she threatened. I don't even know what that means, but I basically shit myself. "People don't forget a first impression, and I will *remember* this." It wasn't until I was back at my desk that I realized today was the second time I'd met her and she doesn't give a shit about me. *Analyst*. Fucking horrifying.

I was never a problem child, so this was new territory. My senior superlative in the high school yearbook was "Most Likely to Have Actually Done the Homework." I got the lead in the sixth-grade musical, not because I was talented, but because I was the only kid they could count on to memorize all of the lines.

After Vivienne released me, I felt so shitty about myself that I actually did email that Princeton High School girl back. I wrote that Princeton did not feel small and she should email me with any other questions. Five hours later, the girl hasn't said thank you. I dignified her terror of going to the wrong Ivy League school, and she can't even say *tx*.

"Hey, Allie, can I use your charger?" Tripp asks me.

"No, Vivienne," I say. "Get your own."

"Vivienne still has mine."

"She didn't return it?" I ask.

"No, she's using it to strangle puppies," Tripp says.

"Very funny," Chloe says, her tone soaking in haughty morality. She is sticking up for Vivienne at every turn, halfway to leading a Lean In circle.

"Vivienne did this on purpose," Tripp says. "She wants to isolate me socially so that I have no distractions from her comments."

"Sucks," I say.

"Can I please use it?" he asks.

Jason stands at the pod next to ours. He tells Kim Jee to head home. Kim keeps a straight face as he packs his leather Tumi briefcase.

"Tell you what," I say. "You, charger. Me, dinner?"

"Do not insanity plea out of Titan," he says slowly.

"Ugh," I say. "I will let you use my phone charger if you let me take a break for dinner. I really need this." Taking a break for dinner is like missing a day of work at another firm. People demand, *Seriously, WTF? Where were you?*

Tripp side-eyes me. "First you flip off Vivienne . . ." he says.

"Oh my God," I say.

"Now you're skipping out?" he asks. He shakes his head. His tone is light, but there's a kernel of seriousness in there. "If you are trying to make me do everything on this team, no fucking dice."

"One hour?" I beg, knowing it will probably take longer.

"Fine," he says, visibly annoyed. He shoos me away.

"Okay, see you later," I say.

"Ten p.m., and I mean it," he says.

"Okay, be back soon," I say.

I wave goodbye to the pod.

"And then there were three," Tripp mutters melodramatically.

I head for the exits a little woozy from lack of sleep, but I channel my inner Dad. *Get your shit together,* he says in my head. I add, *Sack up for yoga.*

chapter 8

O n my way to meet Skylar, in a subway car packed like a sardine tin, I realize this is my equivalent of "getting fresh air." The woman gripping the metal pole next to me applies deodorant with her free arm. As we whir around a bend, I'm pushed into her parka, which gives way beneath my weight. In more than one way, I am headed to a better place.

Meanwhile, I lose and gain service over an interval short enough that my phone stays warm. Tripp emails me that he feels "used and abruised," and I draft a reply picking up on his rhyme—"lose the bluessss"—but I delete it, because I actually do feel bad about leaving him.

Tripp belongs at cocktail parties finger-gunning with CEOs, not crunching numbers. Abandoning him at work is not like skipping out on a numbers guy who will seek out antisocial jobs, amass *fuck-you* money, and vote Republican but pro-abortion for the rest of his life because he hates people and people hate him. Tripp loves people. And I am Tripp's main social outlet for most of the day every day, so leaving him at the pod feels almost as heartless as staying in banking.

There's a selfishness to it, too. After two years of banking together, Tripp and I have passively become attached. When something funny happens to me outside of work, sometimes, my head jerks right, as if I'm about to tell him about it. Other times, I hear his voice in my head respond to things that are happening only to me. As I thought about the *so hum* prompt *I am* this afternoon, I heard Tripp finish: *I am . . . dope. I am . . . the man*. If we're having a hard time with this "dinner break," then my goodbye email is going to be a sucker punch to both of us.

Mats hang from the rafters of the trendy yoga studio known as Yoga Mala. Lights are dim, and the sound of chanting permeates the air like anesthesia. A couple of women waiting to check in massage their own shoulders. Another lounges by the wall and practices deep breathing with her eyes closed. Tonight, everyone's yoga clothes look like fucking pajamas. This is sleep porn.

"I know you probably don't," I say to the desk attendant, "but do you by any chance have any coffee?"

"No," she says, smiling elegantly.

"Yeah, I figured," I say. "What about, like, organic coffee?"

She laughs, and I pass it off as a joke.

"We have water for sale," she says.

"Fantastic," I lie.

I survey the display of snacks for anything with cacao, which has traces of caffeine. Nothing. They only sell seaweed crisps and peanut butter bars, a mix of foods that are essentially non-caloric or extremely calorie-dense. *Yin and yang*.

During new-banker training, one of the Training the Street instructors gave us tips on how to stay awake for long stretches of time. He told us, eat. When it's the middle of the night and you have to work: eat. "Have you ever fallen asleep while eating?" he asked. "Of course not. Have an apple." So, cacao or no cacao, just the act of consuming food might keep me up. I buy one of the bars and sit on the sofa next to the check-in desk. The couch sinks deeply beneath my weight like a leaky air mattress. *Mattress* . . . The word relaxes me. My field of vision halves as my eyelids droop softly. *No.* I pinch my thigh and watch an haute yogi recoil at my self-harm.

I crinkle back the wrapper on my bar and shove a couple of bites into my mouth. *Eat. Look at shit. Stay awake.* Despite the fifty-dollar-per-class overhead, Yoga Mala is tiny and decorated like an Indian tenement. Each studio has its own niche, and Mala's may be to offer the most expensive experience of poverty in the city. The walls are made of unvarnished, splintering wood. Random holes reveal exposed pipes. I've been here once before, so I know the only bathroom has a single toilet without a seat. And yet, it feels exclusive.

Frankly, this isn't my vibe. Mala—high price tag, stuffy atmosphere—is very different from the yoga studio in Princeton and from the kind of place I want to end up in. I'd prefer more warmth, less austerity, but Skylar must have her reasons. Maybe all profits go to charity, who fucking knows. On the bright side, I'll see her soon and practice, like, in the middle of a workday.

My phone chirps at me.

From: Tripp Thompson
To: Allegra Cobb
Fri 10 Nov 8:57 p.m.

Viv here. I told her you went to the bathroom. She asked if you do that a lot.

I smirk. My loud phone earns another *hmph* from the same chicly casual yogi. Classroom doors open, and women rise to file inside. A few of them might be models and walk on legs that look like long arms. I manage to stand up. I've had five cups of coffee today, and I don't know if that's too few and I'm withdrawing, or too many and I'm dehydrated.

"Allegra!" Skylar beams.

"Oh, hi!" I say.

She waves to the check-in girl and then to a beautiful, olive-skinned student wearing a tasteful white diamond necklace. Both wave back energetically—*OMG hi!!*—breaking Mala's norm of understatement.

Skylar hugs me and rubs my back. She pulls back to hold me at arm's length, one hand on each of my shoulders. We are the same height, five foot four. At least, that's how tall I was when I started this job. But Erg Guy said my lifestyle was causing daily compression of my spinal discs, so I get shorter every fucking day. Skylar wears a cropped hoodie exposing her core—abs—and pastel-blue leggings. Her rolled mat hangs diagonally on her back like a quiver, secured by a glittering silver strap across her chest.

"You look so cute!" she says.

I'm wearing a white tee and black spandex shorts.

"Thanks," I say, flattered.

Skylar tucks a strand of my hair behind one of my ears.

"It's so good to see you," she says, smiling. She hugs me again. Today aside, I can't remember the last time I hugged anyone. Human contact. "I just reread your journal on the way over." She shakes her head. "But we are here now." She rubs my upper arm. "We can practice and talk after class?"

"That would be great," I say.

We cross the classroom threshold. There are only a dozen people here in a space for thirty or more. I grab a rental mat from the stack against the wall. Skylar approaches the olive-skinned student and taps her once on the shoulder.

"Hi!" Skylar whispers.

The rest of the class is quiet. I wait, hip cocked.

"Skylar!" the woman whispers.

They hug.

"It's so good to see you," Skylar whispers.

"Thank you!" The woman's green eyes widen.

"Would you mind moving your mat over just an *inch*?" Skylar slaps the air to say, *This way*. "I'm here with a student, and we'd like to flow next to each other."

"Of course." She obliges.

"Thank you so much," Skylar says.

She smiles and gestures for me to come over. I unroll my mat next to hers as she unzips her hoodie to reveal a crocheted bra top I've seen in her feed. I actually looked into buying it online before I saw the price tag: two hundred dollars Not to-fucking-day. Skylar sits in lotus, closes her eyes, and engages in three deep breath cycles. I settle in, eager. I haven't practiced *with* someone in months, excluding class with Mark—which was more foreplay than yoga.

"Close your senses," the instructor says. His hair is long enough that it could be braided into the cursive phrase *I smoke a lot of pot*. He tucks it behind both ears in preparation. "Now, let us welcome the practice. If you don't like hands-on adjustments, let me know. Just—do it courteously."

This gets a weak laugh.

"You'd be surprised," he says. "Let us begin in downward dog."

The room falls silent, and my mind is as quiet as the classroom. The peace puts me in touch with how I'm actually feeling. I like just being with Skylar. Her positive energy is empowering. It makes me feel like I'm on a higher vibration already.

I savor this feeling as I climb onto all fours. My head hangs, and a state of relaxation begins, so decadently deep that I notice my slackened elbows giving way. I lock my arms in time to prevent a belly flop. When the second micro-nap hits me, it takes all of my mortal powers to keep sweet sleep from drowning me. I recover, for now.

Eventually, I collapse.

chapter 9

I wake up on Yoga Mala's sofa.

"Let's go," I say, sitting up. The phrase is a meaningless by-product of chronic sleep deprivation. Skylar restrains me with a firm palm on my chest. What the fuck just happened? I sift through wispy memories to figure out how I got here. I know we were flowing through sun salutations, and my balance was shit. I remember that much. At one point, I actually woke up in a split, and Skylar was smiling with her index finger tip pressed against my upper arm. She must have prodded me awake. Then there's a memory of Skylar leading me toward the door.

"Are you okay?" she asks.

"I'm so sorry," I say. "That was embarrassing."

"How do you feel?" she asks.

"Honestly? Refreshed."

She laughs.

I should check my phone. This reflex is clear even when I barely know where I am. The wall clock indicates it's been forty-five minutes. Tripp is probably already looking for me. *Work.* I look back at Skylar, who waits for my answer. Right. Feeling.

What am I feeling? She actually wants to know. Without warning, I'm crying. Sitting, heaving, I look down at my toes as my chest wrenches in and out like a fireplace bellows. Skylar stitches her brow together. *I* don't even know why I'm crying. I just said I felt refreshed. Is this a joke? Am I a comedian?

"I'm so sorry," I say.

"For what?" she asks.

"That." I point to the classroom.

"It's okay."

"This." I point to my face.

Skylar squats on the floor in front of me. She looks left and right to double-check that we are alone. We are, minus the desk attendant absorbed in the matrix of her own phone. In another room, the class I passed out in is continuing.

"It's completely okay," she says. "Did you meditate?"

I nod. "But, honestly, I just thought about my boss. The one I . . ."

Slept with.

"That's okay," she says. "This is actually my whole message to you tonight: It's okay." She laughs gently. Her skin is flawless. Up close, I see how perfectly clear and moisturized it is. No surprise that she reps a line of skincare products, too. "I can tell you're being hard on yourself. But it's okay. You can relax. Sometimes what we *think* we want is really just a symbol for something else. You just have to let it be."

"That's what I thought," I say.

"We're all messy," she says. "We all need support."

"Thanks," I say. I mean it.

She smiles. "Okay! I'm glad we agree," she says. "So, if we could talk about your journal?" I nod. She speaks more slowly now. "I read it very carefully, and what it showed was a very harsh worldview. Like, pretty scary." Her tone is tender, and I don't feel defensive. I feel like we are on the same side trying to put together the same puzzle pieces. "You see scarcity, competition, and individualism. As if you are pitted against others, others are pitted against you, and you are fighting tooth and nail to survive."

I nod. "Basically," I say.

"I'm being very blunt," she says. She forces a small laugh. "But what I saw was there isn't real love or tenderness in your life. This is partly because of your job—but partly because of how you respond to it." She touches my upper arm affectionately. "You have a lot of anger. Sarcasm. Criticism for yourself, for others. You're not listening to your body—there were no signs of movement, really—or your soul. We said suffering is wanting to be somewhere else. . . ." She trails off suggestively.

Yep, that sums it up.

"Allegra, I will help you," she says. "I will teach you to see more love and take care of yourself again. You have more power in your life than you realize. I've already seen it. Honestly, just look at your physical yoga practice. I was in awe—*am* in awe—you can make those contortions. They're supernatural, your alignments. At the same time, you jumped through all the hoops to get to Anderson. And I can tell you want to do good." She smiles. "I can bring that side of you back out."

"Wow," I say. "Thank you."

"Your grip on the world is tight right now, like a closed fist. Together, we will encourage you to open your hand again. Okay?"

"Absolutely," I say earnestly.

She smiles. "I'm so happy!" she says. We hug. "So, I did have a plan for you that will help." I'm so full of gratitude, I can't speak. "This weekend, make time for gentle poses during regular mindfulness breaks. I know breaks are not *naturally* part of your day, so please be intentional about creating them. Remind yourself to *stop working*, slip away, and reconnect. And then, if you feel something, let yourself feel it. Don't label anything as 'wrong' or 'I'm a shithead.'"

I laugh.

"Sorry, I'm just quoting you," she says. "That page where you beat yourself up for your sleeping with your boss? And then for being attracted to him? You wrote it at three a.m., I think?" She scratches her head as if she's trying to remember if that section was before or after the Skittles binge. "It was so full of self-hate. You were at war with yourself, trying to beat down these little feelings with a sledgehammer. So I'm asking you to be kind to yourself. Don't judge what you feel."

"Okay," I say. "Just, like, feel."

I sound like a robot.

"Yes," she says. "Frankly, if you flirted with your MD, that would actually be an improvement from where you are now. In your journal, you judged everything. Your mind was in overdrive. But a lot of what you criticize is just part of being a human being. You get lusty in a chicken coop? So what."

We laugh.

"You really think I should flirt with him?" I ask.

"Yes," she says with authority. "Honestly, have some fun. Find something to break up these insanely long days—I'm stressed out just talking to you." We laugh again. She slips her hoodie back on. "Then we can meet again after the weekend."

"Yes," I say eagerly.

She pulls her phone from her pocket and opens Instagram—I catch a glimpse of her 4,165 new notifications.

breathe in, cash out   95

"I should get changed for work," I say.

"Great!" she says. "I'll wait."

Skylar is still on her phone when I emerge from the bathroom. She sits with perfect posture on the sofa as if she is posing for Erg Guy. I crick my neck left and right to loosen the tight grip of my muscles from around my own throat. The check-in girl looks shocked, and her hands flinch toward her ears. *Sorry*, I mouth. Skylar hasn't budged. As I creak across floorboards toward her, her blond eyebrows stay cinched in a state of focus. She scrolls through comments on Instagram.

"Hi," I whisper.

"One second," she says.

She likes two comments and replies to one with smiling emojis while her face stays impassive. Finally, she looks up, phone in hand.

"Hi!" she says. "Sorry, this sucks up so much time."

She points to her screen.

"It shows," I say. "In a good way. I love your posts."

"Thank you! When did you start following me?" Skylar asks.

On our way out, she waves to the check-in girl, who waves fervently back—*OMG bye!!* Outside, my nose hairs freeze. Melted snow glazes the dark sidewalk.

"Years ago, so I've seen . . ." I make a diagonal line up with my hand to mean her catapult to fame. "You always had such spectacular posts."

"You are so adorable," she says warmly. She smiles.

"On another level," I emphasize, enthused by her reaction. "So much of InstaYoga is trash by comparison. I mean, half of it is straight porn. The people who do yoga in heels and underwear on their beds? 'Yoga.' *Totally*."

"Most people mean well," she says.

"Right," I agree, embarrassed at my complete inability to be positive. "Have you had to deal with any weirdos, though?"

"Hm," she says thoughtfully. "I wouldn't call them weirdos."

"Me neither," I interject. "My bad."

"My fans aren't weirdos," she says.

"Right," I say. "Of course not."

"They're all admirers in their own way," she says. "People follow me because they want to learn or connect. Sure, some people do that by commenting the same twenty heart and fire emojis on every one of my pictures."

I laugh.

She stays earnest. "I did have a few guys DM me pictures of themselves nonstop. One kept calling me his Pose Princess. Then he showed up one day at Central Park where I used to tape videos."

"No," I say, my smile gone. "What happened?"

"I turned off geotag on my posts," she says. "Changed up my locations."

"And you blocked him," I say.

She shook her head.

"Wait," I say. "You didn't block him?"

"No," she says.

That is seriously unsafe. I'm pretty sure most big accounts don't even check their DMs. They say that explicitly so no one's feelings are hurt when messages go unread and unanswered. I'm almost worried for Skylar. Seeing the good in people is great, but too much trust can get you hurt. Besides, it's not like she needs the extra attention. She has thousands upon thousands of non-psychos praising her every day.

My phone buzzes. Work.

"What was it about my posts that you liked so much?" Skylar asks. "Why did they speak to you?"

"Oh," I say, "mostly, you just seemed to be doing it for the right reasons. You weren't performing—you were practicing. You had a normal life and did yoga, and that felt relatable to me. And your photos were beautiful—" I catch myself before elaborating. Her photo quality improved dramatically after she started seeing Jordan, but I don't want to mention him. "And I learned things," I continue quickly. "Yoga concepts. Mantras. Philosophy. It was educational."

She looks touched.

"Thank you," she says.

We stand outside the subway platform.

My phone buzzes again.

"Sorry, I—" I start.

"I assume you'll have *some* time this weekend to unwind?"

"Actually," I say, my anxiety growing stronger every time my phone buzzes in my hand, "I'm heading back to the office now. I'll probably be there all weekend."

"Oh my God. I'm so sorry," she says, grabbing my forearm so that I'm forced to linger. "But Allegra, this weekend, even if you struggle with my directions . . . stick with them. Honestly, when we met, in the back of my mind I did hope there would be a future for us." My eyes widen. "I see an amazing teacher in you. Those photos in *Mindfulness* were incredible. Now, you just need to recenter. Then when you do come into the yoga world, I hope we can work together and be a counterpoint to this culture weighing on you. Your asana is so inspiring."

I am speechless.

"Some of my students come from finance, and you can probably connect with them better than I can," she continues.

"That would be . . . unbelievable," I say.

"So stick with it!" she finishes. We hug.

"See you soon," I say.

"Monday!" she confirms.

You are an angel. We wave goodbye to each other.

I cross the street, light on my feet, and spend the ride to work hopeful. The dream that comes to me is teaching a class with Skylar. She's more sugar sweet, and I'm less so, but maybe we could balance each other well. After class, as we put props away, she might tell me, *No, but my stalker has good intentions*, and I would say, *Literally, no! Not everyone has a good heart! Have you seen the people I used to work with?* All I have to do is find my yoga footing again, which I should anyway so close to the finish line.

I exit at my stop. As I forge through icy air, excited about the future for the first time in forever, I feel Dad with me. He was the reason I entered American Yoga in the first place, which led Skylar to me. Dad and I chose my optional poses together. Those were: first, "full wheel," where I bent over backward until I grabbed my own ankles. And second, "forearm scorpion," where I balanced on my forearms and touched my toes to my crown. He made my training schedule during spring of my senior year, where my days began at 5 a.m. so that I could hone my routine for two hours before the dining hall served breakfast.

I want to thank him and realize I haven't told him yet about the megamerger. He's going to be thrilled. Company names out of it, "maybe the biggest deal of the year" will still mean a lot. He'll be proud. I text him an update, just on the potential deal size. It's my roundabout way of thanking him for the coaching that led me to this moment. He texts back immediately: !!!!!! I smile. Sometimes it's possible to connect and not to connect at the same time. *That's my Fast Lane!* I imagine him shout at home as I step into Anderson's empty lobby. *That's my A-Plus.*

As I rise in the elevator, though, all sense of connection to my dad, to Skylar, and to broader humanity, really, is stripped away. My happiness dies one floor at a time. When the doors open to thirty-five, I resume living inside the nightmarish world of my journal. Back in work mode. I exhale dejectedly and spot Tripp through the glass doors before I reach the pod. He looks like Erg Guy's nightmare.

"Aloe, it's ten fifteen," Tripp says. The floor is a quarter full.

"I know, I'm sorry."

"What the el fucko?" he asks.

"I *know*, I'm *sorry*," I say.

I take a seat. Tripp's Thai dinner almost crosses the invisible line partitioning our halves of the desk. With the length of my forearm, I push his half-eaten chicken pad Thai, open takeout container of rice, and egg rolls until they are entirely on his side.

"Real fucking mature," he says. "We have shit to do. *We.*"

Tripp slurps the final millimeter of his bubble tea. He is a loud, suctionless vacuum. He exhales once and resumes. I log back into my computer and survey the scene: Chloe didn't get a pass—*RIP*—and is probably working from home. Puja's pass covers the "shit-ton of shit" she has to do for "the shit company," which apparently she "doesn't even give a shit" about. The rest of the floor is littered with empty chairs facing every which way, each frozen in the final frame of a negligent push toward the desk. I just need a coffee, and then I should be able to put in a full night.

It's what we call on the floor, the "banking nine-to-five." Nine p.m. to 5 a.m.

A new email flashes on my screen:

From: Mark Swift
To: Allegra Cobb
Fri 10 Nov 10:16 p.m.

The new numbers look right.

—MS
Mark Swift, Managing Director, Anderson Shaw, NYC
(O) x4777 (C) 2125552839 (Fax) 2125559384

New numbers?

I jerk toward Tripp on reflex. Maybe he knows what Mark means or could at least make me laugh with a joke at Mark's expense. *I can't read your mind, asshole,* I imagine Tripp stage-whispering. But Tripp's open Outlook is quiet. On his second monitor, he changes the colors of a stacked bar chart to Anderson gray. Across the pod, Puja's right eye twitches. That's been happening to her more often, which our pod googled and learned is a symptom of staring too long at computer screens.

I check the email again. No one else from Titan is CC'd. New numbers? I definitely have not sent Mark anything new, and Tripp hasn't either—he would have complained about it and then made me do most of it. I reread the email. Mark's email signature looks a tad different. It looks clunkier, or more crowded, or something. He has added something. Right between his office and his fax lines are the ten digits of his cell phone number.

I pause. Did my MD just give me his number? Skylar pops into my mind. *Frankly, if you flirted with your MD, that would be an improvement from where you are now.* My heart beats a little faster. Her instructions to de-banking myself were pretty direct. *Honestly, have some fun with your life.* So I decide to allow myself the extremely lavish fucking extravagance of a single sexual out-let while I slave away. I drag the PDF of the annual report I was reading over my Outlook to hide the cipher and walk to the pantry Keurig machine. From my phone, I reply:

From: Allegra Cobb
To: Mark Swift
Fri 10 Nov 10:20 p.m.

Great!

—AC
Allegra Cobb, Analyst, Anderson Shaw, NYC
(O) x4832 (C) 9175554029 (Fax) 2125559384

My phone buzzes an hour later:

2125552839: How is my deck?

Mark. I press the home button again so that the message repopulates. But I'm not sure how to respond. *Have fun. Have fun, dammit. Fucking do something fun. Now.*

Me: I'm on it

"What are you doing?" Puja asks.
"Nothing," I say.
I'm trying to have fun.
"You looked like you were tweeting something clever," she says.
"Yes," I say, deadpan. "You know me. Gotta get my tweets in."
Three *I'm typing* dots ripple on his side.

Mark: Don't get distracted
Me: I won't
Mark: I've been meaning to ask you, why Princeton? Did you not
      get into Harvard or Yale?
Me: Bad alumni at Yale
Mark: LOL

I cringe. *LOL?* Is he the strapping forty-something I thought
he was or is he texting me from his mom's couch and on his
parents' phone plan?

Me: You disagree?

The back-and-forth ceases and I wait. My bouncing knee
rattles the desk slightly, and Tripp shoots me a *stop* look. I throw
him a retaliatory eye roll and head a few steps away to the nearest
window for some privacy.
     Now, with my back to the floor, I stare at our stalled conver-
sation on my phone in an act of sexual window shopping. I yank
my Messages app down again to refresh—the modern equivalent
of opening, closing, and reopening the lid to a mailbox that you

know is empty. I stand, waiting. I am always waiting for comments. My phone auto-locks.

"Marco!" Tripp shouts. He wants me to *Polo*.

"Yeah, yeah," I say.

On my way back to the pod, I nod to the thirty-something ex-military associate with shitty technicals, a wife, and a child. *You and me both, man. We each got our problems.* At the pod, Tripp and Puja hunch in their office chairs, showing signs of life only in their fingertips darting across the keyboard. Tripp has left his plastic cup, with the un-slurped millimeter of bubble tea remaining on the bottom, on the invisible line between our halves of the desk. I think he's fucking with me. The top of the straw looks chewed.

"Are you done with this?" I ask.

I point at the drink.

"Maybe," he says.

I push it an inch right, onto his half.

"Why are you such an only child all the time?" he asks.

Puja sniggers, and I smirk.

I log back into my desktop, resuscitating both of my monitors. A few minutes later, Skylar sends me a list of gentle yoga poses to perform every half hour. *Half hour?*

My stomach sinks. Two days ago, I was on the phone with an MD, and he signed off to get on a plane. By the time he called me back from his hotel in London I had eaten dinner and drunk a one-liter bottle of Coke, and had not gotten up from my chair.

I study Skylar's instructions.

"Amy," Tripp says with a warning tone.

"Sorry," I say.

Since when is *Tripp* telling me to work more?

chapter 10

For the rest of the weekend, I took mindfulness breaks and did a yoga pose roughly every half hour. Meanwhile, Tripp and I were on office arrest for Team Titan, so I took these in the coat closet on the HG floor.

I tried my best. Friday night through Sunday, I crept into the closet, bushwhacked aside the Canada Geese, held a gentle pose for ten breaths, and then left. When the door shut, it was just me packed among overcoats, and I felt somewhat insane. Tripp noticed I was getting up a lot and WebMD-ed my condition as a point of amusement. He asked if I had a burning sensation when I peed.

Meanwhile, Vivienne ran the Titan team like such a finely tuned machine that the sand grains of my breaks fucked shit up. I missed three calls from her due to mindfulness, and Tripp had to conference me in on my cell phone every time. The fact that Vivienne's number is now in my Recent Calls is a disaster waiting to happen. One day, I'm going to ass-dial it and interrupt one of her fifteen-minute power naps on a Tempur-Pedic pillow. She's going to lift her cooling eye mask to glare at my caller ID like, *I knew it was you, Analyst.*

I didn't have enough mental space for the breaks to really resonate. They just became another to-do item, like eating. *Did I fucking eat dinner? Yes, check. Did I mindfulness? Check.* I got frustrated with myself that Skylar's guidance wasn't taking. *This is my dream, right? What the fuck.* The angrier I got at myself, the harder it was to achieve calm detachment in the first place. It was just a downward fucking spiral. Every break worsened my mood.

The only decent part of the whole weekend was texting Mark a few times. The texts were polite on the surface, but I was so desperate that I found them extremely hot. As a normal course of business, MDs don't text analysts asking them how the office is—*good, thank you*—and are we coming along—*yes, thank you*. It was a release, and in our casual texts I felt freer and more present in my own body than at any other point in the day. That's what yoga used to be for me—a foil to regular life where I connected to myself and with other people. Now Mark is my only release, and yoga is the second job.

To make things even more pathetic, Mark didn't respond promptly. Seven hours would pass between our messages. Mindlessly, I built small fantasies about us, about how he might touch me again or eye me as we passed in the hallway. Skylar's voice exonerated me in my head. So I indulged the thoughts. *Hey, Skylar, here's my progress report for the weekend. Want to fucking work together? All right.*

At 11:01 p.m. on Sunday, I reread my half of the deck. Tripp and I are on the home stretch. After I send him my slides, he will slot them into the master PowerPoint and then finally send the book to print.

Tripp hasn't shaved since Friday. His facial hair comes in as only a mustache, and right now, he has a faint blond 'stache that he relishes. Business casual clothes are required during the week, but we are allowed free rein on weekends. "So feel free to wear your velour tracksuits," the HR speaker said during her overview of the rules in training. I think someone actually laughed at that. Tripp wears a WORLD SURF LEAGUE hat backward and Duke sweatpants tucked into untied Timberland boots. He looks good.

I send him my shit.

"Done," I say. "You'll check?"

He grunts.

I can't wait to get out of here. Puja and Chloe showed up at around 4 p.m. full of fucking energy. Puja went to a wedding yesterday and has been going on and on about it. Tripp is riveted, because the only interesting things that happened to him this weekend was getting his arm stuck in the HG vending machine and diagnosing me with a urinary tract infection. My final, unchecked to-do is the last pose on Skylar's list: *savasana*. I just have to wait for Tripp to zone out again, so I can take the break without another pee joke.

"Apparently, the flowers cost half a million," Puja says. "The flowers. Those things are going to die in an hour."

"Where was it?" Chloe asks.

"Southampton."

"Half a million," Chloe says. "That's like, two nice cars."

"It's like a house," Puja says.

"Or like a big donation to charity," I say, just to be subversive.

Pause. The pod exchanges glances.

"Is she fucking with us?" Puja whispers to Chloe.

"Were you guys here all weekend?" Chloe asks.

Tripp makes a *yes* grunt.

I put my earbuds in and open Spotify. On a whim, I search for Mark Swift on the app and check out the playlists he's made. The most recent are labeled "Spa," "Chest Day," and "Leg Day." Jesus Christ. This dude is at war with aging and he is here to fucking slay. Out of curiosity, I look up Tripp's. His last three are labeled "Feeling '90s," "Country Boozin' Y'all," and "TGISummer." I smirk.

"How's Titan?" Puja asks.

"It's a mushroom cloud," Tripp says. He makes an explosion noise.

"I see the 'stache is back," Puja says.

"*Thank you* for noticing," Tripp says, turning to me as he emphasizes the *thank you* to Puja. He pats his upper lip. "Someone cares. Amy over here barely looks at me anymore."

"That thing is so gross," I mutter.

"Pfft," he says. "You love it."

"No, I do not," I say.

"Girls like hair," Tripp says.

"Girls, huh?" Puja asks.

"Pfft," Tripp says. With a small show of melodrama, he adds dejectedly, "And yet the only woman fucking me is Vivienne DeVille."

"Hey," Chloe snaps.

"What?" Tripp asks.

"I said, *Hey*," Chloe snaps.

"What was wrong with what I said?" Tripp asks.

"All right," I say. "Pipe down."

Chloe's whip is apparently good for something. Tripp dons his own earbuds and chin-bops to a beat I can't hear. He seems to be settling back into the zone. When he is finally absorbed, I creep away.

At the far end of the empty hallway, the door to the closet looms. Sunday is Anderson's equivalent of Monday, so the room is more packed than it was yesterday. Chloe's thin Burberry trench coat hangs pancaked between two thick parkas. Maybe she taxis everywhere and is never actually outside. I shut the door, lie on the carpet, and position myself correctly.

I imagine recounting this to Skylar and cringe. How did my life get so out of control?

When I started doing yoga, it was nurturing and fun. Now it's scheduled, approval-seeking yoga that my dream life depends on doing successfully, while I thread the needle of also working nonstop. You can't make everyone happy. Stand up for yourself. I forget what breath I'm on and start over. Earnestly in corpse pose, I inhale and exhale. My mind drifts to the slides I just sent Tripp. Does he realize I sent him my half?

I lose track again.

Fuck.

I give it one last try.

One breath. Two.

A mantra I learned in the Princeton studio comes back to me now: "Are you breathing or are you being breathed?" It floats through my mind like the wind-tossed plastic bag from *American Beauty*. Gradually, my sense that I am breathing fades into the sense that I am being breathed. I guess you don't realize how tired you are until you're forced to imitate the act of sleeping.

Suddenly, light shatters my view. I come to.

I am lying flat on my stomach. The patch of carpet beside my open mouth is damp. In the doorway, Tripp's Timberlands are haloed by bright yellow light radiating from the hallway. Can he see me? Metal hangers screech from side to side. I consider playing dead to save face. Too late: our eyes lock.

"What the—?"

I scramble to my feet and blink ferociously. Tripp's 'stache is now an inch away in a disorienting close-up. We both tilt backward, and I slink into the plush safety net of tens of thousands of dollars' of winter coats.

"Are you in here *sleeping* while I'm out there *working*?" he demands. He rips his camel coat from the rack.

"This is next-level freeloading, A," he says. "Not fucking *bueno*. You know I went looking for you? Like, outside? It's cold as shit. You left your phone at your desk. I thought you died." He shakes his head as he shoves his arms into his sleeves. "You used to be such a perfectionist and now you're a fucking narcotic."

"Narcoleptic," I whisper.

"*Excuse me*?" he asks. "The shit I deal with."

"What time is it?" I ask.

"Two," he says. "Anyway, here is the update on *our* fucking team. Vivienne called and asked for new shit, so I did that, and then I had to look for your shit, which took me half an hour, and I'm still waiting for stuff back from Bang and Prez."

"Bang" is what we call the branch office in Bangalore, filled with analysts I've never met. They churn out any charts and tables that we request, but they require a four-hour minimum turnaround time. "Prez" is short for the Presentations team of middle-aged people skilled in Excel and PowerPoint who sit on our floor and put together flowcharts and other unusual graphics when asked. The shitty part about that shortcut is it involves giving your work to a fifty-five-year-old on their graveyard shift. Prez takes at least four hours as well.

"That shit is due back at five," he says.

"So one of us needs to stick around," I think aloud.

"Yeah, I fucking know," he says.

Mark needs the books before he leaves for the airport at 7 a.m. After the materials get back from Bang and Prez, someone will still need to *look* at them, send them to Anderson's Print and Ship team, and then "flip" the final, printed copies. Flipping means the analyst looks at every printed page to make sure there were no printing errors—i.e., that the printer did not run out of toner and print the last five slides pink. *Then* the books can be sent.

"And when Viv is like, 'Why the fuck did this take so long?' tomorrow, I am *not* taking the fall for you."

He leaves. I head back to the desk, feeling bewildered and shitty that Tripp had to do all of that. At the pod, Puja and Chloe pack their Tory Burch totes for home. Puja is going on about her latest online shopping spree and how much everything cost. Her monologue is so detailed that she may verbalize the silent decimal places in this extremely boring, itemized receipt. Chloe is totally thinking about her own M&A deal.

I wave them both goodbye. Puja waves back.

Three more hours. I can't even nap, because I need to be available if there are any glitches in the process. Sometimes, Bangers have the audacity to ask questions about our typo-laden, rushed, ambiguous instructions. What am I going to do in this office for three fucking hours?

*   *   *

On Instagram at 4:30 a.m.—so close—I hunch forward even more than usual. In order to stay awake, I ate everything in the HG office refrigerator without a name on it. Then I caught up with Kim Jee, who did not seem to enjoy our shit-shooting at all. Now, I feed my eyeballs Instagram content and check Skylar's latest Story, a street view of Mala. She must have taken the picture before class. *Amazing!!* I respond via DM. My body language remains lifeless.

Slow footsteps approach from behind, and I don't have the energy to turn around. Kim Jee walks by my pod carrying a cardboard box under his arm. The plain brown box is bound with a kind of plastic strap I've seen used to handcuff people in movies. I know from our talk that Kim Jee has to ferry books to his MD's Tribeca apartment before he leaves for an international flight. If deadlines are too tight, sometimes analysts become donkeys. Chloe once had to hand-deliver pitch books to her MD in London, for one of her own mega-billion-dollar deals she told everyone about. Anderson paid for her $10,000 first-class flight to bring the guy just three books at the very last minute.

Somewhere, a text message dings. Looking down, I see it's my phone.

Skylar: Have a minute?

I sit up.

Me: Of course!

She really does get up at 4 a.m., I think as Skylar sends me a photo of herself in wheel pose. In the picture, her backbend is front and center against the backdrop of her yellow living room. Her white leggings and sports bra glow softly under overhead lights. It's an idyllic expression of wheel, a pose meant to energize and strengthen.

> **Skylar:** What do you think?
> **Me:** Really, really beautiful.
> **Skylar:** Any suggestions?
> **Skylar:** I want to post it today.

I blink twice, hard. I wipe my eyes and try to focus.

> **Me:** None, honestly. It's perfect!!
> **Skylar:** No suggestions at all?
> **Skylar:** In the caption I'm writing about friendship. You inspire me :)

Oh! My! God!

> **Me:** Wow—I can't wait!
> **Skylar:** But something isn't right yet. . . . Could you make the outfit less shiny? I'm off to teach a private now.
> **Me:** Okay!

What?

> **Skylar:** I'm using it as my morning post :) I'll credit you! Can I tag your Instagram?

I do not want her to flaunt the shit show that is @AllegraHandstands. My profile is a shell that I use for following yoga accounts.

But two years ago, I'd taped myself training for American Yoga and posted the videos to my gallery. It was Dad's idea, a way to track progress on specific poses. That gallery was never meant to be seen. Most of the footage is grainy, shot in gyms, and incidentally captures strangers working out. The final frame is usually a close-up of the ring of fat around my belly as I bend toward my own iPhone to turn off the camera. My only real follower is Dad.

Me: Don't worry about it.
Skylar: Too modest!! Okay. Can you handle the caption too? Something on friendship, relationship meditations . . . Thanks!
Skylar: See you tonight to hear about the breaks :) Namaste.

I feel more awake than I have in hours. My excitement is exactly counterbalanced by fear. Edit a photo? Caption?

Me: When do you need this by exactly?

I scroll through Skylar's gallery looking for guidelines or inspiration. Yes, I'm a millennial, but I'm disoriented as shit. And I don't usually have much time to play around with the latest Instagram features. I scroll deeper until I find the photos credited to Jordan. In an emotional shot taken *with* him, he gives Skylar a piggyback ride on a cobblestone street in the West Village. A camera hangs from around his neck to rest on his white tee. Skylar kisses his cheek. He smiles through a thick brown beard.

The last time I googled him, a month ago, Jordan was getting slaughtered in tabloid headlines. "Messy Split with Yoga Model Destroys Jordan Roca's Career." "Fans Pick Sides in Yoga

Breakup." Apparently, he lost a lot of his followers and was having a hard time finding work. It's ironic that his attempt to use Skylar to help his career ended up doing the opposite.

My computer alerts me that the materials are back from Bang.

Skylar: By breakfast is great :)

chapter 11

wake up bewildered, to an alarm, in a handicapped bathroom stall.

This is not my fucking studio.

I silence the noise coming from my phone. It's 9:30 a.m. on Monday. Skylar texted me, Thanks my love :). Oh, right. After I sent the books to Mark, I edited her wheel pose and wrote her caption. That involved an hour of reading what famous yogis have to say on the subject of friendship. I must have written twenty drafts before I realized, at the tail end of my all-nighter, that my captions were shit because I don't have any real friends anymore. I was trying to package *wisdom* about *relationships*, but I had no recent experience. *Friends, y'all. They are so great, you know? I like to spend time with mine. #TruthBomb #RealTalk.* Eventually I had to just send something, and the final product sounded extremely vague. Then, I came in here for fifteen minutes of shut-eye.

Now I sit on the floor between the toilet and the tiled wall. I massage the crosshatch print out of my forehead, and my nonwork to-do list comes to me involuntarily. There are sewage and gas problems at my studio that I still need to fix. I had yoga books delivered to a girl I sort of knew in college who lives near me, and I have been meaning to pick them up from her for two months.

I emerge and unbutton my blouse to throw bathroom sink water on my armpits, splashing until I can no longer smell myself. On the way back to the desk, I skim the dozens of emails I missed during my nap, including Dad's two Google Alerts—"megamerger" as the key word—which have absolutely nothing to do with anything I am working on. As I step onto the HG floor, I'm dreading Tripp for once, on top of everything else.

"Hey, sorry about last night," I croak.

He stares vacantly at his computer screen, working in Excel.

"I sent the books," I say, a bit louder. No response.

Fuck.

"Are you pissed or dead?" I ask, increasingly worried until I spot a palm-size muffin wrapper in Tripp's trash can. That's his telltale sign of a Stage One hangover. Stage Two is sunglasses and Coke. "Oh my God, did you go out last night?"

"What?" he asks. He eyes the wrapper. "Oh. Yeah."

He doesn't give a shit.

"What kind of muffin?" Puja asks.

"Chocolate?" Tripp guesses. "Or corn."

"What kind?" Puja asks again.

"Honestly?" He pauses. "I don't even know."

"I want one," Puja says.

"You don't know?" Chloe gawks. "You just moaned about it for ten minutes."

"Literally, I am under attack," Tripp says.

Vivienne appears beside me.

Does she make any noise at all?

She waves hello with a single index finger. When it curves, it looks like a periscope raised from a German submarine just itching to blow me up. "Good morning," the pod chirps in disarray behind me.

"Analyst," she says. "My office."

With my tote still on my shoulder, I follow Vivienne into her SVP plot of the floor. She points at the all-glass door, which draws ceiling light to the Hope Diamond wedding ring around her ring finger. I slide the door shut, sit down, and brace myself.

"Why did the books wrap up so late?" she demands.

Her tone suggests that I am the reason why.

"I am so sorry," I say. "The last turn took longer than we expected."

" 'We,' " she says. She purses her thin lips. "Why do I get the impression that Tripp did most of the book himself?"

He's going to love that.

"I was just away from the desk a few times when you called," I say. "But I was in the office all weekend, and I did all of the pro forma financial statement modeling. Honestly, I think the books turned out really well. Exceptionally well. And we finished on time."

"You were *un*responsive last night," she says. "Had you offered Tripp the *favor* of your services, we could have printed the decks at a decent hour, and we wouldn't be here. Do you understand that I end up looking unreasonable if books wrap up at the crack of dawn? Hm? As if I am disorganized, or swamped, or inventing useless work?"

Yeah, basically.

"When I call or email you, it is my way of communicating," she says. "And when you respond, that's your way of *doing your job*. Am I making myself clear? I thought we established that this team was your first priority."

"This team is my first priority," I say robotically.

"Tripp can't do everything himself. *Tripp*. Titan. Alone."

Jesus Christ. I can't tell Vivienne the truth is that my yoga journey and physical need for sleep put a kink in her assembly line, because this lady has 0.0 tolerance for shit that does not make her money. She probably has even less tolerance for shit that values equality and opposes the class hierarchy propping her up every day.

"I will do better," I say. "You have my word."

She flicks her index finger and thumb to shoo me out.

Back at the desk, I avoid locking eyes with my pod-mates. I drop my tote onto the floor. Tripp has Vivienne's LinkedIn profile up on one of his monitors, which he turns to face me. He points at her high school section of the page, which is packed with text. She still has her GPA on there, which is a 4.2/4.0 at Thomas Jefferson High School for Science and Technology. Her list of activities mentions being president of Future Problem Solvers. No well-adjusted adult has high school details on their LinkedIn. There should be a watch list for this shit. Anyway, she definitely fucking hates me now. I am the latest problem she has to fucking solve.

On my phone, a new text from Skylar says, We just hit 10K likes on our post! and then, Can't wait to see what the weekend did for you! See u tonight my love :)

I walk into the yoga studio known as Hamsa Hand, where no surface has been spared from Eastern decoration. Like Mala, it's a premier studio, but unlike Mala, it is seriously fucking elaborate. Tapestries billow from the ceiling. Ficus plants line the walls. Golden Buddhas, big and small, and other yoga-ish figurines cover every tabletop. This place is so afraid *not* to be yoga that it oversteps in every direction. The decorator may have asked fifty different people, "What is yoga?" and here are all of their fucking answers.

I am one minute early to meet Skylar, 8:59 p.m. I smear the bottoms of my shoes across the shag mat more than I need to because tonight, I am rich with time and can blow it on stupid shit. Mark is at the Titan board meeting—he *texted* me to expect follow-ups—and my other teams are manageable. I even took an afternoon nap in the bathroom again. If that's not the definition of luxury, I don't know what is. So the tea leaves say I can meet Skylar without interruption.

I'm alone in Hamsa Hand except for the teenager behind the check-in counter. She is sour-faced, smacking gum, and wearing a hoodie. She must be a nepotistic hire, because she looks way too off-theme.

"Hi," I greet her.

She looks up briefly, then back down. Skylar must still be with her client in the back. I don't look forward to admitting that the breaks didn't change me. I am exactly the fucking same, maybe with less peace of mind than when we started. My only saving grace is that I tried to help Skylar with her Instagram. She used a version of the wheel pose photo I sent this morning, which now has around 10K likes. She altered the lighting slightly, for the better, and posted it with the caption:

@SkylarSmithYoga: Here is what I would say to 15-year-old me: Beauty happens when you accept yourself.

Stop resisting.

Stop fighting.

Stop trying to starve, pluck, squeeze, or fake yourself into anything you're not.

Relax into it.

"If you relax, it comes. If you relax, it is there.

If you relax, you start vibrating with it." —Osho

Be beautiful you.

Love, Skye

Skylar changed the concept of the caption from friendship to beauty, which does sync better with the photo. I mean, she's *alone* in her living room here. Besides, my caption about friendship was shit. We both know it, even though she didn't admit it. She texted me that she will hang onto it for later. If I can find the right moment for it tonight, I would appreciate her advice on fostering good relationships. Writing that caption only left me wanting some.

I scroll through the comments on her photo now, feeling a small sense of ownership over the product. Hundreds of girls have commented on it so far, sharing that they struggle with "unrealistic beauty standards" and "the media" and "perfectionism." But this picture is "pro woman" and Skylar is making strides for "natural beauty." The photo is an enhanced version of Skylar, sure, but she doesn't look overly perfect. It makes me feel good to see these girls happy and supported. *This* means something. I join the flood of comments: Best one yet!! :) Really, really beautiful.

I hear Skylar laugh in the back. Apparently, the client before me is Dan, a forty-something investment manager with an interest in new age spirituality and finding himself. Are there thousands of us? They have been practicing together for five years. I hope my journey to clarity is shorter than that. The thought makes me wonder about the incentives of health professionals. Doctors need people to keep getting sick, right? Do therapists really want to cure their clients and lose them? I don't know.

My phone buzzes before I decide on an answer.

"No phones."

The teen comes to life.

"Sorry," I lie. "It's my doctor."

She rolls her eyes.

Amazing client hands. I check my phone, shaking my head. Work panelist I can ignore. Tripp gets back from Seattle later tonight, where he went for "Azkaban." That's his code name for an IPO, which doesn't sound that bad when you ask what he actually has to do for it. "Nothing, the first-year is so fucking bright-eyed, she does everything," he said. So he won't notice my absence now.

A man emerges suddenly with Skylar. I startle and hide my phone, because my third hand can be alienating. Skylar wears orange harem pants loose at the top and tapered at the bottom as if she is a modern Jasmine, and a black tube top. Tiny gemstones stick to her forehead in a floating crown. She looks beautiful, as always. The attendant finally perks up in the presence of some-one worthwhile.

"Hi!" I say.

I wave at them.

"My student," Skylar whispers to him.

"Nice to meet you," he says, extending his hand. "Dan."

Our greetings miss each other. I stop waving and reach for his hand right as he withdraws it. We force laughs—and I recognize him. Dan *Glasgow*. He manages Glasgow Capital, a hedge fund invested in emerging markets. He is known for being "out there." His firm famously buys expensive companies in some of the riskiest African markets.

"Allegra," I reciprocate.

"Thank you so much, Dan," Skylar says. They hug goodbye.

"Hi, Skylar!" The desk attendant is now buoyant as shit.

Skylar motions, and I follow her down a narrow hallway into the vacated private room. I sink into one of the two beanbag cushions, while she shuts the door. She sits in lotus on the other massive hacky sack and smiles. The mala beads draped around her neck touch her crossed ankles.

"Dan and I love this studio," she says.

"Dan Glasgow," I say.

"Yes," she replies.

"Big yogi?" I ask, skeptical.

He's worth a few hundred million dollars.

"Yes," she says earnestly.

"Sure." I roll with it.

"Thanks again for your help with my photo," she says.

"It came out great," I say. "I was just reading the comments."

She brightens noticeably.

"That's so sweet," she says. "But let's talk about you."

She reaches forward and touches my wrist affectionately. Her skin is warm. But I don't want to talk about me. My weekend was shit. She is the only person in my life not fucking *Analyst*-ing me. When was the last time I was even in a studio before I met her? It's Hamsa Hand, but whatever.

"I did my best," I say.

Quiet.

"I see," she says. "So, the methods didn't help you?"

The silent no. She waits.

"To be honest," I say slowly, "I'm doing worse."

"Hm," she says thoughtfully. "What do you mean?"

"Well," I start, "I missed these calls from my boss while I was in the closet." Skylar looks confused. "Oh, that's the only place I could take the breaks. I had to work all weekend, so I couldn't be too far from my desk. And my boss is—" Vindictive? Psychotic? Obsessive? The devil? "—type A, so she wasn't happy about that. Then I fell asleep in corpse pose, so we didn't finish this work project until five in the morning, and I had to eat a pound of food just to keep my eyes open, and then instead of sleeping, I worked on that photo for your Instagram. Then the only place I could sleep for fifteen minutes was this section of floor in the company bathroom. Then my boss yelled at me in person." I hang my head. "Honestly, I think the only thing I did right was flirt with my married boss."

The air absorbs my words as Skylar takes my hands.

"I hear you," she says. "What we need to do is go deeper."

I stiffen. At Anderson, you can refuse a staffing when you are "at capacity," or don't have enough hours in your day to take on more work. At that point, it's assigned to another analyst. I've never refused a staffing, because everyone finds out when you pass and then people joke for days about how much they hate you. Now I fear "going deeper" may put me over capacity. My phone buzzes inside my tote. My eyes dart toward it.

"Are you with me?" she asks.

"Yes, sorry," I say. "Just, work."

"*This* is work," she says. She points both of her index fingers down at the air in front of her. Since when am I a bad student?

"I'm sorry. I know you are trying. What I meant to ask, Allegra, is . . . is this"—she opens her arms to mean the practice space around us—"something that you really want?"

"Yes," I say. She looks as nice as ever, but unconvinced. I go on. "I mean, I did exactly what you asked. I'm just in a tough place until my contract ends." She is quiet. I take this to mean she doesn't believe me. My tone rises to compensate. "I'm trying my best. I did everything I was supposed to. I did every pose. I texted my boss. It was fun! And I really did enjoy some of the poses you sent me."

My phone buzzes again.

"Sorry," I say. "I mean, maybe we could wait until after my contract?"

The audacity sinks in.

"I am saying this with love," Skylar says. "But asking someone to be who they want to be is actually pretty simple and natural, right? It isn't such a hardship. And yet . . . this feels difficult. It feels unnatural."

"I know," I say.

"I don't think you do," she says. "There is something blocking you from surrendering." She pauses. "And maybe it's because this isn't what you want. I know you have a demanding job. I read your journal. But either you want this or you don't. You said you wanted my help. So pay attention."

I feel like such a fucking shithead.

"I'm sorry," I say.

"It's okay," she says. "I know what you need. The next step for you is a fast."

"Great," I say.

"A two-day pure fast," she continues.

"Great, great."

She pauses.

Fuck. Let her finish.

"That means zero intake," she says. "It's beyond no food. It means ingest nothing at all." I nod before I understand. Skylar goes on to make the word *nothing* clear with complete detachment, as if she knows the script cold from reciting it to other students. "No water, no mints, and no coffee. No saltwater gargle. No rinsing your sinuses with a neti pot. Keep your mouth closed in the shower. Absolutely nothing."

"No coffee," I repeat slowly. "No coffee at all."

"Cutting coffee will help with your *ojas*," she says, brightening to pronounce the Ayurveda term for "energy." "I think this will loosen your grip. Right now, you are holding onto tension and anxiety. But you must open your hands if you are to receive. You must empty your cup if you are to fill it." She smiles, her mood a bit lighter now. "I am so grateful I can share this with you."

Her gaze drops to her lotus. She shapes each of her hands into an acceptance mudra, which looks like an "okay" sign, and rests them on her knees. Fuck. She is trying to help me. *I* am trying to help me. We should be in sync. I shouldn't be showing up with closed fucking hands. I realize, though, that she is not raising her head. She continues to stare at her lotus until I realize that our time together tonight has ended. Fuck. Okay.

I feel compelled to thank Skylar again in person before exiting Hamsa Hand. I wait for her in the doorway and finger-polish a small golden elephant hanging on the wall. It has twenty arms and hands, each in a different mudra. The attendant smiled at me a few moments ago when I passed her. She was a lot warmer after she saw I was here to meet Skylar. Maybe she thought I was in the same celebrity league as Dan Glasgow, or maybe just affiliating with Skylar got me special treatment.

Skylar approaches the desk in an overcoat. I wave to her from the doorway, but she doesn't see me.

"The studio is too cold," she tells the desk attendant.

"What?" the girl asks, frightened.

"Too cold," Skylar snaps.

"Oh," the girl says, looking frazzled.

"Oh what?" Skylar asks.

"Oh, I am *so* sorry."

"Don't apologize, just fix it. I have classes tomorrow. I told you, seventy-six degrees. It was too cold tonight. Dan couldn't loosen up."

I've never heard her so critical before—in fact, I've never heard her critical *at all*. Skylar reaches the doorway and notices me.

"Oh, hi!" she says, back to her bubbly self.

"Sorry, one last thing," I say.

"Of course," she says.

We trot down three flights of stairs to the street.

"What's going on?" she asks.

"I just want to say thank you for helping me," I say. "Again. You have so much else going on, and there are so many other people you could be teaching. I really—*really*—appreciate your time. I am really committed to learning. I'm sorry."

We walk quickly to keep warm.

"Of course," she says. Skylar presses her scarf down from her mouth with her chin. "I remember what it was like getting started, you know. You'll be a great teacher one day. You just need to do a bit of work on your own, okay? Do the fast."

"I will," I say. "Thank you."

"Be patient with yourself," she says.

"Yes, I will," I say. "Thank you, Skylar."

"You're still young," she says. "Believe it or not, you're further along than I was when I was your age. I didn't have any sort of mentor around, and I had money problems. When I moved here, I mean, my first apartment? You could cut your feet on the bathroom tile if you weren't wearing shoes. There was a hole in the ceiling. The shower wouldn't drain, so you had to use Tupperware to remove water from the bathtub."

Oh. Maybe this is why she likes the elite studios. At least those places pay yoga teachers a decent amount. It's not like going to donations-only Yoga to the People. Skylar's financial struggles must have made it salient that yoga is more than a spiritual practice. It's an industry, too.

"I worked hard," she says, "to do and spread what I love."

I feel positive goodwill being restored.

"All that being said," she says, her tone becoming even more tender, "you're not teacher-ready. I'm sure you feel that. You have to help yourself before you can help others. So reflect and stick to the fast. Who knows? You may have an epiphany." She smiles. "I hope you do. I really would love to work with you."

"Thank you," I say.

"I believe in you," she says kindly.

We still have a couple of blocks between us and the subway station. I wring my hands, itching to ask her one more thing.

"Anything else on your mind?" she asks.

"Well, yes," I say. "Since we have a second. I was thinking about friendship this morning in light of your post—which was phenomenal, by the way. I realized I don't have real friends yet in the yoga community. So, I was wondering, do you have any advice on meeting other yogis? Building those friendships?"

"That is such a great question," she says.

"Thank you," I say. "Do you practice in a group?"

"Hm," she considers. "These days, sometimes with my sister, but mostly by myself. I've been so busy teaching and coaching that flowing on my own works best for my schedule. Rosie and I practice vinyasa."

"You two seem close," I say.

Skylar smiles. Rosie studies arts and media at NYU. Whenever she appears in one of Skylar's posts, the photo gets double the usual likes. Rosie has Skylar's blond hair and bright smile, on a slightly heavier frame. Rosie never does real yoga in the posts, but sometimes she strikes a fun pose while Skylar holds a handstand, or they take a mirror selfie together with Skylar's arm around her sister.

"I think we feel the same way about family," Skylar says.

She meets my eyes thoughtfully. I'm touched, because I think she's referencing my midnight journal entry about Dad. She remembers that random part of my rant! Before we can discuss it any further, though, we're at the subway. We hug and make plans to break the fast together on Friday. She tells me I can have a couple of days to recover from the weekend before I start the forty-eight-hour fast on Wednesday night. Skylar reminds me to be gentle with myself before she disappears into a crowd of parkas.

I should turn right toward my own train, but I can't quite walk away just yet. It's weird how much I miss her, so soon. Every time I see her, I like her more and more. Her attitude just makes me feel like I matter—like I'm more than a deck-building, color-coding robot. I imagine us working together again. Maybe we could teach a flow around the theme of family.

Someone shoulder-checks me.

"Watch it!" the stranger snaps.

"I'm fucking standing here!" I shout.

Ow. I must have lost track of time. I come back to my senses. All I have to do to work with Skylar is have a fucking epiphany during my fast. A fast. Okay, a fast. I once survived a full fifty hours in the AS office on nothing but coffee and saltines I found in my desk drawer—I can do this.

chapter 12

I start most mornings with three eight-ounce cups of black coffee in a row, then drink at least three more throughout the day. I dilute each with water until it's tasteless, because coffee gives me a gag reflex. But I need it. Almost everyone on the floor drinks an insane amount of coffee (except for the Mormons). Puja calls it Prozac. An HG analyst passed out in the shower at home from a caffeine pill overdose a few months ago. She was also on diet pills, though, so it's unclear what caused the fall. Point being: caffeine is life.

Not today. Today is pure fast day fucking one.

I shut my phone alarm off, instantly nervous to face the daily shitstorm of my job un-drugged. I deodorant-shower and pack my phone. I try not to spend too much time in my studio because this shit is depressing. It's a sixth-floor walkup roughly the size of my pod at Anderson that leeches almost $2K from me a month. That's despite living on the Upper East Side, where space is cheaper at the trade-off of being "deeply lame," per Tripp.

If I weren't fasting, I'd pack something to eat from my fridge, where I store food bought with only my Anderson dinner allowance. A couple of weeks ago, Jason called a meeting with HG to review which purchases were not acceptable in the allowance. On the "curb your usage" list: alcohol, multiple frozen meals, boxes of cereal, cartons of milk, gum, toilet paper, candies, pancake syrup, and mints. One of the analysts, who was chewing gum at the time, raised his hand to say that he considered gum a reasonable purchase and a food. Jason repeated that gum is not a food. A lively discussion ensued.

The no-food part of the fast doesn't scare me. It's neglecting caffeine that's horrifying, because I have to be productive for twenty hours a day and act convincingly happy as shit at the same time. Junior bankers get sorted into one of three levels based on performance—top, middle, or bottom tier—and everyone in the same tier is paid the same bonus. If I don't convince my VPs that I'm masochistic *and* extroverted, welcome to bottom fucking bonus tier. I've relied on coffee since I started and don't know who I am without it.

On my way out, I pass two pictures on my bureau: one of Mom cradling me at the hospital right after I was born, and the other showing Dad standing next to me at the finals of American Yoga. This is the best part of my morning, where I feel connected to my family. Then my commute is half an hour. This includes twenty minutes on the subway, where I stand, email, lose all sense of connection, and, whenever I see someone sit down, think, *Sitting is for bitches*.

Today, I sit uncaffeinated among the bitches. I am seated bitch number five from the caboose. The first three are in various stages of sleeping. As the 4 train bolts down Lexington, I wobble and remember what Skylar said: on top of the fast, I should reflect to help myself surrender. I will let that unfold. You probably can't rush epiphanies.

I check my inbox. Mark emailed Team Titan that he will be back in the office this afternoon. The "mtg went well," and the client is coming to the office tomorrow to discuss "nxt steps." *Fkn gr8*. More emails hit with new tasks, and every request without a dead-line specified means it's due today. Only exceptions are clarified, and most of those are due tomorrow. Of course, you don't know what else will tunnel up from hell tomorrow, so "due tomorrow" functionally means "due today." Everything is due today.

I turn to my messages for a break, where Skylar wishes me peace in a single text. I'd muted Dad's thread, but read it now, where he has sent several mind-set tips for attacking the massive deal. His excitement shines in exclamation marks. He's also texted advice from New England Patriots coach Bill Belichick on team building for success. Dad takes Anderson's bullshit love of "teams" to heart. But after two years here, I've learned that when people call you "team," they usually mean "bitch." *Got this, bitch? Thanks. Couldn't have done this without my bitch.* Dad suggests a phone call when I have time. I promise to call soon.

By 2 p.m., I've made a week's worth of mistakes. First, I sent Harry an accretion/dilution analysis with a pervasive sign error: subtracting costs instead of adding them for ten years into the future. A financial model is a column of formulas extended right to the end of the projection period, so a single error in this col-umn means enormous, snowballed errors in the final year. I had modeled that the deal scenario would yield a sky-high 250 percent internal rate of return, or IRR. Harry stopped by my desk, addressed me as "Miss Warren Buffett," and sarcastically congratulated me on finding the deal of the century.

"Thank you," I said meekly.

And it's only gotten worse.

Today, Tripp is Stage Two hungover and also out of sorts. He went to Tao after work last night, which he told us briefly about at noon when he finally showed up. The first thing he did was ASIM me, *I'm still drunk.* I snapped at him that compliance surveils everything, and he ASIMed back, *Pfft I am a celebpretty. CELEBPRETTY.* Apparently, he went to a Victoria's Secret party where it was $5K at the door to get in. He was accompanied by a few other associates, they charged everything to the company, and Tripp woke up alone on a roof. He looks blind in his sunglasses.

"Are you guys okay?" Puja asks.

"Not so loud, Chlo," Tripp says.

"It's Puja," she says.

Tripp sips his Coke.

Another one of my associates just stopped by to shit on me for sending him the wrong version of a file. Version control is holy here. Whenever we change a model, we "save up" and rename the file as a different version. This creates a library of backups. It's common for files to get suffixed up to "_v100" for "version 100" before "_vf" for "version final." But when we get stressed, naming conventions devolve. I sent my associate "_vfinal" but the latest was actually "_vf4." So, he visited to ask if my "dick" was in my "hand." I actually answered, "No, it's not." Tripp, sunglasses on, told the associate to "cheel."

A new request rolls in, no deadline specified. My head hurts.

"Fuck," I murmur.

"What?" Tripp asks. "He still being a dick?"

"No, I'm just out of it, thanks."

"Dope."

"Were you there last night, Allegra?" Puja asks.

I shake my head. *Ow.*

"A doesn't go out," Tripp says. "She sticks to NoFo."

It's wordplay on the name of my neighborhood. People abbreviate South of Houston to "SoHo" and North of Houston to "NoHo." Tripp abbreviates the Upper East Side to "NoFo" for "No Fun."

"What building?" Chloe asks me.

I try to focus. My brain fog complicates the job requirement for constant maximum sharpness. At annual performance reviews, everyone gets "attention to detail" as a skill to improve, because turns out there are a lot of fucking details in spreadsheets of thousands of numbers while you field the EKG beep of new emails at the same time. I open the hundred-slide management presentation that I need to revise "ASAP."

"You guys," Puja says. "Robbie update."

Not now. Robbie is a second-year analyst in Industrials. He is well-known in our class solely because of his Facebook statuses. They invariably have to do with banking and, more often than not, broadcast explicitly that he is a banker. His last one was an *Onion* article headlined "Coworker with Two Computer Screens Not Fucking Around." He tagged another banker and referenced "your 8 monitors."

Tripp obediently opens Facebook.

"Wow," he says.

"Today's is so bad," Puja says.

"A, come see this," Tripp says.

"No, I feel like shit," I say.

"Did you wake up on a roof? I think not."

I lean over to Tripp's monitor and read it out loud. "'Q: Why did the CFO never say thank you?'" I ask. "'A: Because accounting rules only allow him to depreciate, not appreciate.'" So far, it has earned one comment—"No"—and that comment has earned forty-five likes. I add one as Tripp, to make it forty-six.

"Robbie's going to Apollo, right?" Chloe asks.

"Yeah, Apollo," Puja says.

OMG private equity. *Awesome.*

"You think when he's having sex with a girl he's like, 'You know I'm an investment banker, right?'" Tripp asks.

"Tripp, stop," Chloe says.

"That's all I can handle today, guys," Tripp says.

He X's out of Facebook and pinches his sunglasses between his thumb and index finger to adjust them. As unread emails pile up in my inbox, I remember the yoga credo "The pose begins when you want to leave it." Well, that would be now. Maybe this is what Skylar meant when she said the fast would help me surrender, because it stole my liquid shield.

Hours later, I'm cold. The office is always cold, but without my metabolism, it's ice. Anderson must deliberately chill the air a few degrees below normal room temperature. There's no way this is automatic. Chloe says Anderson keeps us cold because cooler air makes us more alert and more productive. Today, though, it's getting in the way of my job. I keep returning to the pantry to fix myself paper cups of hot water and use these as disposable space heaters.

At the Keurig, I mix my latest cup of steaming water with a wooden stir stick. I should have finished revising the hundred-slide management presentation by now, but I'm only halfway through comments. Progress is slow, new shit keeps cropping up, and then I need more hot water. The associate, Adam, still needs to review my work on the presentation before we send it to the MD tonight. He's known on the floor for picking up people's slack, and I might need him to pick up mine.

"Oh my God, *hey*," Puja says beside me.

She looks peppy as shit. Her exaggerated hello is almost funny because I see her all day, every day. I wait in silence for her to finish brewing her cup of coffee. I imagine snatching it. It would be so easy. Meanwhile, pimply first-year Brian opens the HG pantry fridge, takes a 0 percent Fage yogurt, and leaves. Puja and I return to the pod together. As soon as Brian is out of earshot, she leans in as if she has a secret to share.

"Do you want to know the saddest thing?" she asks.

"Yes," I say, exhausted.

"It's like the more time I spend here, the more attractive everyone gets," Puja says. "I'm wearing Anderson goggles or something."

"Yeah," I say. "Broo-tahl."

She laughs.

"Were you looking at Brian?" I ask.

"Literally maybe," she says. "What about you?"

Brian has one or two bruises reliably above his collarbone because he pinches himself when he gets anxious.

"Literally no."

She laughs. "Any better ideas?"

"Nope," I say. "No one."

"Oh, come on," she prods. "Not even *Tripp*?"

"Puja," I chide her. "May I remind you, sometimes, I literally rip his phone out of his hands to get him to stop swiping *yes* to every single girl on Tinder." He goes on Tinder whenever he feels slighted in order to boost his self-esteem, but it pisses Chloe off. "Marginalizing women" and stuff.

Puja eyes my water.

"So you and Tripp *didn't* go out together last night?" she asks.

"No," I say. I already told her that.

"Your side of the pod is pretty dehydrated," she says. "Just saying."

"Um, okay," I say.

We're almost back at the pod. Now I understand what she's getting at. "Oh my God, Puja, no. There's absolutely nothing going on between us."

"Mmkay," she says skeptically.

Is she serious? I looked at Tripp that way for a *second* when we started. Now I have a management presentation to do. I'm woozy, and my head hurts from caffeine withdrawal. I wrap my hands around my space heater, and Puja winks from across the pod. I roll my eyes, which makes me dizzy.

Work, fuckface. I stare at the PowerPoint. Could this day get any worse?

"Team." It's Mark's voice.

He tents his fingertips on my desk.

Oh my God, it just did.

"Terrific to see you," Tripp says.

Mark stands at the edge of our pod in an extremely unusual mixing of banking castes. This does not happen. The only time I've seen an MD visit juniors was the day after Mitch seized at his desk at 3 a.m. after he had been up for eighty-one hours straight. Two of Mitch's pod-mates rushed him to the hospital. The next day, one of the female MDs walked the floor and visited everyone to ask, "How are you?" She kept saying, "Things are going to change. This cannot continue." I'm pretty sure my texting invited Mark over. But Tripp, Puja, and Chloe probably think someone in HG has died.

"How is Team Titan these days?" Mark asks.

"I have never been happier than I am right now," Tripp says.

"Great," Mark says. He looks at me as if I am supposed to answer, too. But I am a bit out of my element and can't find any words.

Mark smirks.

"How was your meeting?" Tripp asks.

"Productive," he says.

He nods as he leaves our pod. As soon as his pin-striped suit is out of sight, Tripp leans toward the center of our pod.

"That was the weirdest fucking thing I've ever seen," he whispers.

Yep. An MD making conversation.

Skylar: How are you?
Me: I'm okay! Thank you so much for asking.
Skylar: OMG I know you better than that!
Skylar: How are you really?

Fair. I am still revising the final presentation for Adam and feel extremely shitty after a daylong series of mistakes. Adam won't be happy with my revisions. Most of them are sloppy—e.g., three-line-long chart titles—because my mind is slippery and my vision randomly blurry. So, this is the best I can do. Plus, Adam's one of the good associates, so I know he'll actually check my work and fix shit.

As anticipated, it's the caffeine withdrawal that's been fucking me. Other bankers have proven you don't need food to do this job. Last year, Anderson's Technology, Media, and Telecom (TMT) group had a weight-loss contest. What began as a funny *what-if-we* pod daydream escalated to become the "TMT Hunger Games." The banker in last place, who lost the least amount of weight, had to pay $1K for a group party or walk around the office all day with his shirt off. It got out of hand. The final week before weigh-in, TMT guys were in Anderson's gym working out in trash bags to lose water weight. They were sucking on Jolly Ranchers all day long and spitting out their saliva into a cup, apparently another strategy to lose excess water. The previously normal-weight winner lost sixteen pounds in the last two days and forty pounds in a month. The guy who came in last did not pay up or take his shirt off. Point being: they worked without food.

If I've had a fast-induced epiphany so far, it's that I don't like screwing people over. I'm not a complete asshole. But that's what I've done all day. It's been more than mildly unpleasant.

Me: Fair. I am shit.
Me: Feel like*
Me: Both
Skylar: Come sleep over tonight!
Skylar: It makes me sad to think of you alone in this state. And I've got plenty of space.

Oh my God, can I? I would love to see her. I glance at the clock. Leaving at 11 p.m. on a weeknight is almost asking-for-it early. Almost. Luckily, Tripp is already gone, sleeping off Tao. I *am* tired.

Me: Where do you live?

Me: I could probably leave soon.

Me: Thank you so, so much.

Her East Village address flashes on my screen like a lighthouse beacon. I decide that I'm done revising the presentation and send it to Adam. *Please don't hate me!* Before heading out, I activate call-forwarding from my landline to my cell phone so my colleagues can reach me. My survival reflex kicks in—*Don't leave! Stay here!*—but I have too much momentum headed out the door to fight it now.

I walk to the elevators, to the lobby, outside. I pass the long line of black town cars waiting, engines running, at the entrance and wave to the head attendant. Bankers working past 10 p.m. are entitled to a free ride home, wherever home may be. I cross the street, where a familiar homeless man sleeps beside the pretzel stand. His shopping cart of trash-bagged possessions is parked next to the glowing pretzel hub. This hobo is known for refusing donations. Tripp's offered him leftover food a couple of times, and apparently the homeless man asks what's inside before accepting a doggy bag. He doesn't like pizza.

"Pretzel?" the cart man asks.

Yes. I've never bought anything from him before, given his notoriously bad attitude and all the free food at Anderson. But tonight, I just want to hold one. I take the warm dough and touch it to my nose to savor the sweet smell of bread.

"One dollar," he says, his palm faceup and waiting. I extend my debit card.

"Lady," he says. "Cash only."

"Oh." I only have credit and subway cards in the wallet slit stuck to the back of my phone.

"Lady, you owe me a dollar," he says.

"I don't have any cash," I say.

"No cash, Anderson Shaw?" he asks.

"No, I'm so sorry," I say. Who even carries cash? People are paying for driverless cars with their watches. "Can I pay you back next time?"

"You better, Anderson Shaw," he says.

He points at me with the most threatening finger I have ever seen. *I get it. You hate Anderson.* This is why the HG heads told our group not to wear our AS ID cards in public. People hate us, so hide your affiliation to avoid negative attention. The anecdote they gave was: One guy wore his AS ID on the subway, didn't donate to a beggar in the car, and it became a *thing*. People singled him out and ridiculed him: "This Anderson guy doesn't give a shit about poor people," and "Anderson hates the homeless."

But the pretzel guy's cart faces our headquarters. His customers are likely all AS. If he hates Anderson, why is he here and what is his endgame? I wonder if he too is bound by a contract to stay, and if he is reluctantly sticking it out until it expires and releases him. In any case, he definitely thinks I'm trying to rip him off. In an intentional display of non-asshole-ness, I rest the pretzel in the picky homeless man's collection box.

"Lady, I am not a charity!" the pretzel guy says. "Fuckin' A."

He shifts his weight from his left foot to his right. He removes his backward cap and puts it on again, still backward. The homeless man stirs awake, bites the pretzel, and spits his mouthful out onto the sidewalk. *Worse than pizza.*

"Look, I will be back," I say.

"Fuckin' Robin Hood," he says. "I know where you work. Fuckin' A."

* * *

"Welcome!" Skylar sings as she opens her door.

She wears gray sweatpants low on her hips and a white tee cropped at her ribs. Her doorway frames her sinking expression. She covers her mouth with one hand and hugs herself across her abs—cut like a two-by-four table of cells in Excel—with the other.

"Oh dear," she says.

"Hi," I croak.

"You look awful."

"I'm actually really happy to be here."

She laughs, and we hug.

Skylar gestures *Follow me* and pays me close attention. We walk through the wide hallway hung with framed pictures from her Instagram on both sides. Each is the size of a standard movie poster, the kind on display in front of a theater. I feel like I'm on a Hollywood set. I stop to admire one where she holds goddess pose—knees bent at right angles, her legs spread apart—in beige spandex alone in the Brooklyn Botanic Garden. The earth below her is carpeted with pink cherry blossoms. Cherry tree branches bloom overhead with more pink flowers. The scene is rich with early morning light.

"This is incredible," I say.

"I love that one," Skylar says.

I notice how far ahead of me she stands.

"Oh, sorry," I say.

"Take your time," she says. "You look fragile."

I hurry past her kitchen, which is large and pristine. The transparent cabinets are filled with stick-straight stacks of plates and bowls. Even her ceramics are centered. Skylar waits for me beside a white marble dining table for four. Her manicured hand rests on the surface next to a Canon camera and laptop open to iPhoto, where the gallery shows a series of new shots with Rosie. The dining area opens to another large room. It occurs to me that this may be a pinnacle of material wealth for a yogi.

When I reach Skylar, I see at last her famous living room. Oh my God! It's as magnificent as I always imagined and feels even warmer than I expected. Seventy-six degrees, maybe? I can't believe I'm here, *inside* the videos I've watched for years. I recognize the light-yellow walls, the beige sofa with thick blankets over the arms, and the full bookcases. There is the wicker basket of rolled yoga mats tucked away in the corner. Her tripod faces an accent wall, where she must have held wheel pose for her most recent photo.

"Wow," I say. "This is so cool."

"You're the sweetest," she says.

I inhale deeply and smell cinnamon. *Fuck.* I suddenly notice the handful of white scented candles around the apartment. I am basically surrounded by lattes. The sooner I get to sleep, the less I will be tempted, or tortured. My head starts to hurt again.

Keys rattle in Skylar's front door, and I recognize the smell before I recognize the person. Pizza. The door opens to reveal Skylar's sister, Rosie, carrying a steaming hot cardboard box. I sit in one of the four dining chairs.

"Rosie!" Skylar says. "Come meet my student."

Rosie waves meekly, flopping her fingers twice over her palm like a collapsing dorsal fin. She locks the door slowly with her non-pizza hand before meandering toward us with her eyes downcast. She looks exhausted. The brightest thing about her at the moment is her Skylar-blond hair. She sets her pizza down on the table and takes the seat across from me. She spins the laptop around to face her and starts toggling keys.

"Hi," I say. "I'm Allegra."

Rosie clearly has no interest in me or anything else except her laptop. I don't know if she's shy with new people, or if my zero-calorie goggles are distorting this scene, or *what*. She must be in a mood. *Had a bad day, Rosie? Because then we can fucking talk.*

"Rosie," Skylar prompts.

Rosie looks up.

"Oh, do you want pizza?" she asks.

Her voice is childish. She opens the box and offers Skylar and me some.

"No, thank you," I say.

"It's vegan," Rosie clarifies.

"No," I say. "Thank you."

Skylar shakes her head to refuse. Rosie sets the box down.

"Rosie," Skylar prompts. "Intro*duce* yourself."

"Oh, I'm Rosie," she says.

She extends her hand, and I shake it.

"Right," I say. "I recognize you from Skylar's Instagram."

Rosie smiles for a moment before she resumes typing.

"I'm almost done, Skye," she says.

"What are you working on?" I ask.

She doesn't answer.

"Rosie," Skylar says. The girl perks up.

"Oh, I thought she meant you," Rosie says. "I'm just going through the photos Skylar and I took today. I'm picking the best shots to edit."

"Rosie and I took some *amazing* photos together," Skylar explains. She squeezes her sister's shoulder affectionately, as if she is trying to pump this girl up. *You're gonna need to squeeze harder, Skylar.* "Rosie, you look so good in that one." Skylar points at the screen and then shifts her gaze to me. "Anyway, I asked you over to check on *you*. How are you?"

"Fading," I say.

Rosie looks up suddenly, as if she is concerned.

"Any realizations?" Skylar asks. "How did it go?"

The smell of cinnamon mixes with the wafting hot pizza steam to suggest a cheesy churro turning golden brown in a nearby oven. I don't even know if cheesy churros are a thing but I want one so bad. I imagine its buttery crust flaking.

"Is it okay if we debrief tomorrow?" I ask. I shut my eyes to focus on my sentences. "I had a rough time at work and actually can't remember the last time I felt this bad. Or out of control. I just sent in the worst presentation of my analyst career, and I don't have the brain power left to tax rate. I mean, think straight." I open my eyes. "See?"

Rosie looks even more fearful.

"Tomorrow, of course," Skylar says. "You need rest."

Skylar stands and waves, *This way.*

"Night, Rosie," I say, standing.

She flops her fingers again to wave goodbye. I follow Skylar through the living room and into a cozy bedroom with a canopy twin bed, where a blue pajama set waits folded on the quilt. It is the cutest thing I have seen all day and orders of magnitude nicer than my place would have been. *Fix the fucking sewage problem, Allegra.* Skylar enters with me and shuts the door.

"Thank you so much," I say.

I sit on the bed and sink slightly.

"My pleasure!" Skylar smiles. "Anything else?"

I pause.

"Well," I whisper. "Is Rosie okay?"

Skylar glances at the door, which is closed.

"She's great!" Skylar whispers. "What do you mean?"

"Oh," I say.

We wait in silence. Skylar eventually takes a seat next to me.

"I mean, it's family stuff, really. But I guess I could tell you a little bit."

"Sure," I say. "I don't want to pry. Whatever you think is best."

I'm so ecstatic that Skylar is pulling me closer, into her inner circle, that I almost forget about my tortured physical state.

"She's just having a little bit of a tough time right now," Skylar says softly. "The attention I get can be hard on her. A lot of her friends at school follow me, talk about me. So I try to involve Rosie in what I'm doing, practice with her, and give her space in my posts. She has so much fun when we're shooting. I tag her in the pictures. And she gets excited when she's featured, but she doesn't have many followers."

She throws her palms up.

"Oh, I see," I say.

"I don't know what else I could do to help her," Skylar says. "It just weighs on her." She looks stumped. "Maybe you have some ideas?"

"Wow," I say. "That's tough."

"I know," Skylar agrees.

"I honestly don't have any answers," I say. "It sounds like you're trying the best you can. But you can't force other people to be happy."

"Mm."

"I think you just have to be yourself," I say. "It took you a while to find your niche, and it took me a while, too. I mean, I'm definitely not there yet. Look at me. I think Rosie will find her place. It will just take time."

Skylar tucks a strand of my hair behind my ear.

"You are wise!" she says, standing. "Okay. Time for bed."

She waves good night before turning out the light and shutting the door.

Alone, I blink hard. My room is still almost as bright as it just was. The neon sign of a bar across the street—SHOWSTOPPER—glows through my window like a second sun. There are no blinds. I stare at the sign from my bed and resign myself to the reality that my room comes with unstoppable artificial daylight.

chapter 13

My phone alarm jolts me awake like a taser. I gasp. My throat is a desert. I slap my phone on the bedside table until it's silent.

Good morning, Showstopper.

Not only is my mouth dry, but my head pounds. I'm nauseous. I dress in yesterday's clothes and check my phone. Buried deep in a stack of blasts is Adam's 2 a.m. email to the MD, revised PDF attached. He shortened all of my three-line chart titles and reformatted my graphs. Fuck, he's nice. A separate email asks that I register a new project code for a potential deal. Each code is a randomly generated series of characters used to name the electronic folder of deal materials. We used to be able to name deal folders ourselves, but apparently, we abused this privilege with inappropriate humor. Now, creativity on codes is forbidden.

I put my hand over my empty stomach. How many more hours? Twelve?

Skylar sits at the marble table, her phone in hand. She wears a skintight black tank and leggings that lace crisscross up the sides. She looks rested as fuck. When she sees me, she lowers her mug and phone to the table. Her blue eyes widen.

"Did you sleep at *all*?" she asks.

"I must have," I say.

The cinnamon candles are already lit. Fuck.

"Okay, I gotta run," I manage.

"Have an *amazing* day," Skylar says.

She walks me to her apartment's threshold and hugs me goodbye.

"You, too," I croak. "See you tonight."

I open the glass door to HG at 9:02 a.m. The floor looks exactly the same, except no one is here. I freeze and listen intently but hear nothing, not even the gurgle of my own digestion. No one is fucking here?

I didn't want to draw attention to myself on the floor today—in a Showstopper daze, the same outfit as yesterday, with a nausea that makes the idea of talking to anyone unpleasant—but this is too much. This is a prime example of getting what you wish for and having it turn out to be seriously fucking different from what you wanted. I look for signs of life until Trixie stops me in the hallway.

"Your hair is getting pretty long, isn't it?" She touches my hair.

"Sure," I say.

"Shorter hair is more professional, don't you think?"

Wow, and how about stripper names? Are stripper names as first names professional, "Trixie"? I return to my desk. *Great.* There has been a banking apocalypse, and the only other person who has survived is Trixie. Fucking self-appointed MD of the assistants, Trixie.

I start up my computer. Our pod is littered with candy wrappers, mostly around Puja's desk. The floor is still heaped with extra candy that the MDs brought in after Halloween, even though it was weeks ago. Either they overbought, or they took all of their kids' candy after trick-or-treating in some lesson about the harshness of the world. *See, kids? Life isn't fair, just like we've always told you.*

I can still sort of see Trixie. Both of her desktop monitors are covered by screen protectors. These thin, black, and highly perforated rectangles obscure the content behind them unless you are extremely close. It's something a lot of assistants do, because most of the time, they're online shopping. Behind Trixie's monitors hangs a bulletin board covered in pictures of MDs' kids. Not *her* kids, MDs' kids from past Christmas cards. Most of these are professionally shot photos posed in front of suburban homes.

My phone rings. Caller ID: Trixie.

Oh my God, do I work for you?

"Hi, Trixie."

"Aren't you going to the meeting?" she asks.

My heart catches in my throat.

"What meeting?" I ask.

My computer finishes logging on, and the reminder flashes. Today, HG has one of its semi-regular, global group meetings. The subject is professional responsibility, and Mark is on the list of presenters. I am ten minutes late.

"Oh, right," I say. "Headed down."

"You're late," she reminds me.

I grab a notebook and head to the conference room mezzanine on the tenth floor. At the meeting room, people are still settling in. Fast walks suggest the thought bubbles *Is this really necessary?* and *Do you even know how busy I am?* People creak back and forth in folding chairs, and jittery mannerisms spin the air into one hot heap of early a.m. annoyance. The whole floor has attended in person. HG bankers elsewhere join by phone.

I take the open seat next to Brian.

One of these valedictorians is definitely going to notice that I wore this outfit yesterday. A screwup like this is exactly the kind of petty shit that these people thrive on. Mark sits on a panel of MDs at the front of the room. His head arches back mid-laugh. A continental breakfast—mini bagels and C-shaped cuts of melon with flowering strawberry garnishes—lines the left wall. The global head of compliance takes the podium beside a projected PowerPoint slide title that reads, *Professional Responsibility*. She looks like *Matilda*'s Miss Trunchbull.

"Hello," she declares. "Today's meeting is about reputation."

Whispers die. Nightmares aside, the only other time I have seen this woman was during her unscheduled visit while we were in training to address my class's "unprecedented, sophomoric behavior." We were supposed to be in training from 8 a.m. to 8 p.m. five days a week, plus homework, but it wasn't closely regulated. On Fridays, half the analysts would leave at noon and go to the Frying Pan for sangria. Then the head of HR would come in on Monday and say something like, "If you already know everything, then I'm sure your manager would love to hear it so you can hit the desk." Still, people left. I mean, HR would end sessions with what-the-fuck phrases like "Another hard day—and more to come."

Back then, the instructor, Patrick, taught us Wall Street skills from a podium before the four-hundred-person class of new hires. He projected his computer screen onto the wall behind him and worked out of a shared folder we could all access. One day, in the middle of a session, people started adding folders and renaming them. We had learned that Patrick's wife's name was Martha, so bankers named the folders *Martha's Snapchats* and *Martha's Nude Snapchats*. Everyone watched, shocked or laughing. An impromptu compliance talk was scheduled after that, led by this chick, where she warned, "This isn't college."

"You, as employees of the firm, represent us," she says, bringing me back to the present moment. "You are ambassadors of our brand and legacy. As you conduct yourself, remember: You can do more to hurt our reputation than to help it."

Mark says a couple of words about integrity.

I touch my hand to my stomach, above the nausea.

"Any headline with the words 'Anderson Shaw' in it gets twenty times as many hits as the same headline without those words," she says. "If you do nothing else in your time here, do not damage the firm's reputation. Don't post about Anderson Shaw on social media. If you have the urge to be funny in anything written, remember that being funny is fraught with danger. No one thinks you're funny except for your mom, and no one cares about her."

Mark nods to second her conviction. *Yeah, fuck your mom. Moms are bitches.* Meanwhile, he pats the side of his head to smooth hair that was already smooth. Together, they walk through reminders: Everything done on an Anderson Shaw IP address is surveilled, and there is a zero-tolerance policy for dishonesty.

"Any questions on lying?" she asks.

I lean forward slightly, to ease the queasiness.

"Your use of IM has come to our attention," she says. "As we have always made clear, we surveil absolutely all IMs." She pauses. "Some people in the audience may believe they are exempt from surveillance. They may believe they are 'invincible.' But I can assure everyone, you are most certainly not."

She uses air quotes around "invincible." I look around the floor until I spot Tripp, sitting straight fucking up.

"IMs carry reputational risk. I would like to read several IMs we have identified from your group as unacceptable. We don't care how tired you are. We don't care how much you are working. Do not send these under any circumstances." She displays a PowerPoint slide of IMs and reads aloud. "'Presenting to farmers so this has to be kindergarten-friendly.' 'After the CEO leaves, that company is going down like the Titanic.' 'I was drunk when I did that page. LOL.'"

She displays an unacceptable PowerPoint slide made by someone in the group. The slide mentions due diligence, which is the process of researching a potential target company, as a bullet point in a list of to-dos. The graphic describing due diligence is a picture of someone bending over a minibar beneath the bubble *No vermouth?* She shuts the PowerPoint off.

"I won't dignify a final, especially grotesque example by showing it to the group, but it goes without saying that sorting VPs into categories of doucheness is shockingly juvenile and grounds for a very serious discussion with your managers."

She straightens her blouse.

"Any questions?" she dares.

I can't see Tripp anymore. Somebody definitely just pissed themselves. An associate asks if our telephone calls are recorded, which somehow transitions to a short discussion on what Alexa is and is not listening to and whether or not Siri is on by default and temporarily recording what we say. Meanwhile, I hinge forward at the waist until my torso touches my thighs and breathe deeply.

"You okay?" Brian whispers.

"Great," I whisper.

"You sure?" he asks.

Stop. I sit up and swivel from left to right to see if anyone else noticed. Thankfully not. Everyone else faces straight ahead, scared shitless of Ms. Trunchbull. I am wiping my chin when suddenly I lock eyes with Vivienne. Fuck, she saw. She stands at the end of my ten-person row, among the small crowd leaning against the side wall. Every other head faces the front except for hers. She glares at me, clearly thinking something awful like, *I heard about your 250 percent IRR, Analyst.*

The head of compliance ends the meeting. As Brian and I join the departing throng, an email from Mark says that Titan's management team will be in the boardroom at 3 p.m. Skylar texts me: Feel the light, see the beauty and bliss around you.

Brian looks at me and winces.

"Fuck," I murmur.

"You left at eleven last night, don't even," Puja says.

"You do an all-nighter from home or something?" Chloe asks. The question comes off as if she is trying to size me up. I don't want to pass the ball to her so she can lay up some shot to prove that her pain is worse. People are always trying to outwork each other here. They *want* to win Whose Life Sucks Most.

"I forget," I lie.

Tripp shows up to the pod, now half an hour since the compliance meeting, looking like a ghost. He sits down without saying a word.

"Allegra," Chloe says. *"Hello?"*

"Hm?" I ask. "I just left early. Whatever."

"You are so second-year right now," Puja says. "I can't."

First- and second-year culture is different. The first year is the hardest, because unless you went to Wharton or majored in finance at a state school, you have no idea how to do your job. New-banker training only teaches so much. So when you're projecting negative cash in 2025 for a major transaction, and the model you inherited from some checked-out associate in the London office has thirty tabs in Excel, and it's midnight, good fucking luck with that monkey knot you've never seen before. Plus, you're applying to your next job on the side, and you just left college. You're used to No-Class Fridays and One-Class Thursdays, where that one class was a noon-start, pass/fail survey course on the Meanings of Gender. Your incompetence requires you to give major shits just to avoid being fired. Meanwhile, second-years have built hundreds of models, seen every transaction, and those materials are templates in new deals. Most have an offer signed. By now, we've all learned better, or stopped caring.

"We're all second-years," Tripp mutters.

"Tripp, you're an associate," Chloe says. "You're not one of us."

Tripp cocks his head from side to side as if he's mocking her. Meanwhile, he fishes his phone out of his pocket and opens Tinder. He proceeds to swipe *yes* on every girl's first picture. Across the pod, Chloe locks eyes with me.

"Not now," I whisper.

"Is he doing it again?" she asks.

"No," I lie.

"Tripp, stop objectifying women," she snaps.

"He's having a *bad day*," I whisper.

"I'm fucking desperate as shit," he says. "Go fucking protest manspreading, I can't deal with your shit right now."

"What's manspreading?" Puja asks.

While seated, Tripp lifts one of his legs up at a time and spreads them apart in a slow, exaggerated demonstration until his thighs form a wide V shape with his pelvis as the fulcrum. He leans back in a power pose, with his hands behind his head and his elbows pointed up. Vivienne appears on her phone.

"*Excuse* me," she says.

"Good afternoon!" Tripp says. He man-cinches so fast that his limbs almost blur, and he gives her his full attention. As he leans forward, I realize his outfit looks more put-together than usual: crisp white dress shirt and navy windowpane blazer tailored to his frame. His baby-blue tie looks new, patterned with a lineless grid of Hermès letter *H*'s. It's such a spiffy ensemble, Mark might choose it.

Vivienne stares at her screen, both of her thumbs at work.

"How are you today?" he asks.

"Fine," she says. That's a *fuck-you* fine.

"I wanted to let you know that the meeting with Titan is very important. Tripp, you should wear a different tie," she says. "Something less fashion. Allegra, you should wear a different outfit all together."

"Brilliant," he says.

"Amazing," I say.

"Is there anything else we can do?" Tripp asks.

"Do you have a phone charger I could borrow?" she asks.

Tripp side-eyes the brand-new phone charger gleaming white on his desk. Vivienne extends an open palm, and Tripp hands it over with first-year zeal. She doesn't say thanks.

"I want to underscore the importance of today's meeting," she says. She looks up to stare only at me. "This is not the kind of meeting where you can arrive late and then sit in the back row."

She leaves.

"Man," Tripp declares, "good thing I'm not hungover today."

I sit at a round table with the CEO and CFO of Titan in my sharp-est black blazer, reserved for days when non-AS people see me. The clients are jolly white men from the South who seem pleasant. Everyone is chatting—"Great to see you!" "How was the trip?"—and sipping from glasses of ice water, except me. Tripp's tie substitute is a cotton J.Crew number, borrowed from the Mormon associate who sits behind our pod.

"A?" Tripp whispers.

"Mm?" I respond.

"What the *fuck*?" he whispers.

It's his way of asking nicely and sincerely if I am okay. I unbut-ton my blazer and slouch so aggressively that the top and bottom halves of my abdomen are almost touching. Tripp smiles at the management team and subtly inches my glass of water toward me. The clients thank Mark and Vivienne with a twang for all of their hard work on the board-meeting materials.

We sit on one of the two floors used for entertaining clients, which are both decorated with Zen-like minimalism. The modest decor amusingly suggests anti-materialism. A knock on the door announces two waiters wheeling a silver dining tray of Shake Shack.

"No thank you." I refuse the ShackBurger offered to me.

Everyone else is served a burger and fries. My empty plate reflects ceiling light like a shining prism. From his seat beside me, Tripp leans forward slightly in an effort to make eye contact with me. I shake my head.

"Do you let your analysts eat?" the CEO asks. He laughs.

Mark and Vivienne guffaw.

"Of course," Mark says. "Allegra, eat something."

The waiter serves me a cheeseburger, and I wonder why the more pivotal yoga moments in my life have involved Shake Shack. *Feel the light, see the beauty and bliss around you.* Skylar's words drift into my mind as if she is reaching through the distance to encourage me. Everyone else eats. Analysts aren't supposed to talk at client meetings, so I'm just trying to sit up straight and look interested. Skylar's words now feel sedative.

"Sorry, I'm a bit distracted," the CEO says. "Is your analyst okay?"

"She's fine," Mark and Vivienne both say, overlapping.

I sit up straighter and smile.

"In any case," Mark continues abruptly.

I try harder to blend in. How do people quit shit cold turkey? As the meeting unfolds, I'm surprised to see Mark faltering a little bit. He tells a couple of jokes that come across as abrasive. The brawny, masculine qualities that make Mark sexy don't translate well here. It's as if he's still riding the 1980s power wave of banking and hasn't toned it down to connect with two actually friendly clients. I'm sure he vibes with other Northeast assholes, but come *on*, dude. Think Southern.

Tripp softens some of Mark's edge with well-timed laughter that actually makes me smile. Finally, the guy who loves people is exposed to other humans during the workday. Tripp navigates the soft-skills part of the meeting better than Mark and Vivienne, so I start taking my cues from him. My brain isn't sharp enough right now to allow me to be self-reliant. Every time Tripp laughs, I laugh a beat later.

Feel the light, see the beauty and bliss around you. The words come to me and repeat, like a lullaby. *Feel the light.* I did feel it last night. Showstopper. The sign glowed electric blue as I tossed and turned. The pillows were almost soft. The sheets were smooth. *See the beauty and bliss around you.*

Thwack. I open my eyes to see the CEO's knuckles on the table. I must have fallen asleep, and the CEO must have rapped the wooden dining table to wake me up. *Anyone home?* I wipe my mouth. This can't be happening.

"Really working your analysts to the bone, eh?" the CEO asks.

"Allegra, why don't you wait downstairs," Vivienne suggests.

No one is laughing now.

Wind chimes clash abruptly. I chose "wind chimes" to announce my desktop alerts because that sounded peaceful. Like monks, gentle winds, meditation, *om*. I wanted to feel like I was under a spa canopy every time I got a message, but that's not how it turned out. Every time, "wind chimes" sounds like a one-second clip of a tornado sweeping Grandma off her front porch. CHIME. CHIME. Nothing left of that fucking house. I peel my forehead off my desk.

Trixie: Mark Swift wants to see you in his office.
Trixie: Now.

I ASIM her back.

Allegra: Tx Trixiee
Allegra: Trixiee*

Her name is Trixie—one *e*—but at this point, fuck it.

Mark is going to be pissed. I turn my desktops off and nervously check my reflection on the black screens. I'm sweating into my blazer. It could be from the fast. More likely, it could be from the fact that I just embarrassed Team Titan in front of an extremely important client and now face the consequences.

I grab a notebook and move my body shape into his office. I wave to Trixie, who makes eye contact with me and doesn't wave back.

"Allegra," Mark greets me.

He sits at the head of the table, eerily stern. He touches his fingertips and thumbs together to form a diamond of space between his hands. I take the seat farthest from him. The door opens behind me, and Jason enters. I sit up straight. Vivienne files in behind him, and I straighten further to ruler stiffness. Jason sits to Mark's left, and Vivienne remains standing at Mark's right.

"Vivienne," I say. "Jason."

"How would you describe our meeting?" she demands.

"Not—" I begin.

I freeze. I am too afraid to *words*.

"Hm? Well?" she prompts.

"I'll cut in," Jason says. "We wanted to check in on you and your staffings. Are you feeling overworked?"

"Not at all," I say. "I feel great."

"Was the meeting uninteresting?" Vivienne asks.

"I'll cut in," Jason says. Vivienne crosses her arms. The expression goes, "Speak softly and carry a big stick" and, well, Vivienne looks like Jason's big fucking stick. I dry-swallow. "This does not need to take long," Jason continues. "We just wanted to get together to show you how much we care about your well-being. And if you are not well *here*, then we would like to help you get well."

Today, Jason left his smile in his office. His tone is civil, but this is as outwardly angry as his personality allows. This is Jason shouting. Meanwhile, Mark stoically preserves the diamond shape with his hands. His two subordinates are assuming all responsibility for reprimanding me, and Mark is not lifting a finger. I apologize profusely and mean it. I promise, "Never again."

Jason leaves first, and Vivienne follows. On her way out, she pauses in front of me, apparently deliberating whether or not she should say more. She can't seem to find the right words and leaves suddenly in a heated shuffle. I get the feeling that she just rejected twenty different ways to say *You failed, Analyst*, but none was a cold-enough dagger. Only Mark and I remain. He looks at me, unemotional, as if he were just trying to understand.

"Are you trying to embarrass me?" he asks.

"No, I'm sorry," I say. "I am just on a fast."

"Is this some yoga thing?"

"Yes, it's some yoga thing."

"Cut the fucking attitude," he snaps.

Attitude? I was just parroting what he said because that took exponentially less mental energy than coming up with my own sentence. Mark leans forward in his seat. My posture erodes an inch in response.

"I'm sorry," I say.

He grunts.

"Today, I'm just out of it."

"I'll say," he says.

He makes several micro-adjustments to his tie knot, drawing attention to the initials *MTS* monogrammed on his sleeves.

The dark-green tie hangs straight down from his collared shirt, collecting in a twisted, snaky mass on the gleaming hardwood. He eyes me up and down once in a way that feels primal.

"Get back to your desk," he says.

I obey.

At the pod, Vivienne is waiting for me. I don't want to know what she finally decided to say. Tripp, Chloe, and Puja are clearly not fucking doing anything at their computers. Tripp toggles between the up and down arrows on his keyboard in a blank Excel doc, listening closely.

"Hi, Vivienne," I say.

She prepares herself.

"I don't just *write* reviews," she says at last. "You *earn* them."

"Anyone want my twenty-five dollars tonight?" I ask.

"Obviously," Tripp says.

"What do you want?" I ask.

"Gin and tonic," he says.

"Tripp, what do you actually want?"

"Mai tai!"

"Forget it."

After the Titan meeting disaster, I assured Tripp that I was fine, just normal miserable. He took my word for it. Since then, apparently relieved, he has been upbeat and calling my performance at the meeting "legendary." Chloe and Puja laughed at first, but then got absorbed in finishing as much work as they could before Jason boots everyone out of the office at 9 p.m.

Tripp and I are supposed to be putting together a deck of target alternatives to Sierra in a format known as "strip profiles." Each profile is a row across a PowerPoint slide listing the market cap, revenue, and headquarters location, accompanied by a brief company description. Tripp and I split the list down the middle, and I have done none of mine. It took me twice as long to finish shit for my other teams, and Vivienne's *reviews are earned* warning haunts me like a ghost. *Feel the light* is long fucking gone. Now it's 8:59 p.m. I'm in a faded hoodie to stay warm, typing adagio, and only just started the strips, like an absolute stoner.

I open PowerPoint.

"And, done," Tripp announces. He flips the bottom of his keyboard up in a gesture of triumph. "Where we at, team?"

Tripp looks at my blank PowerPoint file.

"A, what the fuck?" he asks.

Jason begins his closing-time walk around the floor. Tripp and I do not have a pass for the strips, which means we need to start working from home. Tripp digs his heels into the carpet to drag his wheelie chair closer to mine. His tie is swept back over his shoulder, where he kept it clean during dinner.

"You know, just putting some of your shit together," he says, as if he is thinking out loud. "I don't think you're just normal miserable." *Oh, really?* "I think you have something else in your life going on."

"Wow, Tripp," I say. "How did you know?"

"Easy now," he says. "I'm just saying I noticed."

He opens his arms and raises his eyebrows, inviting me to reveal something or vent. He cranes his neck toward me, probing a bit further.

"Another . . . team?" he tries.

"Nope," I say.

"Boyfriend keeping you up?" he asks. He jiggles his eyebrows.

"God, we are so done here," I say.

"Is that a yes?" he asks. "Yes, boyfriend? Some guy feel sorry for you?"

"Har har," I say.

"All right," he says reluctantly. "Fine, fine. Anyway, I told Viv tomorrow, so get your shit to me tonight. K?" He tousles my hair and snaps his hand back as if my hair bit him. "God, when was the last time you showered?"

I might not make it to Skylar's before I collapse.

chapter 14

On the subway to Skylar's, I earnestly try to recall my epiphanies. Oh, right, now I remember: "I'm not a complete asshole." *Groundbreaking*.

With one arm, I cradle a crinkling Duane Reade bag full of snacks. With the other, I grip a subway pole to which arms are tethered like ribbons on a maypole. When the car shakes, my slippery pole hand slides up and down.

Every new AS full-time is assigned a "mentor" to help them through their transition to the firm. I got an MD named Nicole, who wears sequin-covered jackets and works out every night at midnight. Rumor is she "whips her husband's noodle dick." Nicole gave me a lot of advice during our one conversation in the Sky Lobby, including a tip to take public transportation in order to "stay in touch." The memory comes back to me now. I'm still not sure what she meant, because I look way worse than everyone else on this fucking car. I would have better peace of mind taking cabs and staying in touch with a reward from my job.

Skylar has made more of an effort to help me in less than two weeks than the entire AS community has in two years. *Your*

*life advice for today: To select a whole row, use the shortcut SHIFT +
SPACE BAR.* At the threshold to her apartment, I knock and look
down at the pale-pink woven doormat that reads SHANTI, Sanskrit for "peace." I am so close and hug my snacks even closer:
5-Hour Energy drinks and the whole fucking candy aisle of Duane
Reade. I've never had a 5-Hour Energy drink before, but my
caffeine-withdrawal headache feels like a helmet two sizes too
small. I need to down a few of these just to get back to baseline.

Skylar opens the door, cueing me to unwrap the small bottles.
Without her explicit permission, I begin to suckle one of them as
I stagger down her hallway. I never knew a concoction of unpro-
nounceable chemicals mixed in a factory vat could feel so deeply
nourishing. This highly processed *whatever* goes down as if it is the
exact piece missing from my nutritional puzzle. Fucking tonic. I
finger-*tap tap* the final drops stuck to the bottom into my mouth.

"Oh my God," I say, relieved.

"You do not look good," she says.

I lean on her marble dining table. She stands beside me in
beige cashmere pants and a matching cardigan. I focus on the
food. On the table in front of me waits an elaborate spread,
apparently from the to-go counter at a vegan cafe: beet balls over
squash spaghetti, curried pumpkin stew, a bunless tofu burger,
mushroom-walnut pâté next to a fan assembly of Wasa crackers,
and a bowl of fresh fruit. I don't even like this stuff, but I fork a
beet ball and swallow it whole. If she tells me to eat mindfully, I
am going to fucking lose it. Why are yogis so afraid of food? They
substitute the most common ingredients, as if everyone else is
just fucking poisoned.

Where is Rosie's pizza now?

"There's more in the cupboard," she says.

Is there any normal shit in there? Seriously, where is Rosie's pizza? Either way, I go to her cupboard and open it just to *see* more food. The bags of non-wheat pasta are neatly arranged, and I reach for a jar of almond butter in the far back like a caveman in a grocery store. Back at the table, I spread it across crackers and eat. Skylar waits across from me, perched gracefully like a flower floating on the surface of a still pond. God, food is straight crack cocaine when you are hungry. It is sex. It is everyone who owes you a favor winning the lottery.

"You know, how genius was it of the first nut-butter guy to put the word *butter* into his food creation?" I ask. "I mean, 'almond butter' could have been 'almond slop.' Or 'almond mush.'"

I'm actually savoring the food now. Taste hasn't been this salient for as long as I can remember. I have hit reorder on Seamless every night for weeks. Tripp accidentally ate half of someone else's dinner yesterday before he noticed it wasn't what he ordered. (Tripp had ordered a sashimi dinner box and a side of scallion pancakes, and he had eaten a wedge of Todd Thomas's steak panini before he said, mouth full, "Wait a sec.")

"Allegra, I'm worried about you," Skylar says.

"I know," I say.

"*What* happened?" she asks.

"Right, sorry." I pause to reflect on the destruction that has befallen my professional life in the span of less than a couple of weeks.

"You know, shit is getting chaotic," I say.

She gestures gently for *more*.

"Well," I start, "it's hard to overstate the number of mistakes I made in two days. I stuck to the fast, but I fucked up all of the shit I get *paid* to do." I shake my head. "I submitted calculations that were ridiculous. My coworkers started mocking me and making jokes about my dick getting in the way of my job. Then I fell asleep in an *incredibly* important meeting in front of a VP who already wants me dead."

Skylar gestures, *keep going*.

"So my bosses surrounded me in this *pack* and basically threatened to fire me, and it's getting so close to bonuses. One of my bosses said, 'I don't write reviews, you *earn* them.' It just felt out of control, like I can't fucking do everything." Skylar is still paying attention. "Thank you for listening, by the way. That really means something." I pause. "Also, I was thinking about it, and you're right, I do have this people-pleasing part of me that's getting in my way." I throw up my hands. "That's the whole truth. I'm doing my best. Oh, and I owe this pretzel guy a dollar. And I still have more work to do."

The strips.

"That's a lot to take in," she says. "Can I help?"

"With my job?" I ask, perplexed.

She nods.

"In the spirit of our partnership," she says.

I actually run through the help scenario in my mind, even though my gut reflex is to enunciate, *NO. NONONO.* Anderson enforces strict rules to protect client confidentiality. Whenever you visit a client's headquarters for a deal, for example, you can't tell people outside of the office which city you are going to because this could tip them off to a potential transaction. Instead, you have to be vague and say "Washington" or "West Coast" when you are traveling to "Seattle." You are not allowed to read deal-related materials in public places without vigilantly guarding your shit. All email services other than Anderson's are blocked on work computers, and if you send anything deal-related to your personal email, it's a breach of security and grounds for immediate dismissal.

But strip profiles collect publicly available information. Skylar wouldn't be exposed to any MNPI, or "material, nonpublic information." She wouldn't see Titan or Sierra named, and she would be none the wiser about the deal. It's a somewhat delirious judgment call, but it sort of feels okay.

"There is actually some stuff you could help with," I say, resigning to the fact that my job is now officially a shit show. "If you googled some stats on a couple of companies: where they are headquartered, how much they make a year in sales, those kinds of things."

Skylar leaves the room and returns with a laptop. She beckons me to follow her into the living room, where she positions herself on the yellow carpet in pigeon pose. Her back leg is split-straight and her front leg is bent 45 degrees at the knee. The full pose would entail bending the knee at 90 degrees. Meanwhile, I sit on the sofa and log into my work computer remotely using a combination of randomly generated and prespecified passwords, until I am staring at my desktop exactly as I left it.

"Okay, so . . ." I begin.

Skylar's finger pecking sounds like a clock ticking. In the background, she plays music from a Spotify playlist—the free version with ads, like me—so that she can simultaneously scan for songs to work into her classes and lessons. She lives under an eclectic taste umbrella that includes the theme to *Star Wars*, chapel hymns, and plain, tribal drums.

"Skye," I say.

"Allegra," she says.

If tonight is any preview of working with her, it's relaxing and pleasant. I finish before Skylar does and open Instagram to her latest post, a picture of her and Rosie on a bench in Central Park. Skylar wraps one arm around Rosie's shoulders and flashes a peace sign while smiling wide at the camera. Rosie is mid-laugh, enjoying something apparently so funny that she's lost self-control. Her eyes are squeezed shut, her mouth open, her teeth bared. The caption is about friendship, but it's not the one I wrote.

@SkylarSmithYoga: A real friend is happy when you are happy.
In Sanskrit, we call this *mudita*.
For my best friend, my sister, Rosie.
Your happy makes me happy.
#mudita.
Love, Skye

Like. I click through Rosie's tag to her profile: 2K followers.

A red notification appears at the bottom-right corner of my app. Weird. Sometimes, though, I do get spam attention. At the moment, I have two new followers, the most recent being @LovePiglet_2. Its bio mandates "Follow us if you love pigs" with a link to a website where I can buy mugs or T-shirts tiled with pig pictures and have my satisfaction 100 percent guaranteed. The next follower is a carbon copy of @LovePiglet_2 but for cow shit: "Follow us if you love cows." Oddly, getting followed like this is always briefly exciting. How lonely am I? These fake fucking people.

"Done," she says. "Just sent."

I open her email's attachment.

"Wow," I mutter.

The company logos are aligned perfectly down the leftmost column. Every line partition between columns is ruler-straight. Every number has the same amount of decimal places. Every bullet point ends with a period. She mimicked the starting template exactly.

"You would be an incredible banking analyst," I say.

"Good to know!" she says.

I laugh and slot her slides behind mine, where it's clear that hers are better. I send the final deck to Tripp and wonder if he will comment on the improvement.

From: Tripp Thompson
To: Allegra Cobb
Fri 17 Nov 11:30 p.m.

 I'm out will look tmrw

Or not. I fold my laptop.

"What a fiasco," I mutter.

"Now," Skylar begins. "To the *real* work."

I laugh and drop my neck back until my head rests on her sofa. That was exhausting. Skylar sits beside me. Her cashmere sweater looks soft. I have an urge to ask her to make me a cup of tea, tuck me in, and say good night.

"How are you?" she asks.

"Overwhelmed," I say.

Skylar smiles as if this is exactly what she wants to hear.

"What?" I ask.

"You're doing it!" she says. She jostles my shoulder, and I wait for the other shoe to drop. "*This* is real openness." She looks joyful. "You're being honest, not ashamed of your feelings. Now we can go even deeper."

"Even deeper," I repeat faintly.

"Yes," she says. "We have good momentum now. As a next step, I will send you some gentle postures you can do right at your desk."

At my desk.

"You can start small," she says. "The right intention, with the right gestures, will open your spirit even more. Gestures like upward-facing cup with your hands." She demonstrates. "Then, breathe deeply. Receive energy through the cup."

At my fucking desk.

"If you feel comfortable, you can raise your arms to welcome possibility." She demonstrates. "Physical gestures have power."

She stands and disappears to her bedroom. When she returns to the sofa, she extends two plastic bottles of oil labeled with brands I don't recognize, subtitled in Chinese. The syrups look thick as shampoo.

"Then, these oils you can rub on your body," she says. "The way you might in *abhyanga*, or a massage, in Ayurveda. The flower smell might seem a bit much at first, but the oils will help calm you. There are instructions on the label. You can wash them off at the end of the day."

End of the day.

"Scalp, face, neck," she says. She imitates the rubbing motion. "If you like, you can massage these onto your chest and back, too. People usually rub clockwise, but I don't think that matters."

"I leave the oils on?" I clarify.

"Yes," she says. "Treat yourself."

Her bottles of amber oil remain untouched in her hands.

"What's wrong?" she asks.

"Nothing," I lie.

She waits, blond eyebrows stitched.

"Nothing," I repeat the lie.

I can't go into work covered in oil.

Skylar takes them back into her lap.

"So, these are not speaking to you," she says.

Yeah, no shit. Titan is up to its eyeballs in Sierra. Mark is mind-fucking me. Vivienne wants to kill me. Tripp is asking about my feelings. *Tripp* is asking about my *feelings*. Jason could staff me at any moment on a triple trans-border fucking reverse merger, and then I'd get paired working with an Anderson team in a whole other time zone and deal with exchange rate bullshit. My schedule twenty-four hours ahead is unpredictable as shit. I am at fucking capacity. Oils?

"Allegra, I am on your side," she says gently. "I thought we were working together to center you. Then we could spread the peace together. Now I feel you resisting me again. I can't teach you if you won't stay open to the process." She pauses. "I thought we would have made a good team, but I won't force anything on you. If this isn't meant to be, it isn't meant to be."

"No, I'm with you," I say. "I just can't go to work covered in oil."

"What *do* you want to do?" she asks directly.

Without thinking, I answer, "Teach."

She reflects. I see the wheels turning in her head.

"You know what? That is a great idea," she says. "Maybe it's in a studio that you really shine. And that's where we want you to end

up anyhow, right?" She laughs. "Sometimes, the right answer is
the simplest one. So, would you like to sub in and teach for me?
Monday night?" The tail end of her question beckons me invitingly. I must be showing my answer, *Yes.* "Great!" she says. She
prayers her hands. "Then you emerge truly as a teacher, or . . .
maybe the time isn't right. We won't force anything unnatural."

I left Skylar's apartment that night with a sense of urgency. She
didn't say it outright, but the Monday class felt like my last chance
to earn the opportunity to work with her. Her patience was wearing thin.

Skylar gave me no parameters aside from time and place—Yoga
Cyclone, Monday, 8 p.m.—so I could structure the class as I saw
fit. Of course, I've never taught a yoga class before on my own,
nor have I trained as a teacher. I've done thousands of hours of
yoga in my life and competed onstage in front of yogi masters,
which should be enough to guide a class. At least, I think so. And
Skylar does, too. But, really, I would be winging it.

I started thinking about the class as soon as I left her apartment
and anticipated using most of the weekend—Saturday—to plan. I
had to think about the flow sequence, the pacing, the modifica-
tions, and my own script. Should I sync the flow to music? What
kind of music and how loud? Then there was the meaning of the
class to consider. I could structure the flow around a mantra or
quote, ideally one that would resonate honestly with students. I
just had to figure out: *How can I teach a meaningful class when my
days are full of nothing but meaningless transactions and dollar signs?*

chapter 15

I woke up Saturday to emails from Mark and Vivienne and a
missed call from Jason. Our last analysis for Titan showed how
much the company would be worth if it bought Sierra, using models
from Anderson Shaw equity research. Titan was intrigued and told
us so at the management meeting, after I left. Now we are doing
the same analysis, this time with models provided by Titan. Mark
phrased this as "moving forward" in a team email sent at 1 a.m.
He wants the deck Monday. We should "back-burner" the strips.

Vivienne sent Tripp and me an outline. Decks are capped at
fifty slides each, as one of Anderson's lifestyle initiatives. Vivienne treats this maximum as a bull's-eye target that must be hit
with precision. Her outline detailed ten slides of what the deal
is worth and forty slides of deal rationale, including a section
called "Growth Potential." This section is supposed to show that
the monster business would have a spectacular growth profile.
It should show, as she underlined, "growth in all segments." A
draft to her was due Saturday night.

I called Jason back. Apparently, he wanted to check in again
and make sure my workload was manageable, but he didn't ask

any questions and spoke only in declarative statements. *I wanted to check in on your capacity. Titan is a very important team. I'm sure Vivienne has been in touch. Thanks.* It didn't sound like he was asking about my workload at all. He was warning me to show up for Titan. So Tripp and I spent Saturday together in the office. He rolled in shouldering a backpack stuffed with his new wet-suit booties and GoPro, as he had been on his way to Newport to surf when Mark's email hit at 1 a.m. Tripp came straight to the office from Grand Central Saturday morning.

Vivienne effectively babysat us with the length and duration of her conference-call check-ins. She ate lunch with us by phone. She slurped her soup with us on the line. At the end of each call, she asked Tripp, "How is Analyst?" He would say, "She's fine," and wink at me. It gave me the sense that not only was this deal under a microscope, but *I* was under a microscope *under* that microscope. Then Vivienne would say, "Thank you, Tripp," and hang up. The *and fuck you, Analyst* was implied.

So I didn't have a long enough leash to plan a class. I told myself, *Okay, Sunday, Allegra. Sunday is your day. Find an hour and plan. Break it up. Do it while you pee.* Then Vivienne showed up Sunday morning wearing a wrinkled Anne Fontaine blouse, undereye circles, and, for the first time, no wedding ring. I told Tripp *immediately*, and he said he was seriously not interested. I wondered how long it had taken Vivienne and her husband to call it off, because she was on the phone with us almost all day on Saturday. I actually felt bad for her. Maybe she wasn't the fire-breathing dragon I thought she was.

Instead of working in her office, she sat at Puja's desk all Sunday long. I didn't see any opportunity to steal away and plan my class. I stayed put, scared shitless of this ghostly apparition who had a deal to push forward in bonus season and who might or might not be getting divorced. Skylar texted me Sunday afternoon that she was "so excited" to watch me "blossom tomorrow."

After several rounds of comments, Tripp and I sent Vivienne the latest deck at 3 a.m. on Monday. Vivienne sent a calendar invite three hours later for an 8 a.m. meeting to give us *more* comments. At *8 a.m.* That rooster time is fictional here. I go to midnight meetings without batting an eye, but an 8 a.m. might as well be in Vivienne's bedroom at her weekend house, which I've heard is on the water in Connecticut. Point being: it's strange, inconvenient, and oddly intimate. I get that this is Titan-Sierra, but come *on*.

So I woke up Monday morning, class unplanned, to Vivienne's meeting request. Her ambush compelled me to backseat drive my taxi to the office—*You can make this light, pass that guy*—and use the full extent of my free will to avoid any penalties awaiting the tardy.

Sitting inside Vivienne's office right now is surreal. So far, Tripp is one minute late. I am still sweating from the final sprint to get here, but I made it on time. My foot crossed her SVP office threshold at exactly 8 a.m. My first lesson from her today: "On time is late."

Vivienne sits across from me at her round table with the intimidating presence of an entire panel of interviewers. She wears her Monday-morning normal—no makeup, taut bun high on her crown, and a pencil dress—with the exception of one key accessory. Seeing her naked ring finger is like glimpsing smoke as it wafts slowly up from dry tinder. Eventually, the fire has to catch.

She starts to tap her foot, the steady thumps muffled by carpet. Her pace quickens. She cups her sharp chin in her pale hand.

"He is three minutes late," she announces.

Tripp needs to get here before Vivienne starts getting creative, or vindictive, or even more desperate for that promotion. The outcome of this meeting determines whether I can plan my class (or make the thing at all).

"Let's just get started, since Tripp is *busy*," she says.

Vivienne starts drafting slides on a blank sheet of printer paper. Each box denotes a new PowerPoint slide, free-drawn with the precision of a ruler. The subtitle to this moment would be: "I'm going to create slides until Tripp gets here [chortle]." She makes more boxes until both of our phones buzz to signal a new email: a goodbye blast.

Whenever a banker leaves, they send a group-wide email with the subject line "Last Day." It begins with a clause where the sender specifies how long they lasted. Example: "After 2 years and 3 months, today is my last day at AS." Then we commemorate our time at the firm and thank our colleagues in an idiosyncratic way. This part tends to feel sincere. The message ends with where the alum will go next, plus contact information. Most analysts start planning what to say in their goodbye blast during training.

But quitting *before* the bonus cycle is a bold move. It suggests, "I hate this place so much that I would rather leave now than stick around for one more month and get paid $100K." Or, "My next gig is so much better than this that I am leaving ASAP. Keep the bonus." It is a giant middle finger.

Intrigued, I read the email. The bold sender addressed her Last Day email to "friends and colleagues." It's not an uncommon way to start, but the phrase has always felt awkward to me.

It effectively labels an entire group of people as non-friends. Someone is going to get this email today and think, *I'm in the colleague category, aren't I, you fucking colleague.* The body of the email is just a thank-you to the group as a whole, without any personalized spin. It feels like I'm glazing over placeholder type, like lorem ipsum, the pseudo-Latin text that fills text boxes. This person gives fewer than zero shits. She's probably dashing out to the lobby right now.

Vivienne sets her phone down. Its scratched, metal ass faces up.

"People need to honor their commitments," Vivienne says.

She draws faster, clearly taking everything personally. She sketches more boxes until the sheet of paper between us looks like a checkerboard. Her two-handed wall clock ticks steadily on. I don't know what the fuck is up with her personal life, but I feel like the only one who didn't disappoint her today. I want to help.

I've practiced yoga to the mantra, "The most precious gift we can offer anyone is our attention," from Thich Nhat Hanh. Right now, that's all I can give her. So, I pay attention, accept her boxes, and it hits me that I *care* about Vivienne. This is new. It may be the first sign I'm improving under Skylar's direction. So what if I fell asleep in the Titan meeting? Today, I was right on time and, here I am, empathizing with the devil herself. Now that's some fucking compassion.

Tripp falls into his office chair at 10 a.m. He places a Starbucks cup of coffee on his desk and rests his head in his hands.

"You know who's the biggest douche canoe on the floor?" he asks.

This better be good.

"Who?" Puja asks.

"Peter," Tripp says. Peter is the blond, Mormon analyst who went to BYU and is married with a son at age twenty-four. His wife is pregnant with their second child. He brought their baby to an analyst dinner at the Mexican restaurant near Anderson. He put the kid in a cradle under the table and left with his wife at 8 p.m. while the rest of the analysts went out to Up and Down, a club downtown. I sat next to him one day in training, where he told me that he saves seventy-five cents for every dollar he makes.

Yeah, total douche.

"What happened?" Puja asks.

"I was just getting my coffee and complaining about the job, you know," he says. "And Peter was like, 'I'm a realist. It's a secure job, and you have to start thinking about these things when you start a family.'"

Puja snorts a laugh.

"Yeah, what an asshole," she says sarcastically.

"Broo-tahl," Tripp agrees.

"Tripp!" I actually smack the hardwood of the desk surface in front of him.

"Easy, Amy," he says. "Rough weekend. Let's talk later."

"Don't hit the desk," Chloe says.

"Are you protecting the rights of *furniture*?" Tripp asks.

"Tripp, focus," I say. "You missed our meeting with Vivienne this morning."

His irritability becomes genuine fear as I detail the latest comments.

"Whose ass does she pull this stuff out of?" Tripp asks.

"That's irrelevant," I snap.

"Are you defending Vivienne?" Tripp asks.

He glances at Chloe, then back at me, as if Chloe fucking multiplied.

A bit softer, I add, "Let's just get it done."

I plan the entire class on my walk to Yoga Cyclone, which is close to the office. We sent the final deck to Mark at 7:01 tonight. He sent it to the client at 7:30, which granted me freedom at 7:31. Class starts at eight.

I am bundled up and booking it. My tote holds a change of clothes and laptop. The fresh outfit cushions my prized computer like packing peanuts. If an ASAP work request hits in the next hour, I can handle it right after class. Meanwhile, with my un-mittened hand, I browse my gallery on @AllegraHandstands and mentally arrange a few video clips into a flow sequence. I Google the poses' Sanskrit names and practice pronunciations, should any student ask.

"*Salabhasana*," I mutter.

I speed walk.

"*Navasana. Padmasana.*"

"Fuckin' nut," the pretzel guy mutters as I pass.

I ignore him and keep thinking through my script.

"Hey, I know you!" he shouts. "You owe me!"

Oh my God, he's right. I stop and face him.

"I am so sorry," I say earnestly. "I will get you cash."

"Oh, you have hard time?" he mocks me. "Oh, you have a shitty roadside food stand, where customers steal from you? Because then I understand. Oh. *Wait* a second. That's *me*. *I* have a shitty roadside food stand, get robbed. *You* have a big fancy job in a building filled with millionaires."

You made your point.

"I will pay you back," I promise.

"Fuckin' A."

I add it to the top of my to-do list: *Get him the dollar. Sewage problem. Gas problem. Yoga books.* I keep walking and return to the fast-approaching task of narrating an hour-long class. What should I even say? I'm a banker who steals from local vendors. How is anyone going to take me seriously?

I scroll through my Instagram feed for inspiration in the captions. What should tonight's class mean? I haven't picked a keystone mantra or phrase. I'm an imposter. I decide to tie the class back to the only moment I can remember that touched me recently. When Skylar and I met, she said, "Part of what I do—and what I do believe you are drawn to—is just show compassion." That resonated, and they say imitation is the greatest form of flattery. Tonight, I can pass on what Skylar showed me. The theme will be compassion.

"Fuckin' A!" he shouts after me.

I arrive at Yoga Cyclone with ten minutes to spare. The studio is devoted half to yoga classes and half to cardio classes. I cross the threshold and stand in the gift shop between two distinct wings. On the left: rooms for yoga. On the right: a stadium of stationary bikes for high-intensity interval training. There are dozens of boutique fitness studios in New York City, so competition is fierce enough to spark unusual novelty. You wind up with a lot of places like this, smashing opposites together for a niche sound bite.

The yoga teacher from the previous class stands in her door-way, bidding students goodbye. She uses the word *like* to indicate the grammatical necessity of a comma, and her enthusiasm is uncannily high given that her task is simply to acknowledge people. The skin of her stomach crinkles like a single layer of Saran Wrap over her abs. She looks like Alec Baldwin's wife.

In the other wing, the inside of the cycling stadium looks like a dark cave of shame. Frankly, it's a crazy place to be if you're not overeating. Those classes torch up to a thousand calories in an hour, so if you're not having cupcakes for breakfast, you may die. The cycling instructor stands in her own doorway, saying goodbye to the exiting bikers. Her dark hair is soaking wet, and her black leather pants gleam. She looks like she could be Tim Burton's wife.

"I'm teaching a dirgey class next," she says to a couple walking out through the door. "Do you know what dirge is?" They don't. "It's like funeral music. Some people like to work out to fun, poppy stuff. I like dark."

This job ruined Top 40 for her.

I shrug my parka off and hang it outside my studio room, where students are already inside. From here, I glimpse a tranquil, middle-aged couple with their eyes closed in lotus on mats they clearly own. The woman has bed-head-wavy hair and wears two dark-purple hair wraps that drape from the nape of her neck down below her shoulders. The shirtless man beside her has the same haircut and wears stud earrings.

Skylar smiles at me eagerly from the doorway, barefoot and in a hemp halter top. Does she get fitter every day? She motions with a fast hand that I enter behind her and, like, fucking set up for class already. I know, it's almost time. On the teacher's stage, I unroll my mat and sit in lotus. My warm hands rest on my knees. Skylar has laid her mat in the back corner, where she alternates her front feet in a series of lunges. She pushes each knee out sideways to open up her hips.

Six minutes remain until we start. I'm wearing my favorite black leggings with cinched bottoms, only a black sports bra on top, and a beaded necklace. The room before me, which can hold up to sixty mats, is half-full.

Another student walks in, and I do a double take. *Do I know you?* It's Robbie from Industrials. *Robbie,* the banking enthusiast known for his Facebook statuses, who told me in training that he wants to send his future kids to "capitalism camp for kindergarteners." (I had to look that up. Turns out, there is a place called Spark Business Academy that teaches six-to-ten-year-olds about "cultivating an entrepreneurial mind-set" and "building a stock market portfolio." The website features kids wearing suits and on cell phones.) I am teaching the capitalist of all capitalists tonight.

Behind him, I recognize another face, also from Industrials: Max. He rowed in prep school and college. Throughout training, he would work out for five hours a day in the Anderson gym. I once saw him riding a spin bike while biting into a device that made it harder to breathe, so that he could build more muscle around his ribs and lungs. His girlfriend enters behind him.

More analysts trickle in, followed by more associates. Somebody actually points at me. Of course they know me. They aren't in HG, but they fucking know me. Training was class-wide and sector-blind. We mingled at the new-banker cocktails. We were in each other's groups for the diversity discussions, where in my randomly assigned group of six, three were white guys from Westchester and two of those three were named Will. Each week, we rotated to a different table of new analysts. The tables were named after financial capitals—New York City, Kuala Lumpur—and together we graffitied over the table-tent labels with better names, like Rack Rack City.

Robbie approaches the teacher's stage.

"Allegra?" he asks.

"Hey," I say.

We pause.

"What are you doing here?" he asks.

"What are *you* doing here?" I shoot back.

"It's bonding night in Industrials," he says. "The staffer said we were all too stressed, so we're doing yoga. A teacher at the studio reached out about a group rate or something. Everyone is here."

A couple of the guys are still in three-hundred-dollar dress shirts with sleeves rolled up past the elbows. More and more heads turn toward me. I feel trapped onstage not as their teacher, but as the night's entertainment. Industrials is the frattiest banking group at Anderson, and that's saying something. This is probably their only free hour all week, and they're going to want to have a good time with their friends. Earnest yoga? Yeah, fucking right. An HG analyst is teaching? They're going to have a fucking field day.

"You're a yoga teacher?" Robbie asks.

"No," I say honestly. It's kind of the truth, but it sounds ridiculous given that all signs point to yes. I'm sitting in lotus wearing a long, beaded necklace that grazes the top of my mat. A couple of other analysts approach us, and I don't quite know their names, but we are familiar enough to say hi. I hug them and try to stay calm like the yogi I want to be.

"Do you have a second job?" one asks.

I part my lips to answer.

"Trying to make ends meet?" another chimes.

The small group gathered around me looks gleeful, chomping at the bit to one-up each other with jokes. *Banking and yoga is a stretch. Get it? Nama-slay.* LOL. I allow them their fun—*har har, guys*—expecting them to take their places and unroll their mats, at least, but their jokes keep coming. They keep going.

"Do they pay you?" one asks. He shakes his head.

"Man, times are tough when Anderson bankers need a side hustle."

"What, you just blowing everything on models and bottles?"

"I hope you disclosed this to HR. Could be a conflict of interest, you know. You don't know what this studio is invested in."

"Yeah, they probably have an extensive stock and bond portfolio," Robbie says. "With billions of dollars in Lat Am."

"This just screams paperwork to me."

Skylar approaches, and finally, they leave. The bankers press their palms together in mock prayer and bow to each other, leaving with their rental mats under their arms. People lumber around. Some thumb away on their phones, shooting off two-word emails in rapid fire. I have no choice but to roll with it.

"No phones," I announce in a calm teacher voice.

"No phones? This yoga is bullshit!" someone jokes in a shout-whisper. On the bright side, two listen and lay theirs blinking side up next to their mats. One asshole in the back continues to glare at his, hammering away. The fitness freak ogles his girlfriend's ass as she bends over playfully into downward dog. "Woof," he says. He gives it a light pat, and I don't think anything bounced.

"Please let me know if anyone is uncomfortable with assists," I say.

"Will loves assists," someone says. Laughter.

"Yeah, extra assists for Will."

"Shut up!" the one who must be Will shouts.

A group of three in the back chants: "Will, Will, Will."

The class that followed, of course, was shit. People raised their hands in the middle of flows to ask questions: "Which pose best targets the glutes?" "Is there really such a thing as a 'yogasm,' and what exactly does that mean for my experience specifically?" "Can Jack get a private lesson, but he's going to need lots of assists because he is a tactile learner?" Two more bankers from Natural Resources filed into the class late, and eventually there was so much disruptive laughter that I wrapped it up with an early *savasana*.

Skylar and I are the last two here, side by side on the teacher's stage. At the back of the room, there's a messy line of prop blocks and blankets that people did not return to the shelves. I'm embarrassed. I did not structure the class around compassion. I didn't structure it around anything other than trying not to cry. I just tried to keep my voice steady and the flow as respectable as possible while the group devolved.

Skylar puts her hand on my back. I stare at my toes. All I can think about is what an insane coincidence it is that dozens of AS bankers showed up to class on the *one* night I teach. Yes, Yoga Cyclone is right by the office and, yes, groups have off-site bonding activities every once in a while, but come *on*. What are the odds? One of those fucking numbers guys rolling up their mats could answer that.

"Can I be honest with you?" she asks softly.

I lift my head.

"I am impressed," she says.

chapter 16

Skylar's impressed? But that class was a total disaster.

"This class wasn't about the students, it was about you," she says. "You can't control what goes on outside, you can only control yourself, and you did! *You* kept your composure. *You* were calm. You were exactly the strong, beautiful presence I knew you would be." She smiles so wide it's contagious.

"Oh, wow," I exclaim. "That's great!"

"I think we can make our relationship more formal," she says. "You and I met during a time of growth for me, too. Next year, I will be growing my little enterprise, and I would love to have you on my team."

My head jerks at the word *team*.

"I've always said I admire your skills, and I know you will be a great teacher one day. But I always imagined us working *together* in a different way." She pauses, which feels like a silent drumroll. "I think you would be a beautiful voice for some of the beliefs of my practice."

"Okay," I say hesitantly.

What does she mean?

Skylar smiles wider.

"So, I would be a spokesperson?" I ask.

"Think of it as, you are an example of what I help people achieve," she says. "Here's the story: you're unhappy at Anderson, unfulfilled despite 'having it all,' but then we meet, and I transform your life with the SkylarSmithYoga method and teach you advanced asana. You are suddenly breathing easier, sleeping better, spiritually centered, a few pounds lighter, and you feel compelled to evangelize my practice. You're perfect for the role. Your poses will be stunning."

I am speechless.

"Really, it is such an incredible opportunity for you. You'll help people live their best lives. You'll get name recognition. And you'll travel. I've already picked some great cities."

"Okay," I say, clearing my throat. "So, I would travel as, like, advertising. . . ." I linger here, putting the pieces together out loud. "And not teaching. Just talking about how much you helped me?"

She nods. A pause grows.

"But I haven't changed that much," I say, asserting the obvious out loud.

"I think you're losing sight of the big picture," she says, still upbeat. "I have such big dreams for you! You will travel to all of the best studios—places like Mala, Hamsa Hand—and be part of the SkylarSmithYoga team. Your practice is so inspiring. What you can do with your body is breathtaking, and adding my story to it is something I've been, well, really excited about. You will be a role model."

"I'm the client other people could be," I say.

"Exactly," she says, smiling. "And it's not just you—I'm building an *amazing* team. Rosie will take on more responsibility. She'll be working for me on the Instagram side, editing photos and writing content. She'll stay up on the hashtag and pose trends, so I don't have to." She laughs. "To be honest, I'll be glad to take that one off my plate. Then I can spend more time teaching retreats and making videos."

"So Rosie will manage your account?" I ask.

"Yes!" Skylar says. She wraps one arm around my shoulder the way she held Rosie on the park bench in #mudita.

"Wow," I say, still processing.

"I know!" she agrees.

"It's just . . . I just imagined myself teaching," I admit.

She swats the air. "You will be *in* the studios," she says. "Think of all the people you'll meet and inspire."

Rustling noises amplify outside the closed studio door, signaling that another class may soon begin in this room.

"I'm really, really flattered," I say. "Honestly. But it's a lot to take in. I'll probably think of more questions after I leave. Can we talk about it again later?"

"Of *course*," she says. "I don't need to go through the whole contract right here and now." We stand, and she hugs me. "Talk again very soon. I think we're going to work well together. You're so teachable."

It doesn't sound like a compliment.

I change in Yoga Cyclone's dressing room. As I zip my skirt, I avoid eye contact with the woman wearing two dark-purple hair wraps. *Yeah, I know class sucked, lady.* I scan my work emails—nothing due *now*—and mark banking Google Alerts from Dad as "read."

I mentally write my to-do list for the rest of the night. Cold air pricks my face as I leave.

Skylar's offer reminded me of a moment from new-banker training. During one of the presentations on company culture, an HR rep projected a slide illustrating the income trajectory at Anderson Shaw. The chart showed a single arrow sloped diagonally up. The y-axis: Money. The x-axis: time, going from analyst to MD. It was an attempt by AS at retention and suggested the caption "Stay here for life and ride this fucking arrow all the way to the top of our line graph. How incredibly fucking dope does that sound?"

Analysts have plenty of high-paying exit options waiting for them after two years here, but one of Anderson's selling points is a "risk-adjusted" path to wealth. Go to the buy side and your income is insecure. Many of the associate jobs that analysts flock to after AS only have two-year contracts, and then the firing rounds begin. Beyond that, investments can fail. The market can crash. Hedge funds close. But companies will always need bankers. Anderson was saying: "You can count on this fucking line graph. You don't need your own dreams when you're building ours, bitches!" I just don't know if my working for Skylar would be her dream or my own.

I stop at a convenience-store ATM and withdraw twenty dollars for a $1.95 fee. I break the twenty into some single dollar bills. Soon enough, with my cash in hand, I see the pretzel cart come into view. It glows radioactive orange in the dark.

Out of curiosity, and because I need a distraction from thinking about my uncertain future, I look up the cart on Yelp. There are apparently several pretzel carts nearby that expose this one to be even shittier than I believed. One a couple of blocks away sells sweet and savory pretzels in flavors like Gruyère paprika, cheddar truffle, and churro. The pictures uploaded by customers are as well lit as acting headshots. The churro-pretzel competitor is described as the "perfect love child between a pretzel, croissant, and biscuit." How is Anderson's pretzel guy even still in business?

He mans his stand while I wait at the intersection.

"You again," he says. "Fuckin' A."

I hand him two dollar bills. He gives me the middle finger.

"Why are you so mean?" I ask.

"I sell you pretzels," he says. "I don't sell 'be your bitch.'"

"Got it," I say, with some admiration.

He may be the only person I know who's not sacrificing who he is or acting two-faced just to make another sale. He is staying true to what he believes—in his case, he seems to believe, *Fuck Anderson*, but still. His main mantra in life isn't *Sell more shit* and, for a second, I like him.

"You have a tip jar?"

"No."

You got a mission, bro. Godspeed. I hope I have *half* his guts in the morning, when I face the bankers I just taught.

chapter 17

As I walk onto the HG floor with unusual trepidation, Tripp is one-earbud zoned into *Game of Thrones*. Chloe is adjusting her shawl. Puja is unwrapping a Reese's Peanut Butter Cup, presumably from the stash of MDs' leftover candy.

"Well, well, well," Tripp greets me.

He removes his earbud. Chloe and Puja perk up.

"Looks like the pod has *another* celebrity," he says, with a thoroughly unmalicious aura of amusement. "Are you in office-chair pose right now? Looks amazing."

Chloe smirks, and Puja giggles.

"Does everyone know?" I ask.

The associates Harry and Alex stop at the edge of our pod. Their impromptu visit is unusual. I ignore them.

"Sorry, are you meditating right now?" Harry asks.

"We wouldn't want to interrupt that," Alex says.

"Yeah, I am, fuckface," I snap.

"Hey, now," Alex says. "Whoa."

"That's not very yoga of you," Harry says.

"Yeah, someone needs a green juice and a flow," Alex says.

"Yum," Puja says.

"All right, all right," Tripp says. "I'm trying to watch *Game of Thrones*, guys."

He waves them away like dust bunnies, and they oblige, sniggering. I mouth *Thank you* to Tripp as Outlook loads. The first email to appear turns out to be an all-HG-analysts blast where the photo above the sender's signature is a gypsy caravan. The wagon is decorated with vaguely Eastern symbols.

Tripp fills me in. Since the class last night, the guys in Industrials have been spreading the word that an HG analyst—me—is teaching at Yoga Cyclone. The news traveled fast because it's extremely bizarre. I now appear to have a whole other, second *identity* that people can't reconcile with my life at Anderson. The fact that I have time for it at all is a point of fascination and attributed to "yoga powers."

Tripp says not to worry. People are just unhappy and jumping on an easy laugh. Right now, it's at my expense, because, "come on, this shit is fun-*nay*." Soon enough, it will pass. Which brings us back to the wagon picture blast. Yep, that's me. I am HG's yoga gypsy in residence, smoking ganja and peddling feathered dream catchers to the clients out of a fucking wagon. I am the butt of a group-wide joke.

"Do you want to get a drink or something?" Tripp asks.

"It's ten a.m.," I say.

"Bloody Mary?" he says.

"No thanks," I say.

"Oh, is it the yoga?" he asks. He winks.

"L-O-L," I spell.

"Leggo," he says. "Come *onnnn*."

I open Instagram for a distraction. The first post comes from a yogi my age sitting in a non-asana on her yoga mat in a leotard. The surface area of her one-piece suggests a profound shortage of latex. The thigh holes run so generously high that she is basically wearing a white version of the iconic *Baywatch* swimsuit. *So yoga*.

A red notification hovers in the corner: +201. *@AllegraHandstands has 201 new followers*. The fuck? The profiles are attached to handles like @LikeCashLoveYoga, @HGUnit, and @BankDatAssUp. My most recently posted video has been viewed over five hundred times and earned twenty-five comments. I read them. The number of banking puns is astounding. There is only one explanation: My colleagues found my yoga Instagram.

Mark walks onto the floor, briefcase in one hand and coffee in the other.

"Morning, team," he greets the pod.

"Fantastic to see you, Mark," Tripp says.

Fuck my life.

I head abruptly for a conference room. The trip unfolds as if I am a television show walking through my own audience. Some people look at me, stare, and lean in to whisper amongst themselves. I steal a random cardboard notebook and use the prop as a deflective *I'm busy* flag. *Oh, you have a yoga joke? Sorry, I'm on my way to a meeting. A megamerger meeting, to be specific.*

I duck into the first dark conference room I see and leave the lights off. Conference rooms like this one are scattered throughout the floor. They are used mainly for interviews and late-night dinners when people literally get sick of their screens. My pod sticks close to home base, but I went to one of those dinners a few weeks ago. A dozen analysts sat around the table, and casual conversation turned into swapping ambitions. People shared how they wanted to change the world. One analyst from Ghana said he wanted to go back with the skills he learned to reform his country. A similar mind from the Caribbean said he wanted to learn microfinance and development economics, and then go home to develop his nation. Another analyst mapped out how he wanted to rise in a private equity firm and then go into policy. Yeah, where are those grounded and respectful assholes now, huh? It's like recess out there.

I turn my back to the door so that no one can see my face. Who even makes an all-glass door? What is the point of that? I know I'll have to come out eventually. For now, I think back to some of the things Skylar has said to make me feel better. *You can't control what goes on outside, you can only control yourself. . . . You kept your composure. You were calm.* This time, though, it doesn't seem to help. I don't know. Listening to Skylar is sort of how I got here in the first place.

Tripp, Chloe, and Puja rise at noon, beckoned by the silent call of the un-discount. I drink the final inch of Keurig coffee waiting room-temperature in my paper cup. Coffee grounds speckle the bottom like a kaleidoscope of shit spray.

"Want anything?" Tripp asks.

"Nah," I say. "Meeting."

"Do you mean nah-maste?" Chloe says.

She giggles. Tripp raises one of his eyebrows.

"*That*'s the one minority we can jab at? Yogis?" He shakes his head. "That's fucked, Chlo, really. I expected better from you."

They head for the door.

"Let's be politically correct, but fuck the yogis," Tripp says.

"Oh my God, so mean," Puja says as they leave.

Thanks, Tripp. He's deduced that I don't want my "second job" in the limelight. Every time someone stopped by and expressed uncharacteristic interest in how my day was, Tripp shooed them away because he was "cranking right now, steaming at the ears, thanks bro." He usually had a window of *Rick and Morty* up at the same time, which made his "cranking" excuse empty but even more appreciated by me.

A familiar, round figure comes into view: my associate, Adam. I'm reminded of the shitty management presentation I sent him during my fast last week. Adam graduated from Columbia Business School in May and has over one hundred thousand dollars of student debt. He was born and raised in Illinois, gets to the office at 9 a.m. on Sundays, and has a deeply internalized sense of subservience. When the companies he covers report their financial results every quarter, Adam proactively emails his MDs on how they performed. At every internal lunch meeting, he clears the place settings of the VPs and MDs. He has gained fifty pounds since he started working here. Of all the associates to burden with shit work, I sent nice-guy Adam shit work.

"Hey, Adam," I say.

"Allegra," he says cheerily. "Ready?"

I follow him to the MD's office, where we take our seats and flip open our notebooks. Adam titles a fresh page "Mgmt Pres Review," and I double-take when I see his wrists. They are extremely slender and pale as printer paper. I look away because they are so fucking sad. I don't want to know that his wrists belong to an 1850s Southern debutante with sun allergies. Thin hairs struggle to assert masculinity. This poor fucking guy.

From my seat, I see down the line of pods. A few analysts have added new decorations to their desks: a miniature Zen sandbox and fork-size rake, a hatha yoga book the size of a brick, and a small electric fountain.

"Is it Diwali?" Adam whisper-asks me.

"Yes," I lie.

The MD, Zena, is a single mom, member of the Anderson Women's Group, and force of nature. She reminds me of Everest Lady, who we reference at the pod every now and then as a personality type. During training, Anderson hosted a day of lectures by alumni including a woman who had climbed Everest *twice*. Apparently, you can't just climb Everest from bottom to top. You have to climb a bit, then trek down halfway, then climb a bit more, then trek down halfway, over and over again in order to acclimate yourself to the altitude. At the time I thought, *Yep, there's an idea: find the worst place on earth and bring to life the myth of Sisyphus.* Everest Lady literally did. Not only that, but she trained while working at Anderson full-time. She used the rowing machine in our gym at night with her eyes closed and said she had brainwashed herself into believing that she was both sleeping and working out. Most of the time, I can't do either, and Everest Lady did both at the same fucking time.

Zena finishes an email at her desktop, hits ALT+S to send it, and wheels herself to the table. Deck printout in hand, she summarizes a phone call with the CEO and his latest comments on our presentation. Zena supplements those with ideas of her own. Meanwhile, Harry stops by the pod with the Zen garden and rakes a couple of squiggles.

"What do you think, Allegra?" Zena asks.

Fuck. They stare at me. I get the feeling that Zena is calling me out because I am a woman. If I were a male analyst, she wouldn't care. But I missed what she was saying.

"I agree," I flounder.

Zena pauses as if there's a glitch in the Matrix before promptly resuming her comments. Words zoom across the table. Adam is scribbling, but I'm slow. I feel out of this flow. The only way to describe it is that I am a full body in between two heads. Harry continues to rake. I can't even hear the wooden tool grate sand, but the sound is as distracting as that of fingernails raking across a chalkboard.

We must be finished, because Adam closed his notebook. Zena signs the upper right-hand corner of the presentation and records the date and time. Some MDs joke about how bad their handwriting is when they return paper markups, with *oh, my chicken scratches* kinds of bullshit. I once spent half an hour trying to figure out if loopy markings were a comment or a doodle, passed the presentation around to other analysts, and took a vote at the pod on how fucked I was. Two to one, I was fucked. At least Zena's cursive is neat.

"Thanks, team," she says. "Goodbye, Adam. Allegra, a minute."

Adam departs with the deck.

"How's it going?" she asks. Before I can answer, she continues, "I couldn't help but notice you didn't speak up in our meeting."

"I'm sorry," I say honestly.

"Why not?" she demands.

"I got distracted," I say. "It won't happen again."

She nods. "This is something we talk about at the Women's Group," she says. "Studies show women in finance have lower confidence in their skills, but better skills. We perform better on written tests than men."

This is clearly a gender pep talk, but she has no idea how low on my priority list my banking skills are right now.

"You have the skills," she says. "Don't doubt them. Stick up for yourself."

"Find my voice," I say.

"Exactly," Zena says.

I remember my first meeting with Skylar, when she told me the exact same thing. *Find your voice and tell your story.* Zena spins back to her desktop. I know Zena is trying to be nice, but I also know that everyone has an agenda. When someone says, *Find your voice,* they already know what they want you to say.

chapter 18

I changed my handle from @AllegraHandstands to @Pretzel Yoga a few days after Yoga Cyclone. Enough already. The jokey comments had deteriorated and were getting plain mean. Most new ones were put-downs to the tune of "this is such a shitstagram 💩 👎." A few called it "slutty." Sure, I'm only in a sports bra in most of the videos, but come *on*. It was a practice gallery.

I thought a new name would thwart more colleagues of mine feeling clever. *Looking to shit on @AllegraHandstands? Surprise, "no results found," assholes.* Still, even with the new handle, my Instagram keeps growing. @PretzelYoga now links to 3,011 followers, a couple of weeks since I taught at Yoga Cyclone. I don't even know who these people are anymore. *Three thousand eleven.* I have 312 friends on Facebook.

I read some of my new direct messages at my desk.

1. I can take picture for you ?
2. Can you lick your own pussy
3. What are you some good beginner yoga moves?

4. 🖤
5. Your hot
6. Do you teach yoga?
7. Do you visit LA ever?
8. Hi PretzelYoga. Enjoying your holidays?
9. My name is Ricardo and I am a professional photographer and videographer specializing in your niche. . . .
10. great job. proude of you teacher. if you have time then you can visit in india. there are so many awesome locations beautiful nature Yoga Meditation Schools. this is not expensive
11. So do you know how to do a lot of gymnastics or what
12. Hi ! I want to do yoga. Can you help me?
13. Hi, I love your flexibility which leads me to ask if you have any tips on which stretches work best to get really flexible. Anything will help x

These are not *I-dare-you-bro* messages from colleagues. The profiles look real. They belong to teenage cheerleaders, gymnasts in training, photographers, and a couple men posting entire galleries of selfies. Once again, I face an enduring question in my life: *what the actual fuck?* To answer that, I research. Turns out, Instagram may be able to "promote" any post to its Discover page, where people see the content without searching for it. It's my best guess that, after a slight organic boost from the AS trolls, one of my videos was promoted, introducing it to strangers who genuinely care about yoga.

Tripp slurps the top of his vanilla soft-serve swirl at the pod. At 3 p.m. every day, the cafeteria opens ice cream machines where the salad bar normally stands, complete with an abundant spread of candy toppings.

"You know my VP called me out for using air quotes today?" he asks.

I did know that. I happened to walk by as one surly VP crinkled slow-motion air quotes in front of him as they stood alone in a conference room.

"How'd you use them?" Puja asks.

"Fucking everywhere," he says. "I have no idea what the deal's about anymore. It's changed so many times."

"Nice," Chloe says.

"'Reverse merger,'" he says. He makes air quotes.

My laugh stops abruptly as I check my phone to see a new email from Skylar. I read it, humorless. Skylar has sent me a map of the United States pinned with red flags in cities from Miami to Seattle. These are the locations of studios where I could promote my SkylarSmithYoga transformation.

"Jesus Christ," I mutter.

"Exactly," Tripp says.

For the past three weeks, Skylar has been flooding my inbox with information about my potential yoga business trips, ending each with a smiling emoji. In another email, she included a script I could use as inspiration in describing the great influence that she had on my yoga journey. The script was a series of bullet points, which left me "wiggle room" so that it would "sound natural."

The first four:

- *Last year, honestly, I was miserable. From the outside, my life must have looked perfect [say: Anderson Shaw, New York City, 6 figures].*

- *But inside, I knew something was wrong [say: unhappy, out of shape, unfulfilled, no friends].*
- *Then I met Skylar Smith [say: we vibed, her message immediately resonated].*
- *Her personalized life coaching and yoga methods changed my life. . . .*

I can only reply to her every so often. I keep postponing our next get-together—blaming work, as bankers can—and it's been nearly two weeks since we've seen each other. The latest plan is to meet this weekend for a chakra workshop.

I don't have my official answer yet and don't want to commit too soon. Skylar clearly expects me to say yes to her offer. All she did at Yoga Cyclone was say *will* and *when*, never *would* or *if*. But I don't know yet. I would love the life she has, but I'm not 100 percent sure I can trust her. And isn't yoga all about intuition? I don't know. I'm not even sure if working for her would be closer to or farther from my dream of teaching in the first place. Skylar texted that she sensed distance between us, and again I blamed work. She called yoga the "real work."

"Oh, how expedient," Tripp says.

The SAT word snares my attention. Tripp is reacting to an email from the *second*-to-last person I'd want to hear from.

From: Mark Swift
To: Vivienne Wood, Tripp Thompson, Allegra Cobb
Fri 8 Dec 3:15 p.m.

Could you swing by?

"Did Mark eat Jason?" Tripp asks.

"We'd better go," I say.

Tripp gulps the rest of his ice cream in one swallow and buttons his top button. I walk a pace or two after him, hiding behind the broad V of his shoulders and back. I haven't answered Mark's texts in weeks. He texted me a couple of times asking how I was, but I didn't respond. Skylar wasn't telling me to flirt with him anymore, and that was the whole reason I'd engaged in the first place. Mark let it go.

I avoid eye contact with him now as I step into his office, as an extension of my ghosting. I doubt he gives a shit, because this job does not leave headspace for drama. Tripp and I take seats across from Vivienne.

"Team, I have some bad news," Mark says.

"What did Titan say about our last book?" Vivienne asks.

Mark waves her comment away like a mosquito near his face.

"We never gave them that book," he says. "The deal is on hold."

Vivienne becomes, if possible, paler. Bonuses are close enough that I can almost see their six-figure shadows in the snow. Delaying the deal means our fees will miss this year's cycle, if they come at all.

"Why?" she asks.

"It has nothing to do with the valuation or any of the work we gave them," Mark says. "They've always understood all of that. It's relationship issues between the companies. They just don't like each other. Who would take over? Where would the headquarters be? We can't throw pitch books at bickering."

Mark's phone rings. Vivienne jumps.

"Excuse me," she whispers.

"I'm afraid I have another call," he says. "I wanted to tell the team in person because I know how much this deal meant to us."

I picture Dad.

"Yes," Vivienne says. "Excuse us."

"Thank you, sir," Tripp says.

We file out behind Vivienne. Is she limping? The last words this woman needs to hear today are *relationship issues*. She turns into her office and sinks dejectedly into her posture chair. On the walk back, we pass Harry. He is actually reading *Yoga for Dummies* in full view as if it is a copy of the *Wall Street Journal*.

Tripp drops his client notebook three feet, where it lands on his desk.

"Bitchtits," he mutters. "The deal wasn't even announced. We did all that work, and I can't even put that shit on my résumé. All I have on there is two shitty IPOs."

"Is Vivienne okay?" Puja asks.

We turn around to look at Vivienne in her office. She curves into a defeated slouch over her keyboard, holding her head in her hands. Her chest heaves. She might actually be crying.

"Jesus, did she get fired?" Chloe asks.

"No," Tripp says. "Titan-Sierra on hold."

"Wow," Chloe says. She doesn't sound sorry.

"I literally don't know how this day could get any worse," Tripp says.

Right on cue, Mark's daughter appears on my left like a terrifying apparition of a twin from *The Shining*. She wears a green uniform and carries a clipboard. *Oh my God, why the fuck are you here?* She stares without a sense of humor.

"Would you like to buy some Girl Scout cookies?" she asks.

"Is that a fucking joke?" Tripp mutters under his breath.

I can't think of a more coercive point of sale. Her brother appears next to her, twitching with youthful energy as if he is possessed. Banking is now literally a horror movie.

"Sure!" Chloe jumps in.

All four members of the pod sign our names across dotted lines on the form jammed into her clipboard and place our orders. I haven't eaten a Girl Scout cookie since the toasted-coconut Samoa days of middle school. Luckily, they still sell those.

"How much do I owe you?" I ask.

"Twenty dollars," she says.

She isn't fucking around. This is a better business model than managed care: mark up your shit to the sky and then sell into a customer base socially obligated to say yes.

"Do you take credit cards?" Tripp asks.

"Cash only," she says.

"Pretzel cart motherfucker," Tripp mutters.

"You eat those?" I ask.

"What, you're never hungover?" he asks.

"No," I say.

"Oh right," he says. "Yoga."

The four of us pull out our wallets and scrounge together crumpled ones and fives to meet our minimum payment. I've never felt as poor as I do right now. Assistants aren't spared either. I watch the Swift girl sell to Trixie next. *Cough it up, Trix-alicious.* Trixie has been bringing her own two kids to the office for every unnecessary school holiday since forever. President's Day, they're here. Columbus Day, they're here. Her kids play a game called Calculator, where they run to different analysts, ask for a number, and then add it to twenty-seven to see what it is. No matter what the sum is, they gasp. Last time they played it, Puja said, "I wish I were a kid. I'm so bored by everything now."

It's par for the course. When we started as full-times, the HG group heads ended our welcome session with a request to treat each other well. This was the same meeting where they told us to hide our badges around the city. The MDs acknowledged that popular opinion of Anderson is extremely low and advised that we stick together. So we tolerate family visits.

"I need a drink," Tripp says.

"Preach," I say.

He slaps the table. "All right, let's do it," he says. He stands and points at Puja, then at Chloe. Neither budges. "Oh my God, come *on*."

"It's three thirty," Chloe says.

"All righty then," Tripp says. "It's you and me, A."

"Now?" I ask.

"Let's go," he says.

At this point, what do I have to lose?

Tripp and I sit at the seriously turdy bar at Samson's, a pub close to Anderson. It shares the block with Gucci, Burberry, and Hermès. There's even a Michelin-starred restaurant nearby, where Chloe went with her boyfriend for the four-hour tasting menu on their two-year anniversary. Samson's, though, is lit like a cave and smells like smoke. Its bar is lined with rickety stools that spark the *aha* moment as to why they're called *stools* in the first place. It's as if this bar was here first, the entire neighborhood was constructed around it, and Samson's is not fucking changing.

Tripp and I are flanked by two disheveled alcoholics. Tripp faces me from his stool, back to the rest of the room. He nurses his IPA and grimaces as if it's sludge. My glass of ice water has left a ring on the countertop, which I use as clear ink for the pretend pen of my straw.

"I should take an online depression test," Tripp says.

I already have this month. I'm not.

"Fuck," he says. "Such bullshit."

"Why do you do it then?" I ask.

"This guy who lives in front of my parents in Southampton was a banker, and now he runs a hedge fund," Tripp says. "He has five pools. Five fucking pools."

I'm not surprised. Put in your banking hours now, go to the buy side, and then literally swim in benefits later.

"Wow," I say, unimpressed.

"How fucking sick is that?" he asks.

"Very fucking sick," I say.

We both check our phones. I have two new requests since we got here: Print five equity research reports on one client and book a dial-in for a conference call with another. Welcome to Trixie's job. The line between analyst and assistant can blur. This shit would take VPs a second to do themselves, but people here are obsessed with saving micro-increments of time and asserting their boss status at every chance.

"You know, I have to be sober to do all of this shit but doing all of this shit makes me want to drink," Tripp says.

He takes another swig.

"Anyway," I say, picking the old conversation back up, "if you live *next* to someone with five pools, aren't you, like, fine?"

He smirks.

"You only have four pools or something?" I ask.

"Broo-tahl," he says. "Broo-tahl."

"Fine, fine," I say. I let it go.

"You mean, why aren't I sucking the allowance teat?" he asks.

"Ew," I say.

"Exactly," he says. "Not today, A. Not fucking today."

"But if you *could* do anything, what would you do?" I ask.

"Make a shit-ton of money," he says.

"No, money aside," I say. "Take the money out of it. What do you wake up in the morning and get excited about?"

"I don't know," he says. He shrugs. "What about you? Yoga?" He continues before I can answer. "Jesus, you're probably judging the shit out of me." I laugh. "Hold on now," he says. "It's not like I think money is everything, by the way. It's really about freedom. I don't want to rely on my parents. I want to pay for my own shit and live in nice places. I want to buy this drink. Well, this drink's definitely on AS, but other drinks. It's about living on my own terms."

"Sure," I say.

"But what about you? Yoga?" he asks.

"Yep," I say.

It's probably obvious by now, but that's the first time I've said it out loud to anyone other than Skylar.

"Nice," he says earnestly. "You should. I mean, you're fucking good at it."

"Yep," I say, deadpan. "I crush."

"You could really do something with your Instagram, too," he says. "People just follow girls in tight pants. It's a thing."

"Thank you," I say. That's actually the most supportive remark I've heard about my account. "You don't think it's slutty?"

"It isn't slutty *enough*."

I laugh.

"Give the people what they want."

"Thanks," I say.

He takes a long sip of his beer.

"Yoga, wow," he says. "Well, I hope you quit ASAP."

"What?" I ask. "Why?"

"Because I can't ask you out if we work together," he says.

For the first time, there's a pause between us that I can't fill with a stupid phrase or grunt. He looks me in the eye, handsome as ever, and smiles. His expression sours suddenly.

"What the fuck?" he asks.

"I didn't say anything."

"No," Tripp says. "Don't turn around. Mark is here."

I slowly swivel to face the entrance where Mark and his elegant wife glide over the threshold. Her face is dewy and her long, brunette hair manages to reflect light in this armpit. My God, she is fucking regal. Their kids race past them suddenly and run in circles, giddy with a Don't Touch Me game. Mark's and his wife's parallel tracks suggest they are playing a version of that, too—Don't Touch Me: Marriage Edition.

I look back at Tripp, who is smiling, waving, and muttering like a ventriloquist, "Yeah, don't bother to fucking say hi to us, you fucker." Tripp rests his beer on the countertop in front of me and leaves his arm there. He more vigorously waves his free hand as if he is scrubbing the patio around his fifth pool.

I turn toward Mark, who finally sees us and waves limply. Tripp's arm stays behind me, positioned as if we are on a date. Mark looks away, reactionless. What else would he do? The guy has a family, and we spent one messy night together. Mark holds up four fingers to the hostess, who tucks four menus under her arm; gestures, *this way*; and guides them to the dining room. Kids eat fucking early. As he disappears from view, he fades from my mind.

Because I can't ask you out if we work together.

Looking at Tripp again, I feel us pick up where we left off before Mark interrupted. This is how it always feels with Tripp—totally natural.

"So that thing I said," Tripp says, "about asking you out."

"Oh yeah?" I ask.

"I shouldn't have said that yet," he says. He removes his hand from where it rested in front of me. "That was me jumping the gun. We shouldn't do anything, you know, while we're working together. That's not right."

I furrow my brow.

"You disagree?" he asks.

"It's a point of discussion."

He smirks as he pays for the drinks with Anderson's gold AmEx.

"Point of discussion, huh?" he asks. "I didn't expect that. Well, can we pick that discussion up again after you quit?"

I wink.

"Look at you, Alison," he says.

"Thanks, Kip."

We smile mischievously at each other as we leave the bar. I enter the password to my phone and *will-do* my way to the bottom of my inbox. Then, I open Instagram, where a new direct message catches my eye from Jordan Roca—Skylar's ex.

chapter 19

hold my phone to my chest. *Skylar's ex-boyfriend?* I process in disbelief as Tripp and I rise to HG. Why would he message me?

"Don't make it awkward now," Tripp says.

"What?" I ask, startled.

"You look like you saw a ghost," he says. "Lucky for you, I am an office romance pro." He smooths his hair back in an exaggerated display of suaveness.

"Oh," I say. "That's great news."

"No one will notice," he says as the doors open. "Not even you."

As soon as we are back at the pod, he collapses into his wheelie the way he does after getting hit with a new staffing. Tripp slouches in defeat while staring dejectedly at his computer screen. He sighs as if the weight of the world is on his shoulders. It looks so normal and natural—as if our bar conversation never happened. He might actually be an office romance pro after all.

Focus.

I read Jordan's message:

@JordanRPhoto: Hello, great photo gallery. I would love to do a photo shoot with you one day if possible. My name is Jordan Roca (click here for more about me). I shoot portrait, event, and movement photography and have shot for @OhmMomYoga, @MirandaYogi, @PranaEnergy, @AviraDance, and the Tribeca Film Festival.

I have a special understanding of asana. I completed a 200-hour training with Lotus Yoga to learn more about the poses and their history. I see yoga as a gorgeous, physical expression of the human spirit. It is as difficult as the most demanding sports, as captivating as performance art, and yet so much more delicate and understated. Many prominent teachers have trusted me to capture their practice.

My portfolio is available on Instagram and my website.

Have a great day. J

Oh my God. I google Jordan. He hasn't made the news in over a month, not since the tabloids said his fans and clients were dwindling after the breakup. Is his career so shitty now that he has to cold-call nobodies like me?

The yogis he mentioned are stars. @OhmMomYoga and @MirandaYoga are massive accounts with hundreds of thousands of followers each. Is he honestly interested in taking my pictures? What is happening? Jordan must have come across one of my videos like the thousands of other random people who did.

I toy with the idea of telling Skylar, of asking her what I should do. But that feels like a mistake. Just *mentioning* Jordan might rub her the wrong way. I think about how to respond—Tripp sighs his *woe-is-me* sigh again—and I realize how much I want to meet him. This man *knows* Skylar, maybe better than anyone else.

*   *   *

The next morning, I'm waiting for Jordan in the French coffee shop near Anderson. It's a narrow slice of real estate designed for grab-and-go. I sit at the only table. The shop is in a lull, the breakfast rush over, leaving me alone with the barista. She keeps glancing at me and smiling uncomfortably.

"Do you want to order anything?" she asks.

"Not right now, thanks," I say.

I know. I'm a fake patron. I'm sorry.

I told Jordan I'd love to meet him, and he offered to come to me. I jolt as a college-aged bro enters the shop in business formal and orders a "tall black drip." He grips a plush résumé folder tightly in one hand and looks stressed as shit. I can almost hear him rehearsing in his head, *I've always had a passion for finance, ever since I was a little kid*. He must have an interview nearby.

As he leaves with his coffee, he holds the glass door open for Jordan. I wave excitedly, identifying myself before I remember I'm the only customer here. Jordan walks slowly, more mellow in person than he seemed in Skylar's feed. He wears an old black parka and dark jeans. His thick beard covers the bottom half of his face, a full-circle extension of the shaggy hair on his head.

"Hi," I say, standing up.

"So good to meet you," he says softly. "I'm Jordan."

"Allegra," I say.

Over a light handshake, he holds eye contact that feels kind and respectful. Of course he's handsome, but I didn't expect him to be so gentle. If I didn't know him, I might have guessed he was a poet.

"I brought you a portfolio," he says.

He lays a slim three-ring binder carefully on the table.

"Great," I say, lowering my tone to match his energy.

He takes his parka off to reveal a gray thermal and sits across from me. I open his binder a crack, and he reaches forward until his hand hovers a couple of inches above mine, preventing me from turning the cover.

"Sorry," he apologizes. "But before you begin, I wanted to say something." He brings his hand back. "These are samples of my work, but every job is custom." He gestures as if he is slowly twisting levels in a Rubik's cube, as if the thought and care he brings to his art are like the extended concentration required to unlock the full blocks of color. "My style is fluid. I don't try to leave a mark or make clear that it was me, Jordan Roca, behind the camera. I try to emphasize who is in the frame."

"Wonderful," I say.

"Please," he says, indicating I can browse.

First is a full-page photo of Stacy Jane—the yogi behind @OhmMomYoga, as big as @SkylarSmithYoga—in a standing split by the East River. She stares at her grounded leg as her ruler-straight split divides the photo in half. Her light-blue leggings blend into darker-blue sky. The picture oozes with soul.

"That's stunning," I admit.

"Thank you," he says earnestly. "The book is chronological, so my earlier work is first. That photo is from a couple of years ago."

I pay as much attention to him as to the photos. He rests two fingertips on his lips as I flip the pages. It's one gorgeous, thoughtful yoga photo after another. He *does* have a special understanding of asana. Every pose here is correctly executed; most of them are advanced; and, in every photo, the setting reflects the spirit of the pose. For postures meant to energize, the scenery is bright.

For postures supposed to restore, the scenery is calm. I recognize every yogi featured, even though these photos are from a while ago—I had no idea Jordan was so prolific before he dated Skylar.

"Also, if I may," Jordan begins. He pauses, as if he is mentally rehearsing his next lines. "I wanted to let you know how much I admire your gallery. Your photos are modest, which is refreshing. Most of the yoga I see today is egotistical, but yours has integrity. If we work together, I would try to honor that humility."

He is so nice. His compliment is so sweet and thoughtful that I almost want to hire him. Then again, sometimes I eat vitamins instead of buying food. There's no way I would pay for a photographer.

"Thank you," I say honestly.

"But that's just my opinion," he says. "It would be helpful for me to know your own vision for your photos. What are you looking for?"

I continue to flip through the book.

"I'm open," I say. "I don't have a specific vision."

The final page is a photo of Skylar from last year. She holds a forearm stand in Central Park while smiling at the camera. I realize, a beat later, that she isn't looking at the camera—she must be looking at Jordan. Her smile appears as radiant as the pink morning light on the skyline.

"Skylar Smith?" I ask, casually as I can.

"Yes," he says.

"Wow," I say. "What was it like working with her?"

"I don't discuss other clients, past or present," he says. He forces a joyless smile. "I would grant you the same privacy."

"Oh," I say. "Sorry, I don't mean to pry. She's just such a star."

"Yes, she is," he says. "Now."

"Now?" I repeat, gently probing.

"We started working together before she was famous," he says. He clears his throat. "In any case, I hope you enjoyed this selection of my work." He turns the page to close the book. "I'm sorry that I don't have anything more recent."

"Nothing since Skylar?" I ask.

Jordan leans back against his chair.

"I took a break," he says. "I just started working again."

I flip through his book a second time, from one yoga celebrity to another all the way to the end. I stop on the final photo of Skylar and leave the book open. The day I met her, she said that Jordan used her for his career. Sitting across the table from him now, I can't imagine him "using" anyone. Besides, this portfolio proves he was established long before she was. Meanwhile, Jordan seems uncomfortable.

"Are you okay?" I ask.

"It's just . . ." He trails off.

"What is it?" I prompt.

He looks from the photo back up to me and squints. "You don't read the tabloids?" he asks. I don't move a muscle. "I suppose it's public knowledge that Skylar and I dated. We broke up. . . ." His voice winds down in a way that pulls at my heartstrings—until, suddenly, he sits up straight.

"You know her, don't you?" he accuses.

The about-face stuns me.

"What?" I stammer. "No!"

He snatches back his book.

"Jordan, I barely know her!"

His eyes widen at the admission. He freezes exactly where he is, with his torso bent forward over the table, about to stand.

"I've only met her a few times," I say hurriedly. "She didn't put me up to anything. Honestly." I feel the need to prove it. "Look at this." I pull my phone out to show him the thick stack of emails from her. "She's been trying to recruit me for her company," I continue. "I've been brushing her off." I point to the rows of messages from her, my sporadic responses—*Work, sorry*—and look back to Jordan. He reads, riveted.

"I barely know her," I repeat.

He sits back down and touches my wrist.

"Allegra," he says. "Stay away from her."

He points at my phone.

"This is what she does," he says. "She uses people. She'll pretend she adores you, she'll make you believe you're special—so long as you're helping her career. Then, one day, she won't need you anymore, and . . ." He slaps his own hand loudly. The barista shudders. "She doesn't feel, like a normal person does. There is no remorse, no conscience. She only dated me so that I would take beautiful photos of her for free. So that I could pour my soul into the videos that made her famous. I loved her. I *worshipped* her. Then, when she was her own brand, she got rid of me. I'm sorry, I can't even talk about it anymore." He looks me in the eye, defeated. "This isn't going to work right now."

He leaves, forgetting his binder.

And I don't know what to believe.

chapter 20

I slip downstairs to meet Skylar in the lobby. Sunday morning, shit to do. I still don't know what to say to her offer, but I can't put off seeing her any longer.

Our plan is to visit a chakra workshop nearby. The seven chakras exist along the spine, and each one has a special power. A chakra is either "in balance," contributing to health, or "blocked," contributing to pain. For example, the first (lowest) chakra is earth. When someone's earth chakra is blocked, they may feel unstable or insecure. The cure: gemstones. Skylar and I will leave this thing with gemstones I can place around my desk and my bed to cure any blockages.

Skylar smiles hello and hugs me tightly in the lobby. Her white parka gives way in the embrace. I haven't hugged anyone in this building before. Skylar has a new tattoo on the back of her neck, the size of her palm. It's the Sanskrit symbol for karma. She wears purple harem pants tucked into winter boots.

"This is amazing," she says.

She looks eagerly around the lobby. A Pollock-esque mural

spans the entire, block-long wall. The high ceilings evoke cathedral interiors.

"Can I see where you work?" she asks.

"You mean, upstairs?" I ask.

She nods.

"Well, sure," I say. Maybe now she'll understand why I was stressed out of my mind during our "training."

As the front-desk attendant takes Skylar's picture for a temporary ID badge, I wonder how much attention she will draw. Her blond ponytail is effectively a yellow spotlight on karma. We get into the elevator with another Princeton alum: thin, brunette, prep school, squash. This girl is known for her vacant stare and for always being on a call. She exits at the Sky Lobby and wanders out of view.

"How are you?" Skylar asks.

"Great," I lie.

On thirty-five, we take the short route to my chair. Tripp's portable stereo plays Sublime from his "Feeling '90s" playlist. He wears two layers of joggers and Air Jordans. His biceps contour his long-sleeve Abercrombie tee. Puja hates Sublime and said Tripp is stuck in a time warp today. She and Chloe look absorbed in work.

"This is it," I say, with a two-handed *ta-da* motion.

Skylar rests a hand on my backrest, compliments of Erg Guy.

"I'm Skylar," she greets the pod. Chloe and Puja wave.

"*Buenos días*," Tripp says. He stands up to shake her hand.

"I teach Allegra yoga," she says, by way of introduction.

"Wow," Tripp says. "You kick her ass?"

He winks at me. Skylar laughs.

"We won't disturb you guys," I say. "Just giving a quick tour."

Together, we round the short edge of the track-shaped floor. It's almost full. The accordion spines of a few office chairs squeak as people adjust to get a better view. Heads turn to eye the fresh meat. Sometimes people bring visitors to the office, but the vast majority of those are family.

Skylar surveys the floor with intention, and I try to see it through her eyes. It looks less manicured than she might expect. The office gets a grunge makeover every weekend, when people work from different desks and personalize their new areas. They adjust the monitor height and eat any food left in sight. My pod is one of the rare exceptions in regard to desk promiscuity, and we stick together at our base. Other people risk walking in Monday morning to a sticky keyboard. Maybe the F1 key will be missing, too, because a visitor ripped it out when they kept hitting it by mistake instead of F2.

"Well, hello there," Harry says.

His gangly legs rest at full extension under the desk in front of him. As Harry turns to face us, so does his deskmate, Alex. Harry's pale skin, red hair, and extremely high opinion of himself suggest generations of deeply inbred nobility. His last name is probably hitched to an inch of Roman numerals.

"You're not going to introduce us?" Harry asks.

He adjusts rectangular, wire-rimmed glasses.

"Harry, Alex," I say, pointing. "Skylar." I gesture.

"Nice people skills," Harry says. "And how do you two know each other?"

"I'm Skylar Smith," she says warmly. "I teach yoga. Allegra is a student."

I cringe, awaiting their response. Harry leans forward from his self-assured recline. His smirk expands.

"Her guru, perchance?" he asks. "Now that is by far the most interesting thing I've heard all day."

Skylar beams despite his sarcastic tone.

"You could say I'm a neophyte," Harry says. He holds up *Yoga for Dummies* from where it lay on his desk.

"A Neanderthal?" I quip.

"No, there's only one Tripp," he says. "Skylar, was it?"

She nods. "Skylar Smith," she clarifies. "From SkylarSmithYoga."

"I've been needing a guru," Harry says. "I feel very lost these days." He flips through the book and pauses on a dog-eared page. He curls the remaining pages behind the spine. "I just have so many questions. For instance, I've been tortured by this concept of kundalini."

Fuck. He actually has been reading it. Kundalini is a kind of yoga that has always been linked to kinky sex.

"Is it true that kundalini yoga can incite a twenty-minute orgasm?" he asks. It's easy when the bullies are stupid. It's tougher when they have done their homework. "I know it's crass," he continues. "My colleague Alex and I have just been reading about it. Call it intellectual curiosity. Apparently, it's like a flower." He gestures to the book. "I could read a testimonial, though I may blush. The body is supposed to fill with light, heat, and energy. Has that been your experience?"

"No," Skylar says, apparently earnest.

"We can go, Skylar," I say.

I touch Skylar's shoulder and push her gently forward. She resists, grounded in her stance. Fuck, she's strong.

"Allegra, please," Harry says. "I am in the market for an awakening."

Skylar glances at Alex, who is nodding along like a bobblehead.

"That's great!" Skylar says. "That open-minded energy is what I look for in new students. I'd love to answer any questions you have."

"Splendid," Harry says.

"And if you have friends interested in the practice," Skylar continues, "here or at another firm, I would be so happy to talk to them as well. From what Allegra's told me, this job can make it hard to stay balanced." She shakes her head. "Maybe I could walk a group of you through small lifestyle changes that may help."

"Tell you what," Harry says. "I have the perfect venue for some introductions. Would you like to be my plus-one at our group's humble little Christmas party?"

Alex sniggers and makes a silent, clapping motion with his hands. The group's annual holiday party is coming up. Everyone will be there—it's HG's only mandatory social event. It also signals Bonus Day is close at hand.

"Rumor has it there will be a mentalist during the cocktail hour," Harry says. "And another rumor has it that he is quite legit. Maybe you and he can swap trade secrets, talk shop, what have you."

"Thank you," Skylar says. "I'd love to come."

"Perfection," he chirps.

Skylar writes down her email address inside one of his client books.

"Email," Harry says. "Ice queen."

"Do you have an Instagram too?" Alex asks.

My stomach curdles. *Too.*

"Yes," she says. "SkylarSmithYoga. I post how-to videos for beginners sometimes, if that's something you're interested in.

Meditations, breathing techniques—everything, really. I make sure there's a lot of variety."

"Okay, that's enough," I say. "We're leaving now."

Harry and Alex turn to their phones, presumably to search for her page. Once we have made enough headway, I lean toward her.

"I am so," I say, "so, so sorry about that."

"It's okay," she says.

"Really, I know this is obvious, but I'll say it anyway," I say. "You really don't have to go to that party. Honestly."

And please don't.

"I want to," she says. "You know better than anyone how much I could help."

We complete the safari. There isn't much to identify without sounding patronizing—computer, person, trash can—so I don't narrate the round. We wind up back at my pod, where we began. The full-screen window on Tripp's left monitor is the landing page for Skylar's Instagram.

While Skylar uses the restroom, I wait for her in the HG pantry. *What the fuck, Harry?* I sit on a banquette and wonder what I am going to do now. Before I make any headway on the question, Skylar is back. She reappears after a lightning-fast pee, smiling, parka zipped up to her chin in ready position, in her purple pants.

"Chakras?" she asks.

Skylar extends her hand, palm up. I take it limply.

I take an armpit shower in one of HG's bathroom sinks. After ten splashes per side, I still reek of incense. Walking back onto the floor, my tote is heavy with gemstones. Apparently, my third-eye chakra is blocked.

Skylar didn't ask me again to join her team. Instead, she acted as if I were already committed. She said I should let her know when I plan to leave Anderson, and told me she'd prefer I quit "ASAP" so that we could begin our "journey together." She kept handing me rose quartz and hugging me every time I opened my mouth. I couldn't get a word in, and then I had to keep track of all those fucking rocks. I knew I'd have to see her at the holiday party anyway, so I figured I'd save any serious conversation for later.

Now, I detour before heading to the pod. I'm headed to the printer enclave, where the machine is allegedly broken. We have a dozen printers in HG, but only two laser-speed, industrial-size units. The broken printer in question is one of the two stallions. This has incited a barrage of apocalypse-themed cartoons on blast. People can't stop reply-all emailing about it.

From: Adam Simmons
To: HG Analysts and Associates NYC
Sun 10 Dec 12:24 p.m.

[*Apocalypse Now* movie poster]

From: Chloe Walker
To: HG Analysts and Associates NYC
Sun 10 Dec 12:25 p.m.

Stop spamming.

Each of the two mainframes has its own enclave, and I reach the one in distress. As usual, the room is a mess. There isn't a naked surface in sight. Every bit of counter is covered with abandoned printouts.

Despite the mindshare this has commanded, nothing is on fire and no one is dead. Brian takes a picture of the flashing paper-jam alert, presumably to send in a blast. I roll up my sleeves while he finishes his shot. He leaves sniggering. An associate enters to kick the "piece of junk," which I half-laugh at to be nice. Turns out there are thirteen different paper jams in the system. This printer's chakras are beyond fucked. Each jam flashes red in the schematic on-screen. I start to un-dam each one.

"Well, well, well," Harry says, walking in. He sips a thimble-size espresso.

"Fixing the printer, I see," he says. "Were you promoted?"

He hovers over me as I crouch. I pull a crumpled "slide 49" from one of the printer wheels, and it rips in half.

"Perhaps you should prana it back to life," he suggests.

Prana is Sanskrit for "breath" or "life force."

I hope all the time you spent doing yoga homework puts a dent in your bonus, asshole.

"No thanks," I say.

"So," he says, "what can you tell me about your guru before our date?"

Oh God. I fish for half of a slide from deep between the printer's wheels and pull it out. My fingers are black with ink.

"She's a public figure," I say.

"So?" he probes.

"So ask Google."

"I am starting my search the old-fashioned way," he says.

I clear the last juncture. Lights blaze and the printer's wheels roar in synchrony, the first leg of a start-up sequence. That was unexpectedly satisfying. I stand to face Harry.

"Printer's fixed," I announce.

"Brilliant," he says, leaving. "Another way to squander your education."

The blasts turn, and celebration memes replace disaster ones.

"Printer's fixed," I tell my pod.

"How is that possible?" Chloe asks.

"I fixed it," I say.

"Oh," Chloe says. "On purpose?"

"Yeah," I say.

"Huh," she says. Her brow stitches. "Thanks."

I sit down for a split second before a collision jolts my desk. Tripp has dropped a plastic food delivery bag to smack the wooden surface between us, and it hit with unusual heft. With dramatic slowness, Tripp pulls from the core of his bag lunch a Saran-Wrapped orange brick.

"What," Tripp demands, "the fuck."

"Hungry?" Chloe asks.

"I ordered a side of queso," he says. "A *side* of *queso*. Some pisswizard sent me this. What the fuck am I supposed to do with this?"

I laugh.

"Pisswizard?" Chloe asks.

"That's nacho cheese," Puja says.

He tosses it disdainfully into the trash, and it clatters in the bin.

"Oh, fucking amazing, now Jason wants me to swing by," Tripp says.

He leaves. Excel fingers pitter-patter. I dump the reply-alls out of my inbox in chunks, until Tripp is back. He takes his seat in slow motion, contracting one discrete muscle at a time. It's odd not to see him animated, and even odder to see such a stark contrast from how frenetic he was just minutes ago. He carries a printout.

"Hey, A," he says.

He jerks his head in the direction of an empty MD office. We walk into the room, which provides a bit of privacy.

"Do you remember those strip profiles?" he asks.

I raise and lower my chin.

"So, you want to tell me what happened?" he asks, uncharacteristically serious.

Blood drains from my cheeks. What the fuck does that mean? He hands me the printout titled *Discussion Materials for Titan—Draft*. The first few pages of my strips are here, just as I remember them. I continue to turn until one pivotal flip—the border into Skylar's first slide.

Beside the pristine column of perfectly aligned company logos, red markings appear like crop circles in a cornfield. The columns are stick-straight and perfectly spaced, and the bullets are perfectly formatted, but most of the words have been circled, crossed out, or linked to underlined question marks in the margins.

"I mean, what the shit," he says. "Headquarters in 'Italy, France'?" He gestures at the page open in front of me. "And the company descriptions are nonsense. It looks fucking random. None of the revenue numbers are right. *None*. Not a single one, and not by a long shot. What the fuck?"

How did I not check this? I try to remember back to that night.

It was right after I broke the fast with Skylar. She offered to help. I did check it. I think I did. But it comes back to me now, and my stomach drops. I only checked the formatting. I trusted her.

The only reason Tripp and I aren't fired right now is because we never actually gave Titan the book—it remained a draft. Mark requested we "back-burner" the strips, as we were "moving forward" with new Titan-Sierra merger analyses that took over that entire weekend. With the deal dead, Jason must have come across this deck while archiving materials for compliance reasons. The damage is contained, but it's still beyond terrible.

Skylar's profiles read like streams of consciousness. It's as if she saw the category labels—market cap, revenue, HQ, and company description—as prompts for free writing. It reflects such a startling lack of concern for my livelihood that I am paralyzed with shock. This is beyond yogi detachment. This is guru narcissism, or even sabotage. Jason must have thought we were just making shit up, cramming ahead of a deadline.

"I told Jason it was me," Tripp says. "PATC is here, and I said it was me." PATC, pronounced "pack," stands for "per annual total comp." Tripp means our imminent bonuses. "I told Jason the book was unfinished and that stuff was just a placeholder. So it looks like I was dicking around with the materials. I can't even think about it."

"I am so sorry," I say.

"'*Italy, France*'?" Tripp repeats. "You mean, like, Italy is the capital of France or their headquarters is just so fucking big it crosses the border and is in both fucking countries?" He shakes his head. "Unbelievable. Right before PATC. This is basic. Were you high or something?"

I have no words.

"You know what? This isn't even fucking 'oops, I'm sorry,'"
he says. "This is asking for it. I know you don't give a shit about
this job anymore, but can you please give a shit about me? This
is just, like, evil."

"Tripp, I was not myself that day," I say.

"I'll say," he says.

"Do you remember? It was the day we met with management,"
I say.

"Zombie Day," he says.

Fuck.

"This will never happen again," I say slowly. "Never before,
and never again. I swear to God that it was not on purpose. Do
you remember how out of it I was? I was not myself. It wasn't me
that did this. You saw me."

A pause grows.

"I have too much shit to do to beat this horse," Tripp says.

He stands abruptly, and I follow him back to the desk.

As soon as we arrive at the pod, Tripp kicks his trash bin, and
the cold, hard block of queso rumbles around in it like a sneaker
in a drying machine.

I've made a lot of mistakes in my time as an analyst. Everyone
does. Half of us went to liberal arts colleges with grade inflation.
But I know that this mistake is different. Before tonight, my
biggest slipup was that I didn't include the number of stores
Starbucks opened pre-IPO in a table. Instead, I put "N/A" in the
first draft. Starbucks went public in the 1990s before the SEC
website posted documents online, so the S-1 registration document where that number *would* be is not available. Still, the VP
pulled me aside and spat, "This is Anderson Fucking Shaw." So I
searched the internet until I found a scanned copy of Starbucks's

first annual report on a random blog. It was yellow, blurry, and did not allow word-search. I read the whole thing until I found the number of shops open at IPO. It took me an hour to fill that square in a table of one hundred data points for draft two.

You don't make these kinds of mistakes with Titan. You don't make *any* mistake with Titan. But worst of all, I hurt Tripp, and he's the one really *in* this business. Even if he *does* watch an impressive amount of TV and claim to be "invinsible," he's the one who will actually stick around. He deserves all five of those pools.

Janitors arrive at midnight. Each wheels a giant yellow bucket lined with a trash bag and filled with our individual trash bags. It is a Russian nesting doll of garbage. Cleaning supplies clatter against the plastic sides.

"Thanks," I say.

I resume work, still reeling from the strips.

Last week, I made a deck for a client meeting taking place tomorrow. Since then, the price of every stock in the book has moved. So, I am "price updating" slides to reflect the latest market. In most cases, this only changes the numbers to the right of the decimal place. Still, I re-paste every chart, output, and table. It leaves me enough headspace to wonder what the fuck is wrong with Skylar.

I stop price updating for a moment—this shit is ridiculous anyway. The meeting will take place *after* the stock market has opened tomorrow, so updating tonight still won't give clients accurate numbers. The task is like painting ocean waves and hoping the ocean looks exactly the fucking same when you give your client the painting. *This is the ocean right now. My analyst was up all night making sure of it.*

I rifle through my top drawer until I find the baseline diary I made for Skylar. The strips were not the first time she messed with my job. I flip past the coffee-stained pages to a fresh sheet and start to tally her offenses. The more I write, the angrier I get: . . . *Yeah, go ahead and meditate right at your desk. You have an open floor plan and conservative coworkers? Awesome . . . And then follow your heart all the way to flirting with your married boss. Let yourself live, right? The soul is meant to be free. . . . And then take breaks all fucking day. . . . Oh, and here's a photo of me, can you edit it right now at 5 a.m. at the ass end of your all-nighter? Write a caption from the bottom of your heart. Now, let's back-burner those. . . . And then pure fast for forty-eight hours no matter what your meetings are. . . . And to top it all off, teach a class to your most closed-minded peers. That fucking work for you?*

And that's excluding the biggest ask of all—joining her team. *So I can end up like Rosie, who looks like you chained her to that beige sofa? Or like Jordan? Everyone you're close to fucking works for you, and no one turns out okay.* As I stare at the page, it's clear that Skylar is more "Anderson Shaw Yogi" than I am, and she's been manipulating me this entire time. It will be easy now to tell her no. I see her show of compassion for what it is: total bullshit. Just like everything I'm doing here.

chapter 21

The pod's bonus countdown began. Tripp hung an advent calendar by our desk to mark the days until PATC or, as he called it, "Money Christmas." Every day, he opened a new paper square and announced the picture inside. Angel turned to Wise Man turned to Crucifixion Cross, and we got closer to cashing in.

Bonus Day would overlap with a few key events. Right before, there'd be the HG holiday party. Right after, I would quit my job. Meanwhile, as Tripp flicked advent calendar squares at the ceiling, @PretzelYoga continued to grow. @JordanRPhoto followed me. Requests rolled in from other photographers, InstaYogis, and small businesses looking to collaborate. People kept liking posts in my backlog and messaging me questions about yoga. Eventually, I got enough interest from potential students that I began to view the account as a professional one.

Until then, I had thought about the path to teaching in a narrow way: quit, then two hundred hours of training, then teach group classes in a studio. But there I was, getting serious interest for private lessons, and it occurred to me that I could get started teaching freelance. My American Yoga gold was a serious credential for knowing safe yoga practices, correct alignments, and poses. @PretzelYoga could connect me with students and create a community of people I had taught, so I wouldn't be a trackless, rogue instructor. Like, *Hey, I'm an uncertified teacher, want to let me into your home for an hour? Sign this fucking waiver first that exonerates me from any injury you may suffer. All right, awesome.* Considering those points, people could then choose to hire me or not.

The more I thought about it, the more attractive this idea became. Becoming a private teacher would be a route where I was entirely self-reliant—I wouldn't defer to any yoga authority, Skylar or otherwise. Skylar could spitefully blackball me at every studio, and it wouldn't matter. If I failed to meet enough students on my own, I could always go back to the conventional route. But this option was worth a shot. Thousands of followers made it feel plausible. The *aha* moment was liberating.

I embraced the app as a tool. I posted more pictures and videos of myself and captioned each with a yoga credo. "Yoga is a way to freedom," came from Indra Devi. "Compassion is the radicalism of our time," from the Dalai Lama. I needed to support myself, but I wanted to make honest connections at the same time, so I kept the captions as earnest as possible. I added a professional bio to the profile.

Over the next handful of days, calendar squares kept flickering down like confetti, and I built up to posting at least twice a day. I gained regular commenters including @2PeaceInAPod which was obviously Tripp. He forgave me for the Titan fiasco (I guess there *are* good people in the world) and started liking all of my pictures within five minutes of my posting them. He'd comment things like, "Brutal," or, "If a tree falls and it doesn't make a sound, does anyone hear it?" The joke made him laugh as he

wrote it. I responded as @PretzelYoga, "Tripp un-mask thyself."
He swiveled in his chair until his back faced me. @2PeaceInAPod
replied, "Nah."

With Titan-Sierra off, I barely saw Mark anymore. Whenever I
passed his office, he was barking at juniors scribbling their wrists
off. Rumor was that Mark had all of his major deals fall through
this year. Talk about his inability to close continued to spread.
People guessed why and passed on semi-credible information:
junior consensus was that he might rub clients the wrong way. *It's
the way he slicks his hair back, some off-color humor, a too-macho
vibe.* He snapped at Trixie publicly on the floor, which made
everyone uncomfortable. That day, I posted about karma.

I haven't seen Skylar since the chakra workshop a week ago.
Still, even without face-to-face interaction, she's made her presence felt. She has been texting me—How is your third-eye chakra?
and What do you think of Houston, TX? and Do you know your last day
yet? You sound so busy!! and I know this must be a tough transition
time for you—but I have not engaged, blaming work. For every five
messages from her, I respond maybe once. We agree to talk at
the holiday party.

I booked my first student, Lucy, for a session a few days before
the event. It was harder than I thought to get internet people to
meet. It turned out most of my followers were only casually interested in yoga, or were young gymnasts or pervs. I *knew* they were
pervs because they DM'ed me to solicit sex, or their bios were
something to the tune of "Just a married man who loves women,
and a man living in a sex less marriage." Was the space between
sex and *less* meant to emphasize absence? #Poetry.

Lucy could be a catfish, but she checks out across multiple sources. Per LinkedIn, she is an SVP of wealth management at Morgan Stanley with a recent master's in archaeology. Per Facebook, she is blond.

I knock on the door to Lucy's penthouse, on time for our first session together. I'd never hit the *PH* button in an elevator before, and something about getting no thrill from it makes me feel insanely free. As footsteps amplify on the other side of the door, a new email hits, from Vivienne.

Fuck. Don't blow up my non-pass Saturday.

Vivienne has been trying to CPR the Titan-Sierra deal back to life with suggestions for new decks as chest compressions. Mark hasn't approved any of them, so the deal's stayed pretty fucking dead. Meanwhile, Vivienne has been floundering. She started asking me to get her lunch for her—small carrot-ginger soup—which I pay for without reimbursement. She made Tripp and me begin every email to her with an estimate of the time it would take her to read it. Like, Est. reading time: 30 secs. She's also started staying in the office later than she used to, pushing deals for other clients. Now she wants me to find an equity research report on Titan. That can wait an hour.

Lucy's door swings open as if on fast-forward.

"You're here!" she says. "Come inside."

Lucy looms several inches taller than I am and glistens with post-run sweat. Her biceps are cut, and she gestures with a strong arm for me to enter. Her career-woman assertiveness is immediately familiar.

"Great to meet you," I say.

"Come on in," she says.

Massive abstract paintings flank us on the way to her living room. She points at the plush sofa, and I sit still as two fluffy dogs twitch and paw at my legs. Framed pictures of the terriers are all over the place. I'd say, never married. A far door opens to her personal yoga room, which has its own bonsai tree and floor-to-ceiling view of the skyline.

"Drink?" she asks.

"No, thank you," I say.

Her tone makes me think she is offering whiskey, but I catch sight of an expensive juicer on her countertop. Lucy crosses her spandexed legs on the chair beside me, with her back to the spectacular view. One of the terriers yaps.

"So, you won the yoga gold?" she asks.

I nod.

"That's impressive," she says. "Anderson, too?"

"Yes."

"Very impressive."

At this rate, we are going to finish the hour in a minute. I'm supposed to be the one interviewing her, anyway, for a baseline. Lucy already looks athletic, with Kate Hudson's peppy smile, Gwyneth Paltrow's Goop-y aesthetic, and Uma Thurman's drive in *Kill Bill*. I see her through a kaleidoscope of famous blondes.

"It really is great to meet you," I repeat, regaining control. I breathe once, deeply, hoping she might take the hint. She swings her top, crossed leg back and forth. "How's your morning?"

"Busy day," she says. "Sotheby's, then drinks, then event."

"I see," I say.

"But first, yoga," she says.

"Of course."

Riiiight. This lady needs more than yoga. She needs drugs to chill her the fuck out. Her vibe suggests she plays the net every Wednesday at a coed volleyball night. Or maybe she misses college rugby.

"So, I thought we might begin by talking about your experience with yoga," I say. "What has your practice been like?"

"Strong," she says. "Started with groups a few years ago, moved on to private lessons. Been doing one-on-ones for a year now."

I breathe again. Maybe I can slow her down. I'd planned to take notes, but Lucy needs to relax. I don't want her to tense up like she's at the doctor's office getting measured with cold metal instruments.

"Okay, that's helpful," I say. "Do you have any injuries?"

"No," she says. "Like an ox."

"Returning to your practice," I say. "Can you speak more to the styles you have seen? Any particular studio?"

"Oh, and I do meditation," she says. "Mainly for success."

"That's wonderful," I say.

"Let's see," she says. "I did the power yoga class three times a week at YogaWorks. But SoHo got to be pretty inconvenient. Cabs took forever. I was following all the Instagram yoga, obviously, and so a while back I got in touch with Skylar Smith and practiced with her."

"Oh," I say. "Skylar Smith?"

My stomach craters.

"I'm not yoga cheating on you," she says.

"No more Skylar?" I probe.

"No," she says, more thoughtful. "Your page caught my eye because it helped me put my finger on something that was starting to irk me about Skylar." As she says, "put my finger on," she gives a horizontal thumbs-up and punches it forward. *Jesus.* "Skylar kept trying to sell me on her videos and other yoga *things*. I ended up buying more gear for her classes than for mountain climbing. Which I do, by the way."

"Oh, good for you," I say.

"It's a great sweat," she says. "But anyway. On your page, it didn't look like you were selling anything. My read was you're not a product pusher, just a genuine teacher." She makes an "OK" shape with her fingers.

"Wow, that's so nice of you," I blurt.

"Right, right," she says hurriedly.

As in, *Let's keep this thing rolling.*

"Okay, so a bit more on the yoga lessons I offer," I say, taking her cue. "I guide a personalized flow to music. We will emphasize flexibility and build up to deeper poses over time. Hopefully, we can move energy from the mind back down into the body. The hour will be a place to do less, think less, and breathe deeper. We can be calm."

"Great," she says. "Can we start now?"

chapter 22

The hour before the holiday party is endured without seasonal cheer. The HG heads leave a group-wide voice mail stating the "imperative" that we be grateful.

"It is critical that we take this time to recognize our good fortune," they said. "We have been blessed, so let us be gratitude champions. Give thanks tirelessly."

Finally, I taxi to our Holiday Cocktails & Buffet, nearby in Midtown. The ballroom teems with bankers and their spouses, who are sometimes the same age. I am the last of the pod to arrive, delayed by comments. I've spent the whole day revising a confidential information memorandum, or "CIM," which I only just sent to my VP. A CIM—pronounced like *Sim* in *The Sims*—is a "reasons to buy me" document that we write when selling a company. Writing a CIM can be like playing *The Sims*, too, where we as authors exist half-alive in a virtual world.

Food calls me back to my physical existence. A buffet table of raw bar, plated first courses, and entrée meats extends the full length of the room. My salivary glands *hell-yes* at the sight of burrata, calamari, carrot risotto, and sirloin. Mark chats with

his wife on the other side of the room. *Hell no.* I turn my back to
them, to see the one thing scarier: Skylar walking in with Harry.
She wears a black satin dress, blond hair coiffed. I hide among
the crowd, not eager to face her yet. Tripp stands in the outer ring
around the mentalist with Chloe and a doughy guy who keeps
whispering in Chloe's ear.

"Greetings," I say.

"Ugh, you sound like that voice mail," Tripp says.

His breath smells like mai tais.

"Have you seen the mentalist?" he asks.

I shake my head. Been busy with another mindfucker. Tripp
fills me in. The mentalist has been guessing people's randomly
chosen three-digit numbers. Some "asshole MD, I mean Tyler"
tried to trick the mentalist by concentrating on the number
010, but the mentalist guessed Tyler's number anyway. Then he
guessed the exact amount of cash that Brian had in his pocket:
eight dollars. The mentalist also asked Chloe to draw a shape
with her back to him, and simultaneously, he drew the same
four-petaled flower and one-leafed stem. It hits me that the man
next to Chloe must be her boyfriend.

Waiters circulate trays of canapés, each served with a quick
description: "Oysters with red-wine mignonette?" "Peekytoe
crab with jalapeño?" Tripp accepts every offer of hors d'oeuvres
with his non-drink hand.

"You can say no, you realize," Chloe says.

"Oh, can I?" he asks, mouth full of food and sarcasm.

"I'm Charles," Chloe's boyfriend introduces himself. Turns
out he is a soft-spoken Virginian and a commodities trader. As
we small-talk, I get the impression that he is extremely wealthy.
He's my age and already managing money. His pool of capital

comes from only two clients, and he works out of his studio in Tribeca. His fund does not have a name, because apparently you don't need an official name until you get to managing $100 million. He is going on about how the markets are like a "puzzle."

"You see a pattern," he says. "You realize what the next piece should be. And then you have to anticipate how fast everyone else will realize it, too."

How does Chloe fucking deal with him?

Tripp nabs another hors d'oeuvre.

"What did you drink to get so drunk?" Chloe asks.

"I was drunk before I got here," Tripp says.

I consider whether what he is saying is true. Tripp shakes the ice in his empty glass back and forth. He tips his head back and takes a dry swig, inclining a column of ice to slide back and hit him in the nose.

"I'll refill," I say.

With water. I head with his glass for the bar, passing the mentalist wowing a new group with the three-digit-number-guess trick. Asshole MD Tyler stands at the front of this crowd, chomping at the bit like, *I'm going to figure you the fuck out, magic man.* The bar is packed with a pulsing throng of first-years itching to get hammered for free. I wait in the back for my turn and lean against the wall. How did I get so old in one fucking year?

"Allegra."

It's Mark beside me. His silver tie knot is massive at the base of his throat, like a second Adam's apple. We are somewhat secluded behind the wall of first-year backs.

"Hi, Mark," I say.

He sips a dark drink from his glass.

"How are you?" I ask, honestly curious.

"Hm?" he asks as if he didn't hear me.

"How are you?" I ask again.

He downs the rest of his drink.

"Sure, that would be great," he says.

Mark lets his arm drift toward me until his drink brushes my chest. He releases the glass, assuming I'll take it. He must have thought I just offered to get him another one. His glass drops to the floor and shatters in one piercing, staccato second. Heads turn, but quickly lose interest. A waiter kneels to brush the glass shards into a plastic dustpan, and I move away as quickly as possible.

I spot Vivienne, Mark's wife, Skylar, and Harry walking to us, presumably tipped off to Mark's location by the shattering glass. Vivienne wears a holiday-red pencil dress, and I can feel her eagerness for MD face time from here. She leads the pack to join us.

"Mark, what a pleasure," Vivienne chirps. "What a coincidence I ran into Mary."

Mary—Mark's wife—kisses me hello on the cheek. Skylar hugs me next, close and comfortably, as if our relationship is completely unstrained. She feels warm and smells like sandalwood. Her friendliness is borderline convincing, and for a moment, I think how easy it would be to submit to her expectations, travel the country, and preach her virtues. Then, I remember the strips. Skylar releases me and shines the light of her smile back to Mary.

"Mark, you have to meet Skylar," Mary says. "She is an amazing yoga teacher. She teaches Dan Glasgow. I was telling her how much we love Dan." She faces Skylar. "He's a *great* doubles partner."

"Mark Swift," he introduces himself.

They shake hands.

"Mark and I try to do yoga a couple times a month," Mary says. "You always leave just feeling so clear. You don't think about what you have to do at all." She snaps her fingers to illustrate her to-do list dissipating. As a public aside to Mark, she adds, "I told her we'd love to work with her. She can come to the studio in our Greenwich house."

"Oh, I love yoga," Vivienne says.

"Skylar has booked ten clients since we got here," Harry says. He puffs his chest as if he is her proud boyfriend, and her success is *their* success. "I was telling her, we must be like fish in a barrel. She's closing deals left and right."

Mark is visibly uncomfortable.

"We do have a lot of friends you could work with," Mary says. She laughs ashamedly, like she just told a sex joke at a garden party, covering her mouth with her manicured hand. "I'll mention your name."

"I'd love to take a class," Vivienne says.

I gaze curiously at Skylar. She flips her blond hair over into an extreme side part, revealing the intricate web of ink strokes in her karma tattoo. I fit the pieces together: Skylar reached out to me right after reading that I work at Anderson Shaw. She invited herself on an office tour where she introduced herself to my coworkers. "Skylar Smith from SkylarSmithYoga," she told them. "If you have friends interested in the practice, here or at another firm . . ." Now here she is, chatting up bankers at our holiday party.

And this hasn't been her first introduction to Wall Street types, either. She teaches Dan Glasgow. I'm almost positive she orchestrated the turnout at Yoga Cyclone, which means she had the banking connections to pull those strings, too. She taught Lucy. It hits me: This line of work is chock-full of people looking to spend serious money to make themselves less miserable. She is literally surrounded by rich people who feel unfulfilled, and she is here to *pitch*. She is her own CIM.

Tripp enters our group with the mentalist.

"These people," Tripp announces in a faux aside to the mentalist, "*need* to see you." He turns to us. "Have you ever seen a mentalist before?"

Vivienne shakes her head no.

"It's unreal," Tripp says.

"Phenomenal," Vivienne says.

Are these two suck-ups going to carry the entire conversation by themselves? As our circle faces the mentalist, I keep my eyes on Skylar.

"Can I talk to you?" I ask. "Alone?"

"Now?" Skylar asks.

"That's rude," Harry says snidely.

"Well, she *is* my student," Skylar says to him.

"No, I'm not," I assert.

Skylar laughs as if I've just told a joke. The mentalist waves his arms in a distracting, elaborate gesture, presumably to signal the end of a trick. Tripp makes a *yeow* noise. Mary claps excitedly.

"Can we do four digits, my man?" Tripp asks.

"I knew you were going to ask that," the mentalist says.

"U*nreal*," Tripp says, beaming.

I turn my back to them, effectively turning myself into a human wedge between Tripp's magic show and my huddle with Skylar and Harry.

"Skylar?" I ask.

"You are being quite rude," Harry says.

"Skylar and I need a minute," I say.

"Apparently, we do!" she agrees. "I'll be back," she tells Harry.

I lead Skylar in a figure-eight weave through the crowd until we find a patch of footless floor. She stands composed on stiletto heels, which bump her up a few inches taller than I am. She smiles and waves at someone behind me.

"Skylar," I say, "I'm not your student."

"Of course you are!" she says.

"No, I'm not," I say definitively. "I've been doing a lot of thinking about this, and I'm not going to work for SkylarSmithYoga, either. I really appreciate your offer, and thank you for all of your help, but I am going to do my own thing."

"What?" she asks, perplexed.

"As in, no thank you," I say. "I sincerely appreciate it, but I'm not going to be able to join your team. I hope we can stay on good terms."

"I don't understand," she says.

I've realized that whether they're banking MDs or Instagram gurus, people with power live in *yes* bubbles. All they hear is "Will do ASAP," "Revolutionary idea, sir," "Fantastic to see you," and, "What a coincidence—your favorite sports team is *my* favorite sports team." But I know what I want, and I'm done with that shit.

"I want to teach," I say. "The only way to do that right now is to go for it alone. I've booked a couple of students already in the city, and I'm gaining momentum. But, as I said, I really want us to stay on good terms."

"Allegra," she says, taking my hand. "This upsets me. I was really looking forward to working together. I care about you."

"Okay, well what about the strip profiles?" I ask boldly. I wait for her to admit something. "Did you care about me when you put those together?"

She hesitates.

"Oh, right," she says finally. "The profiles."

"Yeah, for my job," I say.

"But your job isn't important," she says. "What matters is the practice."

"Look, I have no problem with money," I say. "But let's be real. I mean, look around. You're at the Anderson Shaw holiday party. You're not on a Himalayan mountaintop in rags. Okay? Sorry to be blunt, but call it a business already. Be real with the people who work for you. Respect me as a person."

"I see," she says.

She pauses thoughtfully.

"But do you remember where you were when we started? You were a mess," she says. I nod. At Shake Shack, where I was thinking *fuck you* to a group of lunchers. "I did my best to help you. No matter what you think my intentions are, I think I did some good."

She squeezes my upper arm affectionately, and I do consider her point. Did she actually help me or not? On the morning we met, I woke up in Mark's bed. I had no serious plans for next year, only half-baked dreams that made me feel guilty for disappointing Dad. Now, I am *teaching*. My colleagues know the real me. I even felt compassion for Vivienne. Yes, I'm in a better place.

But come *on*. The strips. I've improved in *spite* of Skylar, not because of her. And there's no way she's going to stamp her trademark all over my journey.

"I'm sorry," I say. "I don't want to be on your team."

She nods, as if my words are finally dawning on her.

"So you're going to teach freelance?" she asks.

I nod. "Working on it."

"In Manhattan?" she asks.

"Yes," I say.

She nods again. "Well, then that's your choice, and I do wish you the best of luck," she says. "It does hurt me that you think I never cared about you, though. Maybe I didn't present myself the right way. I'm unconventional, I know. I'll be sorry to lose you." The cadence of our conversation is slower now, as if Skylar is weighed down by a sense of defeat. She prayers her hands.

"Thank you, Skylar."

"I do expect we'll run into each other in the future." She makes interweaving sinusoidal waves with her hands in front of her. "Teaching in Manhattan is a smaller world than you might think. There are only so many studios and students. So I agree, we should be on good terms!" I can't tell if this is a threat.

"Sure," I say.

"How about one last practice at Mala this weekend?" she asks. "It will be a high note to end on. Then, when we run into each other again, the last thing we remember won't be *this*." She laughs a bit sadly.

"That sounds good," I agree. "A last practice."

"Saturday?" she asks.

"Okay," I say.

"I'll introduce you to the studio owner after," she says. "Maybe that will help you get started? Namaste."

Breaking the news to Skylar is a relief. Her support—or at least her show of it—makes me optimistic. She's let me go and now she can't control me anymore. I finally feel free to enjoy the party and find the only person I really want to see: Tripp. We stand among the bar crowd as Tripp leans one elbow on the counter.

"I got this," he tells me assertively. "Two mai tais, sir."

"Coming right up," the bartender says.

The bartender hands us two tropical-looking drinks.

"Do you think the bartender, like, respects you at all?" I ask.

"Not really," Tripp says.

He winks, and I laugh. I've never had one before, and it tastes so gross that I can only take one sip. Tripp downs the rest of it himself. Gradually, more associates join us, until I am surrounded by drunk colleagues playing Celebrity Crush. Tripp suggested the game, which only entails naming the celebrity you find most attractive. This third time around the circle, the guys ahead of me cited Charlize Theron, Lindsay pre-coke, and Angelina pre-Brad.

"Pass," I say again.

It gets a rise out of him.

"Ace, literally just say a name," Tripp says.

"Isaac Newton," I say.

"Don't fucking ruin my game," Tripp says.

"Albert Einstein," I say.

"Out. Of. *Bounds*," Tripp complains. "Fucking *try*."

"So necro," the ex-military associate says.

Tripp shakes his head, frustrated by the escalating noncooperation. He gestures with a waving hand for the game to continue, as if he is cueing different instruments to play into his Celebrity Crush symphony. I smile. When someone says, "Reese With*or* With*out*herspoon," Tripp erupts into applause, his good humor restored.

As the circle of associates rattles off more names, I spot Skylar on the other side of the room with Harry, talking to an older couple. She's doing most of the talking and gesticulating. It looks like she's trying to sell them something. It hits me that Skylar *can* take credit for something I learned after all—but it's more of a business lesson than a yoga one. She showed me that a place to look for students has been under my nose this whole time.

When big banks visit Princeton to recruit undergrads for jobs, alumni market "optionality" as a selling point. Investment banking gives you "options," because as an analyst, you can learn marketable skills in two years, pin a fancy firm's name on your résumé to signal you're legit, and bank up to $100K in the process, guaranteeing yourself the flexibility to pursue your real dreams. Of course, most analysts end up staying in finance, so the "options" mirage is a bit empty. But, in the most unexpected way, I found "optionality" from Anderson after all. The recruiters had preached, *Take your skills and network* anywhere, which I could now legitimately bookend with, *including a life of yoga*.

Tripp, as the entertainment maestro, guides our group into a couple of other games. He maintains his impressive state of drunk-yet-functional until the senior folk start to leave, and the "functional" part disappears with them. As VPs and MDs exit, eventually, a tipping point is reached that releases the invisible chains constraining juniors, and an exodus begins for the door. Our huddle dissipates. A couple of the associates mention that they have kids to get back to, and a couple of others say something about wanting to get a good night's sleep.

"Allergies," Tripp slurs.

"Not a name," I say.

"Let's play Truth or Dare," he says.

"Nah," I say.

"Okay, my turn," he says. "I choose dare."

"I dare you to do a Netflix cleanse," I say.

"And *die*?" he asks.

Puja, Chloe, and Charles find us on our way out. Charles carries Chloe's Chanel handbag while she thumbs an email. Tripp points at Chloe's phone.

"How are the frenemies, Chlo?" he asks.

"Someone should take him home," she says.

She looks at me.

Tripp fell asleep in the cab to my place. I had to help him up the first five flights to my studio, wounded-soldier style, and listen to him complain about Charles. Tripp got stuck talking to him on our way out, which became the "worst ever ten minutes" of his life. Tripp sobered up the higher we climbed and the deeper he got into his rant. I asked him at one point if he'd read *And Then There Were None*. He said obviously, but he likes *Murder on the Orient Express* better because how does everyone do it, that's genius. Then he turned the conversation back to Charles. Going up the final flight, Tripp takes steps on his own.

"He kept talking about the markets like they were a fucking porno," Tripp says. "I was like, *Have you had one enjoyable moment in your whole fucking life?* Jesus Christ." I laugh. "He was all about 'patterns.' Shit is 'patterns.'"

"Yeah, he told that to me, too," I say.

"Unreal," Tripp says. "This guy has one fucking line."

"He and Chloe have been dating for years," I say.

"That's it, then," Tripp says. "Dude's gone insane."

I laugh.

"That's probably the only thing she allows him to say," he says.

We reach my door, where the red paint chips in four ominous grooves down the front. It's as if Wolverine were here and indicated, *This is my fucking place*, with a downward swipe. As I take the keys out of my pocket, I fumble for the right one. I'm actually a bit nervous to have Tripp over now. He's way more sober than I thought he would be. It feels like the end of a date.

"You don't actually live here, do you?" he says, squinting around. "Or is this where you murder people?"

I nervously use the wrong key. It doesn't turn.

"At least the security's good," he says.

I open the door this time and switch the ceiling light on, though it takes a few start-and-stop flashes to shine fully. Cockroaches scatter. Tripp hits the bathroom fast and pees for longer than it would take to complete a dial-up internet connection. Meanwhile, I make him a bed on the sofa. We pass each other without saying anything as I enter the bathroom and brush my teeth. When I emerge, he is sitting on the sofa, untying his shoes. I change into a pajama shirt and shorts behind the privacy of my closet door. He was supposed to be really drunk.

"Well, night," I say.

I turn the light off, and it takes a few seconds before I can make out his shape on the sofa. He uses the flashlight app on his phone as he finishes untying his shoes. As I walk by, he takes my hand firmly as a request to stay. It's surprisingly assertive, and my heart beats faster. He lies down on the sofa, pulling me with him, and finally, we kiss. He runs his hands through my hair and down my body, learning its outline. His hands stop on my waist. I press my hips into him. Five hungry seconds later, I pull back abruptly.

"But we still work together," I say, half teasing.

"Fuck," he says. "I hate my job."

We linger where we are.

"Hey, Tripp?" I ask.

He nuzzles my neck with his nose.

"Mm?"

"You know my name, right?" I ask.

"Oh my God," he says. He lets his hands drop to his sides, maybe genuinely hurt. "Do you know how much concentration and creativity it takes to say every A-name but yours?"

I laugh.

"Allegra," he says, taking my body again. "Of course."

"Tripp," I say.

We kiss. I rub my hands over his chest.

"How do you work out this much?" I ask.

"Hell yeah," he says to himself. "She notices."

We kiss even more softly this time. Instead of speeding up as time passes, we slow down. Eventually, we fall asleep, completely comfortable under the shrug blanket and wrapped in each other.

chapter 23

Skylar is ten minutes late to our last practice. I wait on my mat at Mala and email Lucy back that yes, next Saturday works, same time. *Send*. Things are falling into place. Lucy has re-booked twice now, and I meet two new students next week. Monday is Bonus Day.

I open Instagram to a new picture from yogi Jessica, @JessicaOlie. She has half a million followers and posts a lot—like, an *industrial* amount, as if she employs her own pod counting down to its own Bonus Day, responsible for posting thirty new yoga Stories a day or it's bottom fucking tier. Another avid yogi, Morgan from @Finding MorganTyler, sometimes appears in her posts, like the one in my feed now. It reminds me of dreams I used to have for Skylar and me, working together.

"Good morning," Skylar says.

"Hi." I stand.

"So sorry I'm late," she says.

She wears gray leggings with a subtle, darker gray stripe down the outside of each leg. Her sports bra matches: gray with shadowlike flourishes. She fetches a mat from the prop shelf and unrolls it next to mine.

"I just came from a lesson," she says. "One of the clients I met at your party."

"How'd that go?" I ask.

She smiles. "Really great," she says.

"The Swifts?" I ask out of curiosity.

"Mark and Mary?" she asks. She shakes her head. "No. Not yet. I reached out to Mary, but scheduling with Mark is going to be a nightmare." She laughs. "He's so busy. In any case, I'll guide?"

I nod, and now we stand on parallel islands. She starts to flow in a hurry, as if she's making up for lost time. I mirror her. We begin with a sun salutation, and I am a half beat behind. It quickly becomes the fastest yoga flow I have ever done, verging on aerobics. We pause finally in *chaturanga*, a push-up pose holding bent elbows. I count the seconds in my head to make it easier to endure. My abs tense with heat. I read once that it takes seven to fifteen seconds to die after being shot in the head, which I take to mean that you can endure anything for seven to fifteen seconds. My knees touch the mat for a moment of rest. Skylar flicks my shoulder with her index finger, as if to chide me, *No*.

"*Adho mukha vrksasana*," she says. "Handstand."

I obey her lead. From downward dog, I keep my palms planted on the mat and jump forward into a stick-straight handstand. To stay here, I engage my core and point my feet. Skylar holds a handstand as well, though she pinwheels back down first. I immediately follow, glad for the break. We rest on our mats side by side.

"How did you learn scorpion in handstand?" she asks.

I shrug.

"I sort of just taught myself," I say.

She looks so dissatisfied that I laugh.

"Sorry," I say. "It's the truth."

"Can you show me how?" she asks. "Your technicals have always been better than mine. I'd really appreciate learning, if you don't mind."

I imagine her taking everything I teach her back to my coworkers, impressing Mark and Mary with this pose on the back porch of their Greenwich mansion. One of us has to have compassion. End on good terms.

The handstand muscles in my arms are already tired. It doesn't take much to fatigue when you recruit every in-between, nameless fiber in whole-body stabilization and you're barely warmed up. I try handstand again, and she watches. This time, I bring my toes down slowly to touch my crown and hold the full handstand scorpion pose. Five seconds later, I pinwheel down.

"Again?" she asks.

Doesn't she know how hard that was? Skylar would be an unrelenting third-base coach, urging her Little League players to steal home base with every breath. *Do it, Johnny, fucking do it, you skinny piece of shit.* The side wall is covered with mirrors, like a floor-to-ceiling eye. It reflects my apple-red face.

"Okay, sure," I agree. "And then I need to break."

"Of course!" she says.

I find my way back into the pose. She stands beside me, her bare arms crossed tightly as straitjacket sleeves across her chest. She appears to be riveted and memorizing the exact alignment of my limbs. I hold my center of balance in the small of my back. The longest I've held this pose is for one minute.

"I'm going to take a photo so I can remember," she says.

She takes a step closer to me. I can feel my body giving out—the weight on my wrists and upper arms will soon be unsustainable. I start to shake and move to dismount. Without me being entirely aware of what is happening, Skylar molds me back into scorpion with *this-way* pushes. She guides my legs down until my feet touch my head. My hands sting with pins and needles. She keeps me exactly where I am, upside-down, and deepens the arch in my back by pushing my feet farther down.

"Stop!" I gasp.

I struggle against her, but she doesn't release me. She seems intent on bending me until something breaks. I open my mouth to scream, but I can't make any sound. I can't breathe. Suddenly, there's a sickening crack, and I collapse.

Right before the American Yoga Championship, I did my last-minute research. By that I mean, I skimmed all the internet bullshit I could find about the competition. It was more a manifestation of nervous energy than any real attempt to prepare. I came across an article about Arjun Patel, the man behind American Yoga.

At first, the article was a more detailed version of my expectations. Arjun was born and raised in India. He dropped out of school as a teenager to soul search, during which time he met Guru Bhavin. Bhavin taught him yoga and methods of deep meditation and, in the process, helped Arjun find enlightenment. Then, Arjun had a vision: his purpose was to spread true yoga to America and his first stop had to be Hollywood. Something about that seemed weird, but I kept reading the article. Arjun proceeded to build luxury yoga studios exclusively for Hollywood's elite before expanding his franchise globally.

Wow, he must be loaded, I thought.

And he was. Arjun's massive corporation has supported his lavish lifestyle. He's collected Ferraris—and then I stopped reading. *Yeah, yogi loves dem Ferraris,* I thought sarcastically. I wrote off the whole website. It had to be clickbaity garbage. But the next article I read about Arjun on a different site corroborated the first. *Yogi loves dem Ferraris* had been an accurate thought. The Google Images search for this guy was insane—he looked like a caricature of Snoop Dogg in *Soul Plane*, but flashier. In one picture, he wore a leopard-fur oversize bomber, and in the next, a velvet jacket with silk pants and burgundy slippers. This was the founder of the major yoga chain? This was the man trying to popularize the practice with American Yoga? Jesus fucking Christ.

Arjun Patel has made millions of dollars a year in fees coming from the thousands of his yoga studios. Every interview that I read with him was a different shade of outrageous. When asked about his company culture, he said, "It's good. It's great. Fantastic. Everyone loves it. And when my employees complain, I tell them they're lucky to have a job at all." Uh, okay. To describe his teaching style, he said, "When people listen to me, I change their lives. When they don't listen, I tell them to get the fuck out of my studio." I wondered, *Do you have to be a piece of shit to be successful? I should just stay in banking.*

I shut my laptop in disgust. I didn't want to pose in Arjun's contest anymore. I showed Dad what I'd found, and we talked about whether or not I should withdraw. In the end, we decided to finish what we started, even if Arjun was a horrible person. We weren't representing him, we were representing ourselves. We wouldn't enter again.

Being that detached from winning actually helped me perform, because judges deduct points for signs of tension. When it was my turn, I stepped onto the focal yoga mat calm. The crowd and panel of judges didn't affect me as I moved through my routine. After I won, Dad and I posed for the photo that remains on my nightstand. We left content that we had represented ourselves. No matter what you do, you'll run into bad people. You just have to do your own thing.

I wake up in a place I don't recognize. There's a lot of white. Colors slowly become shapes with edges until I realize I am in a hospital bed sequestered by a hanging plastic curtain. Skylar stands nearby, holding a bouquet of white roses that I mistake for lotus flowers. She still wears the gray yoga outfit from our last practice. A white-coated doctor leans over my bedside.

"Allegra," he coos.

I blink hard and swallow.

"Good," he says. He pockets a flashlight the size of a ChapStick. "Can you hear me?" I nod. "Good. My name is Dr. Peterson. You are in an NYU hospital."

"Can we be alone?" I ask him as soon as I can.

He turns to Skylar, who leaves.

"No visitors," I demand.

He nods. "How do you feel?" he asks.

The doctor wears a scrub cap like David Foster Wallace's bandana. I take a deep breath, sending pain to my deltoid. My shoulders twitch on reflex, bringing my attention into my hands. I wiggle my fingers. They move, but it's different.

"I can't feel my hands," I think aloud.

Yoga, of course, can cause injuries. Since college I have seen different people seize, tear a hamstring, rupture an Achilles tendon, and uncontrollably start to shit. I practiced with one teacher who overworked her knees until she was diagnosed with "bone on bone." I met another teacher who had a stroke while holding a headstand. It still takes her five seconds to swallow. *Headstand*.

Dr. Peterson asks me more questions and conducts a brief physical exam. He moves my neck and shoulders until there is pain and touches my arm at different points, which leads him to diagnose me with "cervical radiculopathy." He says this nerve damage can be caused by pressure on the root of the nerve near the spine. As in backbending. Some nerves that run down my arms are recovering, so I can't feel properly right now. My back hurts where the nerve roots are inflamed.

"I've never seen this in anyone your age," he says. "This typically occurs in much older people, after discs have degenerated over time. You almost have to try for this injury to get it so young." I remember the feel of Skylar's strong hands pushing me closer and closer to injury as I tried to struggle out of her grasp. "Fortunately, your case is light," he continues. "And, because you are young, your body is already repairing itself. You may feel uncoordinated this week, particularly in your hands. For the pain, anti-inflammatories: Advil, Aleve. If it takes longer to improve, we can talk about steroids or physical therapy. But that probably won't be necessary."

"Thank you," I say.

"You are very lucky," he says.

Soon after, I sign my own discharge papers from bed. My hospital room door opens to a long hallway. Skylar sits nearby on one of the chairs lining the wall, and the sight of her sends a chill through my body. Her legs cross in lotus, and her spine is as straight as in *tadasana*. I walk hunchback to relax away some of the pain. Every time I breathe, it hurts. I try to breathe shallowly.

In front of Skylar stands a middle-aged couple. The man's broken arm rests in a sling. Skylar points to her own arm and crooks it back and forth. She is talking about something, and the man talks back. She points to his arm, and he nods. The woman listens intently. Skylar pulls a business card and pen out of her parka's pocket. She starts to write something on the back. I walk closer.

"Gentle poses will help it heal," Skylar says to them.

Her eyes dart to me. She finishes with a flourish of her pen.

"So wonderful to meet you," she tells them.

"Thank you so much," the man says.

The couple depart down the long hallway toward the exit. I follow in their footsteps, separated by five seconds of distance. Their head start lengthens, as I am walking slowly. My back would hurt more if I moved any faster. So here I am, at full speed, at a snail's pace. Skylar walks beside me.

"Thank God you're okay," she says.

We continue to pass through the same, repeating unit of hallway: a door on either side, four wooden chairs in a row against the wall. It's as if the architect dragged his formula for the decor all the way to the end.

"I was so worried," Skylar says.

"Stop," I say.

I can't believe she's still pretending to be a good person. We walk in step with each other. Hallway unit after unit, I ignore her. She makes a few more efforts to comfort me, as if my injury were a freak accident. I keep my eyes on the red EXIT sign.

Eventually, Skylar seems to realize that I'm not buying her sympathy act. She falls silent. We pass the front desk, close to the end. We step outside through the double doors, where the streets are dusted lightly with snow. Skylar touches my shoulder lightly, and I jerk her off. Doing so brings an intense flash of pain, but I stay expressionless. I wrap my arms around myself to stay warm.

"Oh, are you cold?" she mocks with faux sympathy. "You privileged bitch. I bet you are. Aren't you, princess?"

I pick up my pace. I'd never heard Skylar curse until this moment, and I'm not planning on sticking around for more.

"Oh, are you running away?" she asks.

She grabs my shoulder, hard.

"You leave when I tell you to," she snaps.

I shove her aside, and she slaps my cheek. I clutch the side of my face in horror. All of the kindness in her face has drained away, and the look in her eyes would scare even the most intimidating VP at Anderson Shaw.

"You think that hurts?" she ridicules. "That's why you'll never make it. You have *no idea* what it takes. You lose sleep in your ivory tower and think you've worked hard? You think you're smart? Look at you, cowering. It's pathetic." She raises her hand again, and I flinch. "You have no idea what I've had to do to make something of myself. I look at you, and you don't have it in you. Not even close."

I gape at her.

"If you try to take *any* of my students, *any* of what I've built"—she spits at my feet—"then I will eat you alive."

I try to run away, but I can't move fast enough. The sidewalk is slippery. I keep my eyes locked on her as her gray figure gets smaller and smaller. She watches me leave and remains perfectly, eerily still. As I round the corner onto the nearest street—whizzing with cabs and witnesses—she snarls and bares her teeth.

chapter 24

recover somewhat by Monday. If I hunch my back in one particular way—with my spine curved into the shape of a cane handle—the pain is tolerable. After Skylar, Erg Guy would probably be first in line to kill me today. It's not how I expected to greet Bonus Day, but so be it.

On the thirty-fifth floor, people are smiling, chatting, and bustling in a hopeful whir of energy. Never have so many bankers looked so happy. It's like the only day of the year they like their jobs. Today, the annual ritual goes: Jason will call us into his office one by one, starting with assistants and working his way up the hierarchy. He will reveal the size of the bonus we earned and our total compensation for next year. Sometimes we get feedback. The meeting takes five minutes.

I expect my bonus to fall between $70K and $120K depending on my tier, judging by rumors of how people made out last year. Associates can expect to earn $90K to $180K today, and for VPs and above, who even cares. Their system is more individualized and can cross into the millions.

I take small steps to my desk and brace myself for the imminent shitstorm of other people's emotions. Today, some ninety-pound, first-year analyst is going to make $100K and learn he's on track to be promoted early, meaning he'll make associate after just one year and not the standard two. He'll update his LinkedIn immediately and walk around with a "Big Man on Campus" chest puff, shaking hands with senior people and thanking them for the opportunity. Maybe he'll lose his virginity tonight. On the other side of the spectrum, some VP will make only $200K today and spend the afternoon puppy-eyeing the window ledge by his desk. I keep my back hunched and take a seat.

Puja and Chloe are mid-conversation.

"Morning," I say.

". . . I mean, we are the one percent," Puja says.

"No, that's not technically true," Chloe says. "To be in the Manhattan one percent, you need to make over five hundred thousand dollars per household per year. I read that. There's no way your bonus is that big."

I rub the tops of my thighs with my palms and realize I can't feel a patch of skin on my inner left knee. All nerve cords connect to the spine, and my injury must have fucked up one of them attaching here. Dr. Peterson said I should be fine, but this is fucking annoying. I rub the area in a circle with my hand, trying to map the edges of the numbness.

"You okay?" Puja asks.

"Where's Tripp?" I ask.

"Working out," Puja says. "He wants 'Bonus Biceps.'" She makes air quotes. I laugh, and it hurts my back.

From: Jason Chase
To: Allegra Cobb
Mon 18 Dec 9:34 a.m.

Allegra, could you swing by?

"It's my turn," I announce.

"Good luck," they say, overlapping.

I pick up a notebook and head to Jason's slowly. *So close.* I started imagining my last day at Anderson on my first day of training. Since then, I have tweaked my quitting fantasy hundreds of times, much like an arduous comment cycle with a VP. *What if we revised this one, inconsequential detail? What if we changed the color here? No, change it back.* As my fantasy stands, I envision myself wearing yoga clothes to work. It will be a thrill and a statement. Like, *Goodbye, standard track. Here's my ass.*

Of all last-day-related details, my goodbye email has taken the most time to plan. Frustrations aside, I've spent a lot of time at Anderson, and my goodbye email will eulogize those years. People don't fuck around with eulogies.

"Prolonging the suspense?" Harry asks. I roll my eyes.

"Yep, I'm walking slow," I say. "Good one."

Harry sits at his desk, outside Jason's office. Apparently, Skylar snubbed Harry's attempt to kiss her good night after the holiday party. Since then, I heard he's taken up ax throwing, a hobby I think he chose for being the polar opposite of yoga.

Jason waves me inside.

"Sorry, gotta go," I tell Harry.

"Proceed," he says. "Enjoy your bonus, yogi master."

I shut the door behind me.

"Welcome," Jason says.

Today, Jason's smile finally looks happy. Last year, he told me that PATC day is his favorite day of the year, because he gets to give us something other than work. I sit carefully. "It's my pleasure to say HG has been doing well, thanks in part to your hard work. Your contributions put you in the middle tier. Your bonus will be one hundred thousand dollars."

I sit up straighter, which pinches something. I cringe. *Fuck*.

"Does that upset you?" he asks.

My mouth is a horizontal line of concentration as I re-stack my vertebrae into the one alignment that prevents back pain. I squirm like an ungrateful perfectionist, discontent with her ranking.

"You got an outstanding review from one of your peers for your work on Titan," he says, as if to encourage me. I know that couldn't have been Mark, because I didn't select him in my handful of reviewers, for the obvious reasons. Of course, Jason means Tripp.

"Yep," I say. "Thanks."

I squirm again. *Fuck*.

"Really, thank you so much," I say. I mean it, but my voice is hollow. His disappointment shows on his face, because I am raining on his favorite day of the year. I must look like such a brat, but I'm ecstatic. I am finally fucking here. I will live off of this bonus potentially for years. Of course, though, I can't say that out loud. *I will live off of this for years* would come off like I was straight-up mocking him. Instead, I twitch a crooked smile and leave.

After the pod leaves for lunch, I head to an empty conference room to call Dad. It makes sense to tell him now.

Bonus feedback for juniors is over. Tripp just finished a half-hour rant downloading his talk with Jason. Tripp "only" made middle tier, but after hearing what Jason said—after Tripp *already* took the fall for the strips—I'm surprised he's even employed. Apparently, Tripp went to a client meeting in the Midwest wearing an Armani suit so fashion-forward that it didn't have buttons. The VP had to take Tripp to a Men's Wearhouse and buy him a suit that the client would not find alienating. At that same meeting, which was a pitched sale to private equity reps, Tripp showed up late and told the client offhandedly, "Talking with sponsors makes you want to skip all this and go straight there, ya know?" Jason told Tripp that he overused the word *nah*, worked out at inappropriate times, and over-broadcasted his Chesticles and Testicles Day in the gym. Tripp disputed this last point. Then Tripp got real-time feedback that he is bad at receiving feedback.

From inside the conference room, I dial Dad from my cell.

"Allegra?" he asks, tone upbeat.

"Hey, Dad," I say. "How's it going?"

"Oh, you know," he says.

I hear his TV on in the background. Sports.

"We get ranked yet?" he asks.

"Yeah, I did," I say. "Just now."

His TV goes silent.

"And?" he prompts.

"Middle tier," I say.

"Fuck," he says.

"The bonus was a hundred K," I say.

"Well," he says.

I can feel him caught between two camps. On one hand, he's pissed we didn't make top tier. We are, after all, the Cobbs. On the other, this bonus is more than he ever made in a single year or will ever make again.

"Dad, I want to talk to you about something," I say.

"Did Jason say why middle?" he asks.

"It's not about my bonus," I say. "It's about the job. I've been doing a lot of thinking and decided not to stay with banking." The silence is rough. "You remember American Yoga?"

He grunts yes.

"I've kept practicing as much as possible, and there's a way for me to do that professionally," I say. "I've already booked students, and there's a career path there. The Instagram account we started? I have twenty-five thousand followers now. You know, this is the life I want to live. If you're going to do great work, you have to do what you love, right?" I don't want to end with a question. "So that's where I'm headed."

"Yoga teacher?" he asks.

"Yeah," I say.

"So, no Anderson," he says.

"Right," I say. "I'll quit this week."

A pause grows.

"Is everyone else in your class staying in finance?" he asks.

It pinches an emotional nerve.

"Basically."

"And you're sure about this?" he asks.

"Yes," I say.

After all of my preparation for this moment—the anecdotes, the reasoning—I don't even feel the need to justify myself. I've been through enough.

"Well, that's something," he says. He nurtures a pause. "You know, I've had my suspicions for a while now, that your heart wasn't in this. Talking to you about work always felt a bit . . . short. I knew there was something else on your mind. I just didn't know it was a bunch of yoga."

I laugh in a release of nervous tension.

"You're doing what makes you happy then?" he asks.

"Yes," I say. "It feels right."

"And I bet no one else in your class is going into yoga, huh?" he asks.

"Nope," I say. "Not a one."

"Wimps," he says.

I laugh. "What?" I ask.

"You know how fucking brave it is to do something no one else is doing?" he asks. "'Fuck all my training, I'm doing what I love?'" I imagine him shaking his head. "No one does that. No one. Nobody wants to stick their neck out. Everyone wants to get lost in the herd. But not you."

"Wow," I say. "Thanks, Dad."

"I might not understand this whole yoga thing. . . ." He trails off. "But I didn't raise a wimp. Anderson to yoga. That's for damn sure."

"Thanks," I say. We pause.

"So you've been doing yoga at your job?" he asks.

"Sort of," I say. "I've been trying. Next time I'm home, I'll explain more how this could go for me. And . . ." I remember meditating at my desk, the poses in the coat closet, and teaching yoga to a room full of bankers. "I have a few pretty hilarious stories for you."

* * *

For the next week-plus, I checked my Chase mobile app for the bonus as often as I checked the time. Today, I woke up, sat on the toilet, and saw $60K had buoyed my balance overnight. The rest had gone into my 401(k). My pee felt golden. That made it Quitting Day, and I wouldn't be the only one. The exodus was about to commence.

I dressed in black leggings, white sneakers, and a gray hoodie. At 8:15 a.m., the HG floor is a ghost town. Not even the MDs are here as I take a nostalgic stroll around thirty-five and admire the window panorama. I can see the tops of skyscrapers for miles. This morning, the top-of-the-world view is *Lion King*–esque, the gorgeous stuff of stock photos. People always take in the view after a tough climb.

Eventually, Jason's routine carries him past my desk on the way to his. He nods hello and walks to his daytime plot, holding a crinkly bag of Chobani and Coke for breakfast. It's time. I make the trip to his office without a notebook. I knock on Jason's glass wall, and he waves me inside. His smile holds, unthwarted by my dress code liberties. I take a seat at his marble staffing table, Indian style. I never refused work at this table. Now, I will refuse the entire job.

"Jason, I'd like to quit," I say.

Our roles have just reversed. I am bringing him the news.

"I'm sorry to hear that," he says.

"Thank you," I say.

"Where are you going?" he asks.

"Nowhere," I say. I laugh once at the implications of *going nowhere*. "As in, I don't have a job offer anywhere else."

"Are you quitting on your way to the gym?" he asks.

I laugh. *Seriously*, ouch, *stop laughing*.

"No," I say. "Yoga."

"Right, I heard you were getting into that," he says. He meets my eyes for a moment of personal connection before transitioning into an impersonal Last Day spiel, mostly to do with administrative details. And, just like that, the deed is done. Our meeting is shorter than PATC.

Chloe is the only other member of the pod here, and it's almost 11 a.m. When I told her that today is my last day, she reacted as if someone she barely knew had died: grief on the face, but not from within. *"That's so sad."*

Now, Chloe is on a recruiting call. I can sense this candidate's eagerness from Chloe's animated responses. Here I am, at the end of the life cycle, and Chloe's call reminds me of the beginning. Back when I told one of my Anderson interviewers, "I don't have an extensive background in finance, but I would chew through this table if you asked me to."

"That won't be necessary," she'd responded.

Back then, I was a junior at Princeton making my own round of recruiting lunches and calls. My most productive call was with a VP named Sheryl in AS's Leveraged Finance group. By then, I'd passed Anderson's résumé screen, and my first interview was a month away. Sheryl told me what to expect: first-round interviews would take place on Princeton's campus. If I did well, I would advance to a Super Day at Anderson's headquarters in New York City. Super Day would entail two hours of four back-to-back, half-hour interviews. Each would be conducted by one or two current AS employees.

Sheryl emphasized that Anderson does not care if its interns have worked in finance before. They hire art-history and comp-lit majors along with the econ grads. First and foremost, the firm wants a specific personality type: high-energy, positive, and driven people who are also genuinely likable. Interviewers use an "Airport Test," where they ask themselves, *If I got stuck with this person at an airport, would it be a pain in the ass?* They can mark *yes* or *no*. Kids with 2400 scores on the SATs get cut when they fail the Airport Test—but, honestly, does any 2400-er *pass* the Airport Test?

Background aside, I would still get grilled on finance. In my case, given that I was a non-Wharton kid, my answers would show how fast I could learn and how badly I wanted this job. To prepare for the technical questions, she suggested I study IBankingFAQ.com and case questions for private equity interviews. I should also be able to talk about current events in such detail that I might be asked the current price of gold and rate of a T-bill. To prepare for that part, I should read the front page of the *Wall Street Journal* every day.

Snippets from Super Day come back to me now. During one interview, I saw another candidate pass by in the hallway crying. She had been asked to multiply 100,000 by 10,000 in her head and could not do it under the pressure. My next interviewer opened with, "I'm only going to ask you three questions. First, why are manhole covers round?" I was blindsided. He cut me off mid-answer. "Wrong," he said. Apparently, manhole covers are round because that is the only shape that will not fall in on itself. His next question was, "What is the first derivative of x^2?" I got that right: $2x$. His last question was, "I have six socks. If I choose two, the chances that I draw a white pair are two in three. What are the chances I draw a black pair?" I got that right, too. A two-in-three chance of drawing a white pair meant there had to be five white socks and one black sock ($5/6 \times 4/5 = 2/3$).

One black sock meant zero chance of drawing a black pair. His three questions took five minutes, and he spent the remaining twenty-five on his phone. I just sat there.

After I'd spent two hours getting grilled, my last interviewer asked if I had received offers to intern at any other banks. I said yes, I had an offer from UBS. "Well, that would really be a step down, wouldn't it?" she asked. She looked at me as if that was a legitimate question that I was supposed to answer. "Anderson is my first choice," I said. We shook hands, and I left with the other Princeton kids.

"And make sure you say *team*," Chloe says.

I remember scribbling that tip down at breakneck speed. When I was on the other side of that call, like my dad, I viewed the analyst job as my ticket to power. I thought it would take me places. I imagined climbing my way up to the next levels of life. Now, though, I see those next levels as nothing but smoke and mirrors. The only place I ever really *am* is inside my own body, so I should take care of my inner life the way I feel is right.

When Chloe hangs up, I break out of nostalgia. My AS email will deactivate in an hour, at noon, and I need to send my goodbye email and leave before then. Where is Tripp? He doesn't know I'm quitting today. If he is Stage Two, I am so going to sober him up.

I endure an exit interview with HR and dispose of all client-related materials. Then I walk the floor to say my goodbyes. These handshakes are a rite of passage. Last year, after a star analyst on track for associate-promote quit, the head of the group refused to shake her hand when she did her own round. But nobody's pissed when a middle-tier leaves.

I pull some people aside for a proper goodbye, wave at others, and ignore the rest. Adam definitely gets a handshake. I snag Zena, too, and she ogles my leggings as if I'm picketing, SUPPORT THE PATRIARCHY. I shake Vivienne's hand, and after, she Purells at her desk. If she was serious about loving yoga, as she claimed at the holiday party, maybe I'll see her around. I hope so. When I wave at Harry, he says to remember him if I ever need help with rent. Trixie gets a handshake. All she has to say to me is, "You're welcome."

I find myself at Mark's empty office. His chair faces out as if he has just left. On his desk is an open to-go carton filled with hard-boiled egg whites in one half and their yolks in the other.

"Good morning," he says behind me.

I swivel around to miss him entirely as he steps inside.

"Hi, Mark," I say.

"Come in," he says without inflection. He sits in his desk chair and reads a one-sentence email on his desktop.

"I'm saying goodbye," I say. "It's my last day."

I walk closer. His phone rings. Outside, Trixie's voice answers, "Mark Swift's line." Mark holds up a *one-second* finger to her.

"Two years up, huh?" he asks. "Where to?"

"Yoga instructor," I say.

"Ah," he says. He eyes my outfit. "I thought it was just buy side and tech poaching you. Now we have to compete with meaning."

I imagine a new set of rules titled Anderson's Meaning Initiatives. *GMI #4: 1 percent of your salary has been donated to charities teaching financial literacy to Manhattan youth. . . .* Meanwhile, the wrinkles in Mark's forehead preserve a mask of frustration and focus. Behind him, emails accrue in Outlook, subject lines colored unread blue.

"I heard you're working with Skylar?" I ask.

"Who?" he asks.

"Skylar Smith," I say. "For yoga."

"Right," he says, as if nothing resonated. "Mary thinks it's good for me."

His phone rings again. Outside, Trixie answers, "Mark Swift's line. Please hold." Mark holds up another *one-second* finger.

"If Mary gets bored with Skylar, I can give her your name," he says.

"No thanks," I say. "I just meant good luck. And—be careful."

"Whatever I do, don't relax, I suppose?" he asks, amused.

"Sort of," I say awkwardly.

"Allegra, if I can't relax on a yoga mat, then I am fucked to high heaven."

He turns to face his phone, where two lines flash activity-red. He picks up an egg white, chews, and swallows. I wish him the best as I leave.

Puja trudges in at 11:30 a.m. wearing business formal, a clear tip-off that she's been interviewing for a job somewhere. Chloe's back zips up straight. Puja glares at her screen. Behind her, Tripp strolls in at a leisurely pace, as if he is an hour early to a beach picnic.

"Where have you been?" I demand.

"Bonuses are in, baby," he says.

Tripp falls into his office chair, wheeling it into the wall and completing the four-piece puzzle of our pod. He looks from Puja to me, then from me back to Puja.

"What the fuck is dress code today?" he asks.

"You want to go first?" I ask Puja.

"Yes," Chloe responds for her.

Chloe knows I'm leaving. She wants to know where Puja might be going. Puja drops her head in her hands.

"First of all, it's a hedge fund of thirty men," she says. "Only men. The only woman there was a secretary. Anyway, so the first question he asked me was, 'You're from Dartmouth, did you see the game last night?' and I totally didn't. So I panicked and said I didn't like sports."

"That was your angle?" Chloe asks.

"Yeah," she says. "I mean, I was expecting accounting questions. I had been going through my index cards on equity investments, and then all he wants to talk about is sports and the personal section at the bottom of my résumé."

"What's even on the personal section for you?" Tripp asks.

"Exactly," Puja says. "I made that whole line up. I don't know anything about photography. Literally. I said my favorite camera was an iPhone, and he asked which one, and I didn't know. Like, an 8? And apparently the secretary gets a free membership to Equinox, but no one else at the firm does."

She shakes her head.

"Fuck 'em, Pooje," Tripp says.

"You wouldn't want to work there anyway," Chloe says.

"Well, what about you?" Tripp asks. "Where'd you interview? Booty Barre?"

"I'm leaving," I say.

"To work out?" he asks.

"No, I'm quitting. Today is my last day."

"Oh, *really*?" he asks.

His eyes sparkle.

"Yes," I reply.

He and I both know what that means.

"Well, thanks for the A-leg-room," he says. He stacks his feet on my lap and lounges backward in a mock recline. I laugh and toss him off of me. Puja comes over and hugs me. It's actually sweet.

"I'm so jealous you're leaving," she whispers in my ear.

A couple of minutes to noon, as I proofread my goodbye email, Tripp declares that he is a genius because he finally figured out call forwarding from his desk landline to his cell phone. He calls it the "greatest thing since delay-send." That's the Outlook function allowing an email to be delivered at a specific time in the future. Tripp was a fan of delay sending as much of his work as he could for 4 or 5 a.m., to give the impression of an unrelenting work ethic. Now, Tripp leans forward toward my computer screen and inserts his nose an inch away from my goodbye email.

"You should reduce the font size," he says. "Freak all the MDs out. They'll think they're getting old."

"Nah," I say. "Is it good to go?"

"Yes," he says with conviction. "It's time."

All,

After two years and two months, today is my last day at Anderson Shaw.

I feel very fortunate to have started my career at such an outstanding firm that is truly exceptional in many ways. I am grateful to have learned from such a remarkable group of people. In particular, a heartfelt thank-you to my pod and fellow analyst class.

I will be teaching yoga. My contact info is below if you are interested in a private class. It may seem crazy, but it beats working yourself to death—I promise.

Warm regards,

Allegra
(I) @PretzelYoga (E) Allegra@PretzelYoga.com (C) 9175554029

I send.

"Guess that means we don't work together anymore," he says.

"Guess not," I say.

He winks.

On my way out, I approach the pretzel stand, which gleams in the sunlight. Tripp has already texted me three times in a row to ask me out tonight. So far, he has suggested drinks ("to wash down that cake we got today? #$"), or dinner ("pro is that's longer than drinks"), or a trip to Pier 1 Imports to redecorate my studio ("jk you have great taste—in men"). I can't wait to see him again. I'm smiling as I reach the stand.

"Hey," I say.

"You again," says the pretzel-stand man.

I pull out my phone and show him the latest landing page for @PretzelYoga, which has a few hundred posts and 25K followers.

"I named this after your stand," I say.

"Does that make me money?" he asks.

"Well, no," I say. "I thought it would make you happy."

"What, you make money, and I feel good?" he asks. "Get the fuck out."

I pocket my phone. He waves me away.

"You know, I quit today," I say.

He looks at me sideways. His forehead wrinkles with thought, as if he is figuring out whether or not he still hates me.

"Quit, huh?" he asks.

"Yeah."

"To do what?" he asks.

"Teach yoga," I say.

"Yoga?" he says. "Yoga. You know I'm from India, lady?" He shakes his head. "Leave Anderson Shaw and tell the Indian man, 'I teach yoga.' I used to think you were a smart asshole. Now I see you're not so smart." He fixes me an extra-large pretzel with every topping. "Take the pretzel, lady. You need it more than me."

As I hold the pretzel, I don't feel like the clown he thinks I am. Instead, I see how my practice has already changed someone. The ultimate miser just gave me a free pretzel out of the goodness of his heart. That's got to be a start.

acknowledgments

Special thanks to Suzanne Gluck and Eve Attermann at William Morris Endeavor for believing in me and for leading a seamless process. This book would not have been possible without Lara Blackman, my editor now at Audible, who really got this story and helped me focus the narrative. For her ideas, jokes, and guidance, I am extremely grateful. Kaitlin Olson, my editor extraordinaire at Atria, has also been instrumental in making this book a reality. I am on team pink cover!

I benefited tremendously from the counsel of Tom Distler at Brooks & Distler, of Robert Stein at Pryor Cashman, and of Jennifer Weidman at Simon & Schuster. Thanks to Emma Parry at Janklow & Nesbit and David McCormick at McCormick Literary for their early reads and advice. Thanks also to authors Jill Davis and Wednesday Martin; to photographers Lucy Brown and Bradley Lau; to copy editor Polly Watson; and to my Yale English professor Alfred Guy for his lessons senior year. Last but not least, thank you to my dear family—Jody, both Emils, and Parker—for their unconditional support, and to Dave Alexandre.

about the author

Madeleine Henry worked at Goldman Sachs and in investment management in New York City. She graduated from Yale in 2014, where she wrote comedy for *The Yale Record*, America's oldest college humor magazine. Now working on her second novel, she shares more information about her life, writing, and yoga practice on @MadeleineHenryYoga. *Breathe In, Cash Out* is her debut.

breathe in, cash out

MADELEINE HENRY

*T*his reading group guide for Breathe In, Cash Out *includes an
introduction, discussion questions, ideas for enhancing your
book club, and a Q&A with author Madeleine Henry. The suggested
questions are intended to help your reading group find new and interesting angles and topics for your discussion. We hope that these ideas
will enrich your conversation and increase your enjoyment of the book.*

introduction

In this sizzling debut for fans of *The Devil Wears Prada*, Wall Street banking analyst Allegra Cobb plans to quit the minute her year-end bonus hits her account, finally pursuing her yoga career full-time. But when she forms an intense relationship with the #InstaFamous guru who may hold the ticket to the life Allegra's always wanted—she's not sure if she'll be able to keep her sanity intact (and her chakras aligned) until bonus day.

topics & questions
for discussion

1. The novel starts with Skylar asking the question "Are you okay?" (p. 1). Why do you think Madeleine Henry chose to begin the novel this way? What does this scene accomplish?

2. Allegra's dispassionate night with Mark leads to an uncomfortable morning. What does this sequence of events tell us about Allegra?

3. Allegra's colleagues Chloe and Puja are described as "the emotionless fake blonde" and "the heiress," respectively (p. 11). They play a large role in the book. Do you think they serve as foils? If so, how do they enhance the various aspects of Allegra's story?

4. How does the banking lifestyle—the grueling hours and the high pressure—come across in this novel? Does it match what you believed about the financial world before you began the book?

5. Allegra and her colleagues spend a lot of their time concerned about Bonus Day. Do you think this incentivizes them to work harder? Or is it just a reality of the job that they expect?

6. Of her dad, Allegra discloses, "When I was young it made him happy whenever I talked like him or won anything. In general, he thinks the world is way too politically correct and way too sensitive: he wasn't going to raise a wimp" (p. 17). He equates her prestigious job with success. Do you think he will come to accept another metric for success as Allegra strikes out on her own?

7. The book includes nontraditional narrative forms like emails and Instagram comments. Why do you think Madeleine chose to include these? How do they enhance the story?

8. Skylar's pseudo-mentor relationship with Allegra is a huge part of the book. How does Skylar earn Allegra's trust?

9. Tripp is introduced as "the devil-may-care associate known for keeping an earbud in his right ear and watching Netflix on one of his two computer screens all day" (p. 11). How does he change throughout the novel? What do you consider the turning point in Tripp and Allegra's friendship?

10. Different characters have distinct views on money and income. How is the meaning of money different for Mark, Tripp, and Allegra?

11. Vivienne and Allegra have a tense relationship, although it softens by the end of the novel. What do you think Vivienne represents?

12. The novel leaves the reader with the impression that the yoga world can be as cutthroat as the banking world. How does this contrast with the idea of yoga as a stress-reducing activity?

13. At Anderson Shaw, Allegra technically works on a "team." In the end, Allegra becomes a free agent. How does this novel portray working in groups in a corporate setting?

14. The book explores a common tension between one's desire to fulfill personal dreams and the reality of having to earn a living. Is the novel optimistic about resolving this challenge?

15. At the end of the novel, Allegra succeeds in manifesting her vision for her life. What personal limitations did she have to overcome in order to accomplish this?

enhance your book club

1. Think back to your first job. Did you love it? Hate it? Was it in an industry entirely different from your current job? Discuss these experiences with your group.

2. In the novel, Allegra and her coworkers play a game, Whose Life Sucks Most. Try playing a round with your book club. Or try the opposite game, Whose Life Doesn't Suck Most.

3. Allegra says her dad "supplied me with a steady stream of quotes to keep me in a 'winner's mind-set,' including, 'Winners do what losers won't'" (p. 24). In your own experience, are mantras useful devices? Discuss whether there are any mind-set phrases that members of the book club try to live by?

4. The novel depicts Instagram as a tool that can sometimes be deceiving. Have members of the group had any notable positive or negative experiences with the app?

5. Visit author Madeleine Henry's Instagram @MadeleineHenryYoga for more information about her yoga practice and the book.

a conversation with madeleine henry

You worked in finance right out of college. How did that job inform this novel? How does Allegra's experience differ from your own?

This book—its setting at Anderson Shaw, the lifestyles of its characters, the conversations they have at the pod—paints a realistic picture of working on Wall Street today.

I worked at Goldman Sachs and then in investment management primarily in healthcare in New York City. Almost all of my friends worked in finance or consulting right after college. Those experiences gave me a feel for what can reasonably happen in that environment. I wanted the Wall Street backdrop of this story to feel authentic, and my history allowed me to create that. Now, anyone who's worked in finance can read this book and enjoy amusing moments of *Yep, that nails it*, and *That happened to me.* That being said, Allegra's story is not my personal story. For example, I didn't start practicing yoga until *after* I left investment banking, so I never had to try and reconcile the two worlds at the same time. Also, how many f-bombs do I drop on a daily basis? Way fewer than Allegra. Like, wayyy fewer.

So much of this novel focuses on Allegra's relationships with her colleagues—both at Anderson Shaw and in the yoga world—instead of on romantic relationships. Was that something you were particularly sensitive to as you wrote the novel?

I wasn't trying to avoid romantic relationships as a subject. My book reflects the reality that Wall Street isn't a very romantic place. I believe the phrase "it takes time to fall in love," and people in these all-consuming, fast-track professions are time-poor. They often don't have enough time to fall in love. So, you can end up with long-term relationships on pause (e.g., Chloe and Charles) or random flings (e.g., Allegra's with Mark and Hillary). Yes, Allegra's relationship with Tripp deepens, but her primary focus is work, as it is for most people in her shoes.

What was your favorite scene to write? Were there any scenes that were particularly difficult?

I loved writing the scene at Yoga Cyclone where Allegra teaches a class to her coworkers. That sequence is hysterical because it encapsulates the clash of worlds at the heart of this book: yoga versus finance. In this studio devoted to health, *aparigraha* (non-possessiveness), and humility, enters a squad of investment bankers trying to make as much money as possible so they can buy Ferraris and big Hamptons houses. I took an English class in college where the teacher taught us that "humor is incongruity." The incongruity of this book is at a peak in that scene.

On the other hand, I found all intimacy between Allegra and Mark (her married boss) hard to write because it feels so wrong. It's hard to write about things I personally find immoral.

This novel satirizes the banking and yoga worlds. Is satire a genre that you're often drawn to?

I choose genres that relate to what I'm currently writing about, so I can learn from how others approached the topic. My second book is a love story, and it's more heartfelt and tender, so right now I'm drawn to delicate, emotional stories and poems ... More about that in the last question.

Yoga and finance are seemingly disparate worlds. How did you balance your interest in both while writing this book?

I believe we need to feed our souls in order to feel happy. While I was working in finance, yoga and writing were the outlets I needed to do that. So, yes, it was hard to make time for everything, but it would have been a lot harder without them in my life.

This novel paints an unhealthy portrait of life as an investment banking analyst. How true to life do you think this is? As more companies try to invest in wellness initiatives, do you see any change happening?

Breathe In, Cash Out is realistic. The fact is that investment banking is a strenuous job and so banks have rolled wellness initiatives (e.g., forbidding bankers from being in the office on weekends) to improve the lifestyle. In my own social circle, however, I don't know anyone who has had a dramatic change in his or her life as a result.

Do you have any favorite books that inspired you in the writing of this one?

There is a little bit of *The Catcher in the Rye* in here, in the sense that both books involve an "I" narrator who dismisses virtually everyone else. Where Holden Caulfield calls people "phonies," Allegra might call them "assholes."

There is also a little bit of Gary Shteyngart's *Lake Success*, as both satirize the financial world. Ben Stiller joins Shteyngart to ask in the book trailer, "Hey are you white? Are you a male? Did you play lacrosse at one of these fourteen schools [Harvard, Cornell, Duke, Brown, Georgetown, Columbia, Johns Hopkins, Notre Dame, Princeton University, UPenn, Stanford, Yale, Dartmouth]? Then the exciting world of hedge funds might be right for you."

But what made *Breathe In, Cash Out* so exciting to work on was that I thought that it was unlike anything I'd read before. To me, it's a very brave book. Allegra speaks truth to finance power, and it's very cool to see someone serve up real talk to a Goliath in our society.

Yoga is a very personal practice and yet so much of this novel illuminates the social media (mostly Instagram) component that has become so huge. How do you think we (and Allegra) can balance the very personal with the very public?

It's hard for me to view any intentionally shared content as personal. There can be an illusion of voyeurism, but everyone who posts *chose* to do so. They've invited you into that moment with them. So, I have to believe that the only really personal moments are the unshared ones. Everyone has their own formula to dictate which those should be.

Aside from personal/public, another interesting contrast on Instagram is introvert/extrovert. I've noticed the app can be an emboldening tool, where introverts can act more extroverted than they do in real life. I'm friends with another yogi Instagrammer who has a million followers and, despite her omnipresence online, she describes herself as a quiet loner. I think this is because the app allows you to share information about yourself without ever putting you on the spot and, in a way, no one else is really there. So, introverts can feel more comfortable.

We've spent the last several years reckoning with toxic work cultures for women. Where, if at all, do you see this novel and Allegra's experience fitting into that?

I know there's been a wave of "Me Too" novels, but I didn't intend this novel to be one of them.

Where did the game of Whose Life Sucks Most come from?

Bankers love to hate their jobs. For some reason, banking culture grants you more social status the more overworked and miserable you are. So, at the junior level, everyone is always complaining—so much so that, one day, it occurred to me that people were already playing this game. I just gave it a name.

We've outlined several differences between banking and yoga. Do you think they share any similarities?

Counterintuitively, in New York City, both tend to involve affluent people. Yoga is free, but urbanites have turned it into an expensive hobby: each class can cost forty dollars, special outfits up to two hundred dollars each, and retreats can cost thousands.

What do you hope readers take away from this novel?

First: entertainment. I hope people enjoy the audacity of Allegra's inner monologue which speaks truth to power. Second: education. For people who want to know what investment banking feels like, *Breathe In, Cash Out* is it.

What's next for you?

My second novel, which has the working title *The Love Proof*, is part love story, part exploration of space and time. I imagine it for fans of *The Notebook*, *The Secret*, and *The Alchemist*.

I'm excited about the transition from *Breathe In, Cash Out* to *The Love Proof* because it reflects a duality that's often taught in yoga: head and heart. The head symbolizes ego, fear, and selfishness bred from a false sense of scarcity. *Breathe In, Cash Out* is very head. It takes place entirely in Allegra's mind. It's about Wall Street. Most characters are just trying to get rich. But the heart involves intuition, sharing, and the human potential to do good and be good to each other. *The Love Proof* is more heart. It's full of soul and very visceral.

I'm really excited to share both.